A KIND OF ANGER

The Paris Bureau told Piet Maas: find Lucia Bernardi. Don't fail. This is your last chance . . .

With no enthusiasm, Maas travels south to the French Riviera. How he finally meets the adorable, extraordinary Lucia; matches his wits with a sharp, witty and extremely crooked blackmailer; deals with agents and double agents of vulgar and violent tastes; and at last experiences an entirely new kind of anger—are told with Ambler's cool, spare, breath-taking skill and charm.

ERIC AMBLER

A Kind of Anger

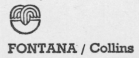

FONTANA / Collins

First published by The Bodley Head Ltd. 1964
First issued in Fontana Books 1966
Sixth Impression September 1973

© Eric Ambler 1964

Printed in Great Britain
Collins Clear-Type Press London and Glasgow

CHAPTER 1

The weekly American news magazine *World Reporter* goes to press at eleven o'clock on Friday night. As a rule there is not much work left to be done that evening, except by the proof-readers and checkers; but the atmosphere in the New York editorial offices is still tense.

It is understandable. A daily newspaper is committed for only a few hours and can always retrieve or cover its mistakes fairly promptly. But when a magazine as forthright and prophetic in its judgments as *World Reporter* is confounded by events, it looks foolish for several days. There was, for instance, the unhappy week when a South-east Asian general, hailed by the magazine on Friday as " Asia's new strong man ", had by Monday, when the magazine reached the news-stands, tamely surrendered to a mob of unarmed students and been hanged. Fortunately, such mishaps are rare. The editors are able men and as wary as they are well informed. Every possible precaution is taken. The major wire service machines are watched continuously. All around the world, in a dozen different time-zones, those who staff the magazine's foreign bureaux are at their posts, monitoring regional news services and radio broadcasts. Private lines and teleprinter circuits connect the main editorial offices with the printing plants in Philadelphia and Chicago. Electronic type-setting equipment has been installed. Stories can be re-slanted, punches pulled or converted into pats on the back, bets hedged and faces saved right up until the last moment. If there is tension, there is also calm and quiet confidence.

At least, there is in New York. In the foreign bureaux the weekly vigil before the Friday night deadline is accompanied by a gnawing anxiety that has nothing whatever to do with the work in hand. It has to do with the editor-in-chief, Mr. Cust.

By nine o'clock in New York on a normal Friday evening, most of the senior editors feel sure enough of themselves and their work on the new issue to go down to the restaurant on the ground floor of the *World Reporter* building and eat dinner. With Mr. Cust, however, it is different. Unless some extraordinary emergency arises, he has nothing more to do or decide until the Monday afternoon editorial conference about the next issue. As the principal shareholder in the magazine as well as its editor-in-chief, he has nobody to whom he must report. He could, conveniently for all concerned, go up to his penthouse at the top of the building and join his wife and her guests for dinner and bridge. He knows this, knows that it is a desirable state of affairs and that he himself has brought it about ; but he also resents it. Accordingly, instead of going up to the penthouse, he remains in his office and sends for smoked salmon sandwiches and a bottle of Blanc-de-Blanc. Then, with the aid of a private file and the undivided attention of an overseas switchboard operator, he proceeds to nourish his self-esteem by bedevilling the foreign bureaux.

It is the only time he ever calls a bureau direct, and he selects his victims for the evening with care. They will be those—no more than two or three as a rule—for whom he has been able to devise what he calls " planning suggestions."

He devotes much time and thought to their preparation. For his purposes, a sound planning suggestion has to possess three qualities : there must be no chance of its having been anticipated by the bureau chief ; it must always seem to be based upon exclusive inside knowledge cleverly obtained by Mr. Cust ; and, finally, it must so surprise, bewilder and exasperate the bureau chief concerned that he is stung into making protests which Mr. Cust can have the satisfaction of quashing. In other words, the suggestion must be eccentric, illogical and perverse.

It is said that he is suffering from a type of cerebral circulatory disturbance characteristic of senility, and that recently the deterioration has become more marked. That may well be true. No editor in his right mind could have issued a directive as stupid and as malicious as Mr. Cust's planning suggestion on the Arbil story.

II

It was received by Sy Logan, the Paris bureau chief, at 3.15 a.m. (French time) on a cold Saturday morning in February. I was in his office when the call came through.

The conversation began, as such conversations always did, with a polite inquiry by Mr. Cust concerning the bureau chief's health and that of his wife and family. Sy replied with the required brevity, switched on the tape-recorder and waved to me to listen on his secretary's extension phone.

Mr. Cust's voice is both loud and indistinct, like a defective public address system at an airport. Though deafened by it you have to strain to hear what is being said. He also eats his sandwiches as he talks, which doesn't help either.

". . . fine thanks, Chief," Sy Logan was saying.

"Great. Now, Sy, I've been thinking about that Arbil business last month, and what we ought to be doing about it."

There was a pause; then, just as Sy was opening his mouth to reply, Mr. Cust went on: "They haven't traced that bikini girl yet, have they?"

"No, Chief."

"Christ!" Although it was said mildly, the tone expressed more than concern over a state of affairs; it managed somehow to suggest that Sy personally was to blame. "What *are* we doing about it, Sy?"

"Well, Chief . . ."

"Now don't tell me we've been taking Reuter's coverage on the story, because I already know that. I mean, what are *we* doing?"

"Chief, there's not much we *can* do. The girl's been missing for six, seven weeks now. Her pictures have been run in pretty well every paper and magazine in Europe. She could be in France, Spain, Portugal or Italy. Probably she's in France, but the police just haven't found her yet. Until they do . . ."

"Sy!" There was a plaintive note there now.

"Yes, Chief?"

"Sy, I don't want *Paris Match* or *Der Spiegel* beating us to it."

This is a good example of the Cust needling technique. He

did not mention *Time-Life* or *Newsweek* or *U.S. News and World Report*. The implication was that, while there was no chance of *their* beating *World Reporter* to anything because of the unceasing vigilance of the New York office, the Paris bureau, in its leaden-footed way, might well permit French or German competitors to steal a march on it. As they *had* stolen marches on at least two recent occasions, the admonition was particularly annoying. Sy leapt to his own defence.

"Beating us to what, Chief?" he demanded sharply. "There's no angle on it for us yet. Not enough to go on. Until the police trace the girl, or she decides to come forward, the story's dead."

"Is it, Sy, *is* it?" In my mind's eye I could see Mr. Cust placing a skinny forefinger against the side of his nose. "I think that's a pretty dangerous assumption for us to make."

"Not dead then, only sleeping."

"That's very funny, Sy, but you're not taking my point. We know there's a political angle back of the story. We also know that there are political reasons behind the inability of the police to trace her. Or perhaps you *didn't* know that."

"I know that's the left-wing line on it here."

"It's more than just a line, Sy. I've dug up some pretty solid evidence that it's a fact."

"What sort of evidence, Chief?"

"I can't go into that now. Let me just say that the C.I.A. are very, very interested." Another standard ploy that. "And we ought to be interested, too. I think we ought to get out and find this girl, and get her story before somebody else does the job for us."

Sy cleared his throat. "I'm sorry, Chief, I didn't quite get that. When you say 'find' do you mean . .?"

"I mean what I say—*find*. Until you find her you can't get the story, can you?" There was a touch of impatience now.

This was all fairly meaningless to me. I had been in Portugal getting interviews with exiled royalty when the Arbil affair had started. As I understood it, a man named Arbil had been murdered in Switzerland and the police were trying to find some woman who wore a bikini and had witnessed the crime.

Sy had been fumbling with a cigarette. He paused to light it before he replied carefully: "I quite agree, Chief. If we could find her, we would certainly have a story."

"Good. Now, who are you going to put on to it?"

Sy put the cigarette out again. "Well, to be honest, Chief, I'd as soon put nobody on." There was a dead silence the other end. Sy went on grimly. "Before I came into this organisation," he said, "I was a newspaper man."

"And a very capable one," the voice conceded graciously. But there was a hint of amusement there now. Mr. Cust was beginning to enjoy himself.

The back of Sy's neck was getting red. "Capable or not," he ploughed on, "one of the first things I learned from you was that I had to change my thinking. I remember some of the things you said. 'Never try to do the newspapers' job.' That was one. How did it go on? 'We are a magazine. We don't compete with newspapers and television for beats and scoops. They record the news. We interpret the news and make it history.' It's a bit late to be changing the ground rules, isn't it?"

"Nobody's changing any rules, Sy." The voice was glutinous with pleasure now. "We're just trying to bring a little imagination to bear on our job. At least, I am, and I'm hoping I can take you along with me. Now, think. The newspapers haven't come up with even a smell of a lead. Why not? Because all they've done is suck around after the French police. We now know that the police have been dragging their feet. It's time we moved in."

Sy was as belligerent as he dared to be. "Move in with what?" he said shortly.

"You know your own people best. Where's Parry now?"

"In Bonn covering the talks. You told me to send him there, remember?"

"So I did, yes." He tried, unsuccessfully, to sound as if he had forgotten.

"Chief, what I'm trying to explain is that we'd be wasting our time. All the big news outfits have had their teams working on it and they've had to give up. As for the police, their attitude makes no difference. If they have really tried and failed, we don't have a hope. If they know where she is and are stalling, we don't have a hope either."

"Not even if I tell you where to look?" You could almost see his fatuous grin as he said it.

It brought Sy up short, but he recovered quickly. "Would that be C.I.A. information, Chief, or can't you say?"

"You're damned right, I can't say. Not over an open line anyway. You'll get all the information you need in The Bag to-morrow. Now, who are you going to put on to it? What's that German psycho of yours doing at the moment?"

Sy transferred the telephone from his right hand to his left. "I don't seem to recognise that description, Chief," he said after a moment.

"Oh for God's sake! The one who did that sick story about the fag night-club. Pete something . . ."

Sy gave me a haggard look. He said: "If you mean Piet Maas, you could ask him yourself, Chief. He's listening on the extension."

"And I'm Dutch, not German," I said.

"My apologies. Dutch it is." He did not withdraw the word "psycho," however. That still stood. "Well, now . . ."

I said: "I'd better tell you right away, Mr. Cust, that I wouldn't be any good at all at playing detectives."

"I agree," Sy added. "What we need for . . ."

"Who's asking him to *play* at anything?" Mr. Cust bleated back. "He's supposed to be working for us, isn't he? What's his current assignment?"

"Automobile production in the Common Market, Chief," Sy answered promptly. "The latest facts and figures, and a three-year growth projection."

In fact, I was working on a piece about new French painters who were being bought by American art museums; but Sy was trying to bluff his way out. Mr. Cust is against the Common Market, and *World Reporter*'s policy is to attack it. Naturally, the Paris bureau is one of the main sources of ammunition for the campaign, and Sy had successfully used the fact before to counter New York office pressures.

This time he didn't succeed, though. Mr. Cust merely hesitated.

"Who requested it?"

"Dan Cleary."

"Well, I'll speak to him. You can forget it for the moment. This has top priority."

Sy had one more try. " Chief, if this tip-off is as hot as you say it is, I think I ought to pull Bob Parsons in from Rome, or maybe get after the story myself. After all, Piet Maas is basically a researcher and . . ."

" And that's just what you need for this, Sy, a researcher." There was finality in the voice now. " Pete, you shake the long hair out of your eyes, get your ass out of there and find that bikini girl. Sy, you see he finds her, quick. Okay?"

Sy mumbled something and the conversation ended. He switched off the tape-recorder and looked across at me.

He is a greying man in his middle forties, with a long, thin head and a bleak look about the eyes. He smells of after-shave lotion. I didn't like him, and he didn't like me. I had never done daily newspaper work ; I wasn't his idea of a pro. I had been educated in England during the war years, and, although I had acquired some American usages since working in the bureau, I spoke English with a British accent. And, of course, there was my personal history. He tried to pretend that it didn't exist, but it made him uneasy all the same.

After a moment, he shrugged. " Sorry, Piet. I did my best. I could have gone on trying to argue him out of it, but it wouldn't have done any good."

He was right about that.

Sy had been second-in-command when Hank Weston, the former bureau chief, had hired me as a researcher. It had been pure kindness on Hank's part. I had badly needed to be hired at the time, and would have taken a job as an office boy if he had offered it. The research thing had not lasted long. If you can write at all, writing for *World Reporter* is an easily learned trick. After a month or two, Hank had put me on the regular staff and given me a year's contract.

The trouble had started soon after he had left to go to a Washington job with U.S.I.A., and Sy had taken over.

Every so often *World Reporter* appoints itself the conscience of the world and goes on a moral rampage. The enemy is always announced as " the spiritual sickness of our time " and *World Reporter*'s method of fighting the good fight is to take a close, prurient and self-righteous look at some social phe-nomenon held to be symptomatic of the sickness. Juvenile delinquency of one sort or another always yields rich material, of course ; but it tends to become monotonous. With the idea that some adult depravity, especially European depravity, might make a change, Sy sent me to Hamburg to scout the *Nachtokale* there.

I found plenty of depravity of the usual sad, depressing kind; but, unfortunately, I also found something that entertained me.

The place was a transvestite night-club with a floor-show of men dressed as girls. It would have been commonplace enough but for one thing: the star of the show was exceptionally good.

Men in drag usually look just that: the false breasts are set too high, the calves bulge in the wrong places, the beard peers bluely through the pancake make-up. This man really looked like a woman; and a very attractive, amusing and talented woman at that. A rather drunken, and plainly heterosexual, ship's officer, who had strayed into the place by mistake, became so enthusiastic that, when at last a waiter felt obliged to tell him that the star wasn't a girl, he yelled back: "I don't give a damn which it is—I want to go to bed with it!"

I made the mistake of reporting the incident, adding that the fellow had my sympathy. I thought it might amuse the office, and it did; so, instead of cutting it, they left it in to amuse the people in New York. Mr. Cust happened to see it and was not amused.

He had decided to have me investigated.

What he had expected, and probably hoped, to discover, no doubt, was that I was a homosexual. He is rabid on that subject. Instead, he had learned that I had been the editor and part-owner of *Ethos*, an experimental international news review which had gone bankrupt, and that I had spent several months in a French mental hospital following a suicide attempt. The investigators, a Paris firm of private detectives, had even managed to worm out of the hospital authorities the fact that I had received shock treatments.

It turned out that Mr. Cust is just as rabid on the subjects of bankruptcy and mental illness as he is on homosexuality. I was finished. If Hank Weston hadn't taken the Washington job, he would probably have been finished, too, for having knowingly hired a man with my record.

Word of this soon got back, and I told Sy that I wanted to leave. But with *World Reporter* things are not that simple.

Mr. Cust is a jealous god, and at that time my contract still had five months to run. In that organisation, if you have an enforceable contract, you aren't allowed to quit, whatever the circumstances. If you go before the contract expires, you go, not because you want to, but because he has fired you for incompetence ; and if the incompetence isn't real, then it will be contrived.

Sy knew this as well as I did.

"What happens if I refuse?" I asked.

"If you do, Piet, you're suspended and go off salary. But you still can't go to work for another magazine until the contract expires. Of course, if you want to take a five months' unpaid vacation, okay."

I couldn't have lived five weeks without salary, much less five months. He knew that, too.

"I'm sorry, Piet," he said again ; "naturally, you'll get all the help I can give you."

Naturally. My failure would to some extent discredit the bureau. Besides, he had been told to see that I succeeded. It was possible that he too was being disciplined ; perhaps for not having warned New York about me earlier. He wouldn't get fired for my shortcomings, but he might get a black mark against his name.

I said: "I take it we can assume that this confidential information of his will be worthless?"

"Not necessarily."

"But probably."

He sighed. "The old man's not entirely stupid."

"I question that."

"I know you do. You also overrate your own importance, Piet. We all know you wouldn't win a popularity contest where he's concerned, and we all know that he can be a vindictive old bastard, but he's still a pro. He hears a lot of high-level scuttlebutt from people who feel it's worth while doing him favours. If he says he knows where this girl is hiding out, then the probability is that he has *something*. It may not be enough, but there'll be something. He likes playing hunches. And besides, there is such a thing as a long shot, you know."

"I know. You don't bet real money on it, just the torn ten-franc note you've been trying to get rid of anyway."

He shrugged. "It's no good belly-aching, Piet. You heard what I told him. You heard what he told me." He went on quickly before I had time to say any more; he'd had enough of me for that night. "I tell you what to do. We have a complete file on the story, with clippings, pictures and the Reuter coverage. Take it home and get some sleep. Then read it, and meet me here at twelve-thirty. We'll have the mail from New York by then. When we know what the score is we can figure out what you have to do. All right?"

III

I went back to the apartment off the Rue Malesherbes, and took two sleeping pills. They didn't work.

After an hour I got up and flushed the rest of the pills down the toilet. It was just a precaution. I never buy more than twenty at a time now, even though I get them through the black market, and there were only a dozen or so in the bottle; not really enough. It takes at least thirty to do the job properly; otherwise the stomach pump gets rid of too much of it. Then there is the long, nasty return to life, and the psychiatric ward. I don't want to go through that again; but I know myself, and I take no chances. In the grey early hours of a bad day, I could be stupid enough to make the same mistake twice.

I made some coffee and looked at the file Sy had given me.

The first reports of the Arbil affair had appeared in the Swiss newspapers, and these were included in the file; but they were mostly scrappy and contradictory. The most complete account was in a French illustrated weekly called *Partout*.

It was entitled, in lettering formed out of revolver bullets, MYSTERY IN ZURICH. Below this, embedded in a lurid washdrawing of a car hurtling down a mountain road with a naked girl at the wheel, was a sub-title: *All Europe Seeks the Beautiful Young French Girl with a Bikini and a Key*.

Partout likes to dramatise, and the men who work on it cultivate a breathless, exclamatory style. They also work in teams. Although there was only one name in the by-line of

the piece, it was obvious that at least three different writers
had contributed. The opening was the work of someone with
left-wing opinions and an unfortunate taste for the historic
present. It read like an old silent film script.

THE PLACE: Zürich, Switzerland.

THE DATE: January 10th.

THE TIME: 22.00 hrs.

*At the central electricity switchboard on this cold winter
night sits the duty Controller, Martin Brünner (54). His eyes
flicker ceaselessly over the meters and indicators on the control panel before him as he sips his cup of chocolate.*

*Earlier that day there has been a partial thaw followed by
a sharp freeze-up. He is expecting trouble.*

But not the kind of trouble he is to get!

Suddenly, a warning light flashes.

Emergency!

*The Controller's fingers move swiftly, precisely. The warn-
ing light has indicated an interruption of service in the wealthy
Zürichberg district—there is a breakdown at a transformer
sub-station. Within seconds the Controller has operated the
switching necessary to by-pass the breakdown and restore
electricity to the area.*

The rich must be inconvenienced as little as possible.

The ordinary guys, therefore, must work.

*Controller Brünner suspects an insulator fault. A standby
repair crew must go out to deal with it. The Controller gives
the order. A minute later the boys are on their way, swearing
philosophically, to do the job.*

*In charge of the crew is Hans Dietz (36), a married man
with two children. He sits beside the driver of the repair
truck. The other two members of the crew sit in the back
among the tools and line tackle.*

*The sub-station is located below the crest of a high hill near
one of the outer radar installations serving the Kloten-Zürich
International Airport. To reach the short track leading to it,
they must drive up the Waldseestrasse, a winding mountain
road with a precipitous drop to a lake on one side and the
boundary walls of some old villa properties on the other.*

*The gateway to Number 16, the Villa Consolazione, is
within a few metres of a hairpin bend. As a safety measure,*

the municipality has set up a large mirror on the lake side of the bend so that descending traffic can be forewarned of cars turning into or out of the villa driveway.

To-night, however, the mirror is obscured by frost.

On the way up, they encounter no cars on the road. That's a bit of luck, because the frozen snow is banked up on both sides of the road and there would be difficulty in passing. The surface is glacial and they are obliged to go very slowly. The Villa Consolazione is barely visible from the road. They do not notice whether or not there are lights burning in the villa grounds.

Why should they notice? They have a job to do.

They reach the sub-station just before 23.00 hrs. It takes them over two hours to locate and deal with the fault. When the job is done, Dietz reports to the Controller over the truck two-way radio, and asks for a test. It is now 01.35 hrs. Three minutes later, assured that all is well and that the sub-station has been switched back into service, the weary crew begin to reload their truck in preparation for the return journey. It is almost exactly 02.00 hrs. when they reach the Waldseestrasse again.

They go down in low gear as slowly and cautiously as they have made the ascent—at 10 k.p.h., no more.

Suddenly, Dietz sees danger ahead!

A car is coming down the driveway of the Villa Consolazione. It is going at an insane speed! He can see its headlight beams on the banked snow. My God! He shouts a warning to his driver. Foot down. The brakes go on hard.

Too late! The heavy truck swings its rear-end and then slides on over the ice with all four wheels locked. An instant later, the car erupts from the villa driveway, skids across the road and catches the truck's front fender.

It is only a glancing blow, and does little damage to the car. But for the sliding truck it is disaster.

It spins broadside on, slams into one of the massive stone gateposts, rides up the compacted snow banked along the wall, and crashes over on to its side. It comes to rest against the snow bank on the lake side of the road.

The car goes on down the hill without stopping. But, at the moment of impact, Dietz has seen both car and driver clearly in the truck headlights.

The car is a black Mercedes 300 S.

The driver is a young woman.

Neither Dietz nor his driver is much hurt. The lads in the back, however, have been less fortunate. One has a broken collar-bone, the other a scalp wound which is bleeding badly and needs stitches.

While the driver does what he can with the first-aid kit for the injured men, Dietz climbs back into the cab and tries the radio.

It is undamaged, and he is able to call Controller Brünner and tell him what has happened. By the time the Controller calls back to say that an ambulance and the police are on their way, Dietz has had time to think.

He failed to get the number of the Mercedes, but, as it came from the Villa Consolazione, he reasons that there must be somebody there who knows the driver's name and where she can be found. He proposes to go up to the villa and demand the information.

"Better wait for the police, Hans," Controller Brünner advises him.

But no. Dietz is feeling his bruises and is an angry man now. He is going to get that madwoman's name.

He goes up to the villa alone.

At this point, *Partout*, heavily laden with hindsight, began to describe Dietz's thoughts as he went up the driveway. They also gave him a strange sense of foreboding which made him hesitate.

According to a local reporter's account, Dietz had stumbled half-way up the steep driveway, lost his footing on the frozen snow, decided that maybe the Controller had been right after all, and turned back.

It had been two traffic policemen in a patrol car who had eventually gone up to the villa.

A photograph showed it to be a two-storey building in a pseudo-*schloss* style of the twenties, with two small turrets. When the policemen reached the top of the driveway, they found the place in total darkness. The garage doors were open, disclosing spaces for two cars. One space was empty and there were fresh tyre-tracks in the snow outside it; the other was occupied by an old 2 cv. Citroën. The policemen got out and went to the front door of the villa. They found that open, too.

They rang the bell several times without receiving any answer. They had no authority to enter the place uninvited. After a bit, one of them went round to the back to see what he could find there. He returned, some minutes later, with an elderly man named Ernesto Bazzoli. Bazzoli and his wife Maria were the villa servants, and lived in a cottage some fifty metres away by the vegetable garden.

The old man had been asleep in bed, and was shivering, querulous and alarmed. At first, the police were given no chance to ask him questions; he was too busy bombarding them with questions of his own. Why were the big lights out? They were never to be out at night; that was Herr Arbil's order. And where was Herr Arbil's car? Why was the front door open? It should have been double-locked, and with the chain on, as it always was. Where was Frau Arbil? What had happened?

By this time he had led the way inside the villa out of the cold, and the fact that there was more to inquire about here than the identity of a hit-and-run driver was at once apparent.

In the main living-room every drawer, every cupboard and cabinet had been opened and its contents scattered on the floor. It was the same in the dining-room. In the library all the books had been swept from the shelves. Even the kitchen had been ransacked.

Upstairs the situation was different in only one respect. On the floor in one of the bedrooms, there was the half-naked body of a man whom Bazzoli identified as Herr Arbil. He had been shot three times, twice in the stomach and once through the back of the head.

Here *Partout* switched tenses, and a crime reporter with a more matter-of-fact approach took over.

One of the traffic police telephoned the news to headquarters. The detectives, who arrived soon afterwards, took a quick look at the scene inside the villa, briefly questioned Dietz, Bazzoli and his wife and came to a conclusion which, at that point, seemed the only one possible.

There had been a violent quarrel between Arbil and his wife, during which one of them had ransacked the house looking

for something hidden—money, jewellery, letters from a lover,
a weapon. At the height of the quarrel, the wife had killed
the husband and then fled in his car.

At 03.05 hrs. the night duty officer at Zürich police headquarters authorised a general call to detain Frau Lucia Arbil.
The registration number of the Mercedes had been supplied
by Bazzoli, and this was circulated along with her description.
The nearby frontier post at Koblenz was specially alerted.

The Mercedes was found four hours later in the car park of
the International Airport. A check of the passenger lists of
outgoing planes at once began. There was no Frau Arbil on
any of the lists. But a clerk at the Swissair counter remembered selling a ticket to a young woman answering her description. It had been for a 6.00 a.m. business flight to Brussels.
She had had a French passport in the name of Mademoiselle
Lucia Bernardi.

The police were in a difficulty now. The Swiss extradition
treaty with Belgium requires that a strong prima facie case
must be made out against an accused fugitive before the person can be arrested and returned for trial to the country in
which the crime has been committed. Before Zürich could
ask Brussels to act, they had to be certain that Frau Arbil and
Mademoiselle Bernardi were the same person.

The aliens' registration department supplied the answer. Contrary to what Herr Arbil had told the Bazzolis, there was in
fact no Frau Arbil. Lucia Bernardi had been Arbil's mistress.

It took until ten o'clock to establish that, however, and by
then the Brussels plane had long ago landed and its passengers
dispersed.

Late that day, the Belgian Bureau Central came through
with the information that a woman answering Lucia Bernardi's
description had hired a car at the Brussels airport and been
driven to Namur. It was believed that she had taken a train
from there to Lille.

If this were true, Zürich had a new problem. We French
do not like to extradite our own nationals. She could only be
tried for the murder in France.

IF she had committed the murder, that is.

By this time, Commissioner Mülder, who commands the
Kriminal-polizei of the Zürich canton, was having second

thoughts on that subject. He had had the results of the autopsy on Arbil's body, and the whole case was up in the air.

According to the doctors, Arbil had been gagged and bound before he had been shot. He had also been tortured. The state of the genitals left little doubt of it.

More. The two revolver bullets which had inflicted the stomach wounds were of a calibre different from that of the single bullet which had entered the head.

The only gun found in the villa was a Parabellum pistol belonging to the dead man, and that had not been fired!

Two revolvers of different calibre suggested two persons. The crime laboratory technicians were able to state that the ransacking of the villa had been done by two men. One had worn cotton gloves, the other leather. They had forced an entry through a skylight in the roof.

Who were they?

Not ordinary thieves, for they had apparently stolen nothing.

Then, who was Arbil?

A third member of the team supplied the answer to this question. He used longer sentences, and had a mildly sardonic way with him. He sounded older than the other two.

The dead man's full name was Ahmed Fathir Arbil, and he was an Iraqi. He was also a refugee.

Three and a half years earlier, as Colonel Arbil, he had been the delegate from Iraq to an international conference of chiefs of police at Geneva. The conference had still been in progress when the Baghdad government of Brigadier Abdul Karem Kassim was shaken by an army revolt in the Mosul area. The revolt was put down after savage fighting, and executions of suspected ringleaders followed. Instead of returning to his fatherland when the conference ended, Colonel Arbil had asked the Swiss authorities for political asylum, on the grounds that, if he were to return to Iraq at that time, he would immediately be shot.

The reason he had given for his sudden fall from political grace had been that he was known to be sympathetic towards the Kurdish nationalist movement which had instigated the Mosul revolt. In support of his contention, he had produced an order for his immediate recall to Baghdad transmitted to

*him by the Iraqi Legation in Berne. Though it was formal
in tone, both his military rank and his title of Director of
Security Services had been omitted. The significance of the
omissions was accepted. Subject to the usual proviso that he
refrain from political activity while in Switzerland, asylum
had been granted.*

*Until a year before his death, his residence in Switzerland
had been relatively uneventful. Unlike many other political
refugees, he had never been short of money. When he had
leased the Villa Consolazione and bank references had been
required, he had had no difficulty in satisfying the owner's
representatives of his financial reliability. It was understood
that his income came from a family business in Iraq. He had
not sought any kind of employment, paid or unpaid, and had
not engaged in any political activity. He had professed to be
working on the history of Kurdistan; but this had not been
taken too seriously. Most political refugees planned to write
books—or said they did. In Arbil's case, it had soon become
obvious that his social life would take up most of his time.*

*A lean, powerful man with the aquiline good looks of his
race, he had been very attractive to women. On his part he
had had a taste for buxom, athletic, unmarried blondes in
their early twenties. A number of reports from the police
des mœurs attested to the fact that during the first two and
a half years of his residence in Switzerland he had been able
to indulge that taste with remarkable frequency. The women
had not been prostitutes. However, since none of them had
complained, since the affairs had been conducted with discretion, and since, above all, the man was a foreigner, no
official notice of these moral offences had been taken.*

*Then, with the entry of Lucia Bernardi into his life, his
tastes, as well as the situation at the villa, suddenly changed.*

*According to the dossier, a précis of which we were per-
mitted to inspect, Arbil met her at St. Moritz during the
winter sports season.*

*Her application for a residence permit notes that she was
born in Nice twenty-four years ago, that her height is one
hundred and fifty-five centimetres and that she has blue eyes
with dark brown hair. Occupation: modiste. No distinguish-
ing marks.*

A great many photographs of her, taken by the infatuated

*Arbil, have been found in the villa. In most of them she is
wearing a bikini, although there were some winter sports pictures, too. With clothes or without she is, in a slender, grace-
ful and most unbuxom way, quite beautiful. She also looks
as if she liked the man who took the photographs, and enjoyed
being his mistress.*

However, Commissioner Mülder's reluctance to accept the
fact that a smiling girl who looked well in a bikini could also
conspire with others to commit murder was only nominal.
His second thoughts about her guilt were based on the evidence he had accumulated on the case.

Further questioning of the Bazzolis had produced suggestive
facts. Some weeks earlier, Arbil had taken a number of
precautions, in the Bazzolis' opinion bizarre and unwarranted
precautions, against burglary. Floodlights had been installed
in the villa gardens and kept switched on from dusk to dawn
by a photo-electric time-switch. Special locks had been fitted
to doors and ground-floor windows. A contractor in Zürich
had been asked to submit an estimate for the installation of
electrically operated gates.

More and more it looked as if this had been a political
assassination, and as if the victim had received some prior
warning to be on his guard.

Who, then, were the assassins?

There was the evidence that they had worn gloves. A patch
of oil on the snow near the driveway gates suggested that they
had come and gone by car. They had left no other clues. A
police check on the whereabouts of other Iraqi nationals in
the canton at the time was unproductive. The Iraqi Chargé
d'Affaires in Berne undertook to find out if Arbil had any relatives in Iraq who might wish to have the body returned there
for burial, and to arrange for the disposal of his estate, but on
the subject of the assassins he was silent. That, he said, was
a matter for the police.

Commissioner Mülder did his best to deal with it, but there
were too many questions and not enough answers.

What was Lucia Bernardi's part in the affair? Had she been
an accomplice of the assassins? It seemed unlikely. An accomplice would have made it unnecessary for them to force a
skylight in order to get into the villa. They had also had to
short-circuit the floodlights in order to put them out. She

*would have switched them off from inside the villa if she had
been in the conspiracy.*

*But if she had not been an accomplice, why had she fled
after the killers had gone? What had really happened in the
Villa Consolazione on that cold winter night?*

*There was, and is, only one person who could answer all
these questions—Lucia Bernardi herself.*

*Nobody knew this better than Commissioner Mülder. Late
on January 11th, twenty-four hours after the murder had
been committed, he made a request to our police authorities,
through Interpol, that Lucia Bernardi be traced and asked to
make a deposition.*

He also invoked the aid of the press.

Results to date? Nil!

Lucia Bernardi had completely disappeared.

Partout described the search in some detail. The press had
gone to work with a will, and not only in France ; there were
reproductions of front-page stories from Italian, Spanish and
German newspapers, too. The French police had seemed co-
operative enough. Along with the photographs supplied by
Zürich they had given all the news media a full dossier on
the girl and the results of their latest inquiries about her.

Her father had been an electrical contractor in Nice until
1958, when both he and her mother had been killed in a car
crash on the Corniche. She was an only child and had inherited her father's estate. It had amounted, after the executor
had sold the contracting business, to some two million (old)
francs (about six thousand dollars) and had been held in trust
for her until she was twenty-one. For a while she had lived
with an aunt, her mother's sister, in Menton, and worked for
a millinery designer as an apprentice. When she became
twenty-one and had gained control of her money, she had gone
into partnership with an older woman named Henriette
Colin. Together they had opened a high fashion beachwear
shop in Antibes. After two seasons it had become clear that
the business could not be made to pay and they had sold out.
Henriette Colin had gone to work in a department store in
Nice. Lucia had decided to go to Paris. She had had about a
quarter of her inheritance left.

During the next two years the only word from her had been
her name on Christmas cards. Both the aunt in Menton and

Henriette Colin had received the same ones. The first year they had come from St. Moritz, the second year from Zürich. Neither woman had attempted to get in touch with her. The aunt, the police thought, had had a suspicion that the girl was leading an immoral life and had feared to risk having the suspicion confirmed. Henriette Colin (there was a coy suggestion of lesbianism in *Partout*'s account) had been hurt by Lucia's sudden neglect of her after their close personal and business friendship. Other French friends had been found and interviewed, with similar results. The inquiries in Germany, Italy and Spain had been just as fruitless.

The inevitable conclusion was that if Lucia Bernardi were still in France, she was living in disguise under an assumed name with false identity papers.

As *Partout* sonorously summed up: " *Somewhere—in a cottage in the country, in the fastness of a rich man's house, or unnoticed among the teeming millions of a great city— Lucia Bernardi may read these words and smile. She holds the key to a mystery. The question now is, will she come forward and let that key be used?"*

The answer to date had been an unequivocal " no."

There was some biographical material on Arbil in the bureau file, but only two later news items of any interest.

A news agency report quoted a Jordanian government official as saying that the Arbil murder had undoubtedly been the work of Egyptian terrorists.

A Reuter message from Berne said that Arbil's body had been claimed by a nephew living in Kirkuk, Iraq, and that it would be sent to Baghdad by air as soon as the necessary arrangements could be made.

IV

" Have you considered the possibility that she might be dead?" I asked.

"Wishful thinking, Piet." Sy was looking as tired as I felt. The plane from New York, carrying what Mr. Cust pretentiously referred to as " The Bag," was late that day, and we were waiting for the messenger to return from the airport.

" It's one way to disappear, and I seem to have read some-where, that statistically, quite a percentage of adult missing persons prove to be suicides."

" Why should she kill herself? She was running away from something, I agree—the police, involvement as a witness, who knows? But she made it. So why suicide?"

" Depression following panic." I could see that it embarr-assed him to hear me discussing suicide so casually, but I went on anyway. " We don't know much about her, of course, but what we do know is suggestive. She loses her parents, she becomes involved with a lesbian, she loses her business and most of her money, she separates herself from her relatives and friends. Whether or not she turned to prostitution after that we don't know for certain. Anyway, she ends up as the mistress of a political refugee twice her age. And then he gets tortured and killed. Not exactly a happy history."

" If she were ten or twelve years older I might buy the suicide idea, Piet, but look." He pulled a photograph out of the file which I had put on the desk in front of me, and held it up. Lucia Bernardi, her hair flying, her arms stretched out appealingly, was laughing up into the camera. " Suicide? That one?" he said.

" ' She had everything to live for ' is quite a common epitaph."

" Not when they're young and as well stacked as that." His secretary came in with the airmail package from New York. " Now let's see what the master has to say."

He shuffled through the usual clutter of galley proofs, photo-graphs and inter-office memoranda until he came to a sealed envelope with the Confidential stamp on it. The secretary took the rest away for sorting and distribution.

He took a long time opening the envelope and reading the paper inside, but finally he handed it to me.

It was headed FROM THE DESK OF THE EDITOR-IN-CHIEF. It went on:

To: *Paris Bureau, pro Logan.*
On story of missing Bernardi girl, I have received the fol-lowing information from a private, repeat private, source.
When Arbil met, picked up, or was picked up by, Bernardi at St. Moritz, she was there in the company of a man, appar-

*ently American, calling himself Patrick Chase. " In the com-
pany of" means that they had separate but adjacent rooms
in the same hotel.*

Now hear this.

Chase was under Swiss police surveillance as a suspected
con man. Suspicion was that he and Bernardi were in partnership and that Arbil was marked down as the sucker. The St.
Moritz (Grisons canton) police checked with Interpol on Chase
and Bernardi, but got back indecisive reports on both. Chase
was " known" but unconvicted, the girl was a " nothing
known." However, Chase had apparently become aware of
the surveillance. With two weeks of his hotel reservation still
to go, he skipped suddenly to Italy. Bernardi stayed behind
and moved in with Arbil.

Of course, Zürich will have gotten all this from the St.
Moritz boys. But what they didn't get, because Interpol didn't
know it at that time is the following:

" Patrick Chase" is an alias. The man is a con artist who
has been operating in Europe for the past eight years, especially in West Germany and Italy. Although raised and educated in New York, and hence able to pass successfully as an
American, he was born in France and is a French citizen. As
" Chase" he has been picked up for questioning on occasion,
and a couple of years ago our Bonn Embassy was asked to
put a trace on him through the F.B.I.

Now, six months ago (early September), there was some
trouble over the circulation of counterfeit U.S. twenty-dollar
bills in Europe. Our people investigated. During the investi-
gation they ran across " Chase." Though later cleared, he was
for a time under suspicion of being a distributor. During that
period a clandestine search of his possessions and examination
of his correspondence revealed an interesting thing. He was
negotiating for the purchase of a house property at a place
called Sète in the South of France. And he was doing it in
the name of Phillip Sanger. A check established that this was
his real name, and that he was born in Lyon, France, in 1925.

Need I say more?

Yes, maybe I should.

Although it is over a year since St. Moritz checked on Chase
and Bernardi, it is always possible that some conscientious cop
in Zürich will start reviewing yet again all the evidence in

*their dossiers, and decide, because he can think of nothing
better to do, to run a double-check on Mr. Chase. If he does
he will undoubtedly get on to Mr. Sanger, because our people
filed a copy of that Sanger report with Interpol. For all we
know it may be happening right now!*

Not a moment to lose, eh, gentlemen?

There was no signature or initial. I gave the paper back
to Sy, and waited.

" Well," he said doubtfully, " it's something."

" Is it? I'd say that long shot you talked about isn't even
in the race."

" Oh, I wouldn't go as far as that." He smoothed the paper
out firmly as if that would somehow improve what was written
on it. " It does look as if he's had a tip-off. From someone
in the Department of the Treasury, I'd say."

" The Treasury reports to Interpol?"

" Sometimes. The United States isn't a full member of
Interpol, but the Treasury and the Bureau of Narcotics maintain contact with it in the counterfeiting and drug areas. I'd
say the tip-off was authentic, definitely."

The " definitely " made me laugh. I said: " If you'd known
what the hot tip-off amounted to last night would you have
suggested pulling in Bob Parsons from Rome?"

He waved the question away irritably. " All right, let's cut
the jokes and see if we can't evaluate this." He stared at the
paper for a moment before he went on. " At its best, I'd say,
it amounts to this. We have a line on a friend of the girl's
who lives in France and who might conceivably, for old times'
sake, be prepared to help her to hide out from the police. On
the other hand the man's a crook, so that the old times' sake
wouldn't mean much to him if it also meant risking a mix-up
with the police. The whole thing's very iffy, but it's worth
checking out. Any thoughts?"

" No constructive ones."

He sighed. " Look, Piet, you asked me if I'd have pulled
Bob Parsons from Rome to follow a tip-off like this. Frankly,
the answer's no, I wouldn't have. We have a stringer in Marseille. Most likely I'd have had him check it out. As it is, the
old man's handed you the job. We both know why—because
he wants to chalk one up against you. Okay, so you don't
let him. He's not expecting miracles. All you have to do is

find this Sanger and make sure he couldn't be a lead to the girl. Then we're both in the clear. Right?"

"How do you suggest I go about it?"

He grinned. "That's better, buddy boy." He glanced at his watch. "There's a plane to Marseille around six or seven. Tell Antoinette to get you a seat on it, and a room for the night at a hotel. In the morning, rent a car, drive to Sète and start digging."

"It's Sunday to-morrow. The *mairie* will be closed."

"The hell with the *mairie*. You might as well go straight to the police and tell them why you're there. No, start with the cafés and gas stations. Don't tell them you're a reporter. They might pass the word on, and some local paper will start sniffing around. Make up a story. Tell them you're an insurance claims man looking for a missing witness. Your French is good enough for that. Or tell them you're trying to look up an old army buddy. They might like that better."

"And if I draw a blank?"

"Try the stores. Hell, it's not that big a place, Someone must know him."

"Do we know anyone at the Quai des Orfèvres?"

"Why?"

"What I'd like to know is whether that thing about the police dragging their feet on the case is true or not."

"What difference does it make?"

"Supposing that, by some remote chance, La Bernardi really were hiding out with Sanger. Supposing the police knew it, but have orders from on high to forget about it. Never mind the reason. Sanger would have what amounts to police protection. *If* I find him and *if* I talk to him, I'd like to know what I'm up against—a crook on the defensive, or a virtuous-seeming citizen who can tell me to go to hell."

He considered that, then shook his head. "You have a point, but I don't think it's any use my calling up the Quai des Orfèvres. I know the Deputy Director pretty well, but I also know the answer I'd get. 'You've been reading the wrong newspapers, *mon cher*. Admittedly, we are no longer breaking our heads over this matter. The young woman is wanted by our Swiss colleagues for questioning, and we have done what we can to oblige them. But now our belief is that she found herself some new papers and went to Italy'." He shook his head again. "No, if it comes to that, Piet, I think you'll just have to play it by ear."

He is always telling people to play it by ear, and the expression always irritates me. I prefer to read the music.

CHAPTER II

I took the plane to Marseille that evening and stayed at the Hotel L'Arbois. In the morning I walked around the corner to the air terminal and rented a car. By late afternoon I was in Sète.

Unless you happen to be a policeman, or have a stuffy objection to lawbreaking of any kind, the picture conjured up by the description " a successful confidence man with a house in the South of France " should be a reasonably attractive one. You see the man instantly. Sun-tanned and smiling, in a chic Italian sports-shirt and sipping a dry martini, he takes his ease on the terrace of a villa at Cap d'Ail or Super Cannes. He is middle-aged, perhaps, but he has kept all his hair, and his young wife is faithful to him. His illicitly accumulated wealth is all safely invested in blue-chip stocks, he has a numbered Swiss bank account and a holding corporation registered for tax purposes in Curaçao. He is the visible proof that crime can, and often does, pay handsomely.

But mention that the house in the South of France is near Sète, and you get a very different picture. That is, if you know Sète.

It is on the Golfe du Lion two hundred kilometres from Marseille, and is, after Marseille, the leading seaport of southern France. Sète serves the wine-growing area of Hérault, which produces the kind of wine that is transported by tanker rather than barrel and is often more valuable converted into industrial alcohol. There are some manufacturing plants, a fishing fleet, a shipbuilding yard, and an oil refinery. The coastline is straight, the countryside flat and almost featureless. The only landmark is Mont St. Clair, a high hill, with a lighthouse and coast defence installations on it, overlooking the port. Most of the town is criss-crossed by waterways connecting the various dock basins. There are a few small commercial hotels. On the coast road outside the town there are two or three family *pensions* which cater in the summer for those hardy enough to brave the shadeless, windswept beach and the icy currents of the gulf. But the town makes no effort to attract tourists. It is a place of business, useful but ugly, and content to remain so.

It was raining heavily when I arrived, and very cold. Sète might have been on the Baltic instead of the Mediterranean. I found a hotel with lukewarm central heating, and then dined at a brasserie adjacent to it.

I had no intention of conducting the kind of inquiry Sy had suggested. If there were in fact a man named Phillip Sanger living in Sète and he owned a house, there was a simpler way of finding the address. Montpellier, the administrative capital of the Hérault *départment*, was only twenty-nine kilometres away. I could go to the Hotel de Ville there and ask to see the title deed records for the Sète area. Or I could look him up in the telephone directory.

I tried that first. There was no listing for anyone named Sanger. I asked Information and got the same answer. There was no more to be done that night. I called the Paris office, gave the duty operator the name and number of my hotel, and went to bed.

Next morning I went to Montpellier.

The *archiviste* in the Hotel de Ville was helpful without being inquisitive. It was quite usual, apparently, for a man to want to find out what another man owned.

It took me just over an hour to find out that Phillip Sanger, investment consultant, of 16 Rue Payot, Sète, owned three small properties on Mont St. Clair, described as numbers 14, 16 and 18 Rue Payot. He had bought them, six months earlier, from the widow of a local grocer for seven thousand new francs apiece. Each was about a tenth of a hectare, approximately a fifth of an acre. The *archiveste* said, with a tolerant smile, that the houses were only " *baraquettes*," old garrison hutments for which the army no longer had any use.

I drove back to Sète and went up to take a look at the Rue Payot.

The original forts and the citadel on Mont St. Clair had been designed by Vauban as part of a system of coastal fortifications stretching from the Spanish border to the Iles d'Hyères.

Until the end of the nineteenth century, the entire hill had been a military cantonment. Thereafter, as defence needs and techniques had changed, the garrison had shrunk in numbers. Part of the Mont had become a village, and the *baraquettes* had been gradually abandoned. Local shopkeepers and small-holders had bought them for use as storerooms, or to house livestock.

The Rue Payot was a steep, narrow lane with high stone walls on both sides. At regular intervals along the walls were wooden doors. Each door gave access to a small yard, at one end of which was a stone two-roomed cottage with a tiled roof and earthen floor.

Number 16, which Phillip Sanger had given as his perma-nent address, looked and smelled as if it had been used for many years as a pig-pen. Half the roof-tiles were missing and it had no doors. Number 14 was in roughly the same condi-tion. Number 18, however, was in the hands of workmen. A water main had been trenched in from the street, and in the yard they were working in a deep hole which looked like the excavation for a septic tank.

None of the workmen had heard of Monsieur Sanger. The *baraquette* was being rebuilt as a little villa, they said, with plumbing, a bathroom, a kitchen, a tiled floor and a terrace. The architect, Monsieur Legrand, was in charge of the work. The owner's representative was Monsieur Mauvis of the Agence du Golfe.

The sun was out that day, and the view from the *baraquette* out over the coast road to the sea was impressive. The terrace they were going to build would be a pleasant spot. I guessed now the reason for Phillip Sanger's purchase.

Monsieur Mauvis, the agent, confirmed my guess.

" Ah yes, it is happening all along the coast. People with money to invest buy up the old peasant houses—anything with four walls and a morsel of freehold land—and make them into villas for the people from the cities. Anywhere where there is sunshine and the sea. Now, even in Sète. You will see. By the time Monsieur Sanger has finished with those *baraquettes* they will be worth ten times what they cost him to buy and rebuild. But one needs imagination and one needs capital."

" And Monsieur Sanger has both, I take it."

"Ah yes. He has properties in Mougins and Cagnes-sur-Mer and Roquebrune, many properties. He does not sell, he rents them furnished. But along the Côte d'Azur and the Corniches there is much competition now and the prices have become absurd. The Belgians, the Swiss and the English are in the business now. Here in Sète you would be in at the beginning of the development. But it is necessary to move fast. Already the little people who own these old properties are becoming wise."

At the outset, I had given him the impression that I was looking for investment property, so I let him go on with his sales talk. He was a short, wispy man with bright eyes like a terrier's. He had a terrier's disposition, too. It was a long time before I could get him back to the subject of Phillip Sanger, and I had to endure a conducted tour of the properties he had on his books first.

When at last I managed to get away, I returned to the hotel and called Sy.

He was only moderately pleased with what I had to tell him.

"Couldn't you at least get Sanger's mailing address from him?" he asked.

"I did. It's care of a bank in Marseille. Sanger doesn't encourage a lot of correspondence apparently. Every week he telephones Mauvis or the architect for a progress report."

"Where does he call from? Did you get that?"

"No. Mauvis was getting cagey by then. Too much interest in his client, not enough interest in property for sale. I tried to get a description of Sanger. 'I wonder if that could be the same Monsieur Sanger I met in Cannes last year. Tall and blond?' It didn't work. He only said 'Perhaps,' and went on trying to sell me an apartment house."

"What next then?"

"I can try getting his address out of the bank in Marseille."

"They wouldn't give it to you. They'd just tell you to write him a letter and they'd forward it. You'll have to do better than that."

"I haven't had time to see the architect yet. But he probably knows no more than Mauvis. I could ask him for a description of Sanger."

"How would that help?"

"You could cable it to New York. Show we are taking things seriously."

There was a hostile silence, then he went on, too patiently: "Piet, if Sanger has all these properties along the coast it's a cinch he lives in one of them himself. We want to know which. That means that you have a lot of legwork to do and not much time in which to do it. I'd like you to get started to-night."

I was getting tired of Sy. "Look," I said, "why don't you just tell the old fool that I've fallen down on the assignment? That's all he really wants to hear."

"It's not what *I* want to hear, buddy boy. He wants results. It's my job to get them for him, however difficult he likes to make it. I can't tell him that you've fallen down on the assignment, because you haven't, yet. You're just expecting to. I don't say hoping to because that would make you too much of a jerk." He suddenly became genial. "So let's have some action, eh, Piet—*and* a little positive thinking?"

"All I need at the moment is an emetic."

He hung up before I did.

I spent the night at Arles, and drove on in the morning through Aix-en-Provence towards Cannes. Mougins is a mile or two outside Cannes on the road to Grasse. I arrived there in the early afternoon.

It is a charming small town perched on a hill. Cannes lies below, and the sea and the Iles de Lerins beyond. Once it was simply a market centre for the farms surrounding it; but in recent years it has become fashionable. In Mougins, the brassy amenities of Cannes are accessible without being unavoidable; and in the season it is noticeably cooler there than in Cannes. It is also quieter. Picasso has a house there.

I parked the car outside the *mairie* and went into a café. There was an old-fashioned zinc bar at the back. Two men in black suits were standing at it drinking red wine. Another man, obviously the *patron*, was behind the bar. There was nobody sitting at the tables.

I went to the bar and ordered a *marc*.

The men in black were discussing a car smash in which one of them had been involved. The *patron* was being appealed to for legal advice.

B

He was a stocky man with a paunch. His manner was breezy and his eyes shrewd. The legal advice he gave to the man who claimed to be the injured party, and who had carried insufficient insurance, was unorthodox but sensible. He told him to forget about lawyers and lawsuits ; instead, he should play " *couche-couche panier* " with his wife that night and take her in an unusual position.

I was allowed into the laugh that followed.

Madame, the wife of the *patron*, appeared behind the zinc. She was a squat, sturdy woman with gold in her teeth and a ready smile. She wanted to know what the laughter was about. The injured party gave her an only slightly watered-down version of her husband's suggestion, and there was more laughter, in which she joined heartily until she noticed me. Then she pretended to scold her husband.

" You are bad," she said. " What will people think?"

" Madame," I said, " I was about to ask your husband for advice, too. Perhaps I should ask you instead."

That got me a polite chuckle and their attention.

" Monsieur?" It was the *patron*.

" I am looking for a furnished villa to rent for the summer," I said. " My wife would like it to be here in Mougins. I am wondering which is the best agency to go to."

He shrugged. " Oh, there are several. But it depends on the property."

" Many are handled through the agencies in Cannes," Madame put in. " It is a small villa you want, or . . .?"

" Oh, small, Madame."

" The Agence Mortain?" the injured party suggested.

The *patron* shook his head. " For a small place the Agence Littoral would be better."

As I wrote it down the men began to discuss other agencies. I thought I might as well try one of Mr. Cust's long shots.

I said: " Madame, some friends of ours who stayed in Mougins last year had a villa belonging to a Monsieur Sanger. Do you happen to know which agency handles his property?"

She shook her head. " No, Monsieur. But since you are here, it is easy. You can ask him yourself. Or, better, Madame Sanger. It is she who arranges the business of their houses."

" Monsieur Sanger is here?"

" Naturally. He lives here." She turned to her husband. " Albert, what is the name of Monsieur Sanger's house?"

" Valentine."

" No, no. He changed it when he built the terrace on." She snapped her fingers. " I remember! It is La Sourisette now. I remember because that is not truly a French word at all—La Sourisette."

It was as simple as that.

II

La Sourisette was a converted farmhouse on the outskirts of the town, and stood on the hillside looking towards Grasse. The old cart-track leading down to it had been paved and lined with oleanders. A screen of juniper and pepper trees hid most of the house from the road above. There were no gates, but a neat, professionally-painted sign warned that this was private property and that a bad-tempered dog was kept. The place had an air of well-tended and possibly elegant seclusion.

I stopped the car on the road and wondered how I should tackle Sanger.

If I just went in, stated my business and asked to see Lucia Bernardi, all I would get, presumably, would be a total denial. If I persisted I would be told to leave. If I refused, he would either throw me out himself, or get the police to do the job. If he called in the police that would mean that he was very sure of himself; it would also mean that the police would want an explanation which I couldn't give without compromising the whole assignment. If he didn't call the police, I would be stuck with his denial, while he would have been warned that he was under suspicion.

The problem was made no easier by my having to assume, for the purpose of arriving at a solution, that my employer's hunch was a sound one, when in fact I didn't believe in it at all.

I thought of going back to the centre of the town, reporting to Sy and asking for instructions. Then I remembered his sickening pep-talk of the day before, and changed my mind.

Besides, I *had* done something; I *had* found out where Sanger lived. I didn't want anyone telling me what to do about it at that stage.

I drove to one of Mougins' inns, and took a room. Then I got the telephone number of La Sourisette from the operator and called.

A woman answered. She had a strong Midi accent and sounded like a maid or a housekeeper. I asked for Monsieur Sanger. When she asked me who wanted him, I mumbled something and hung up. At least, he was there.

I tried to put myself in his place.

Forgetting about Lucia Bernardi for the moment, here was a professional crook who had made a good thing out of his profession and invested his takings wisely in house property. He might or might not have retired from the confidence game; but, for the moment at any rate, he was living, comfortably and respectably, under his own name, a French citizen in France. And why not? According to the information from New York, nobody had been able to convict him of anything so far, not even in Germany and Italy where he had operated. In France he would be entitled to feel reasonably secure.

But there would be weaknesses, vulnerable areas, in such a man's position. I already had an indication of one.

When he had bought the three properties in Sète he had given the address of one of them as his own address. There was no legal reason why he should not have done so, even though the building on the land was uninhabitable; it was a valid postal address. It was also, quite clearly, a cover-up; just as the bank forwarding address in Marseille had been a cover-up. Although Sanger had used his real name in buying the properties (a false one would cause trouble if title later had to be proved), he had, by instinct or design, made himself just a little bit hard to find.

He might feel reasonably secure, but he was also cautious and valued the additional protection of obscurity.

I thought I saw a way to use that weakness.

Darkness fell just after six o'clock. I called Paris and reported my telephone number, but did not ask to speak to Sy. I had a drink and then drove back to La Sourisette. As I went down the driveway I could see lights through the screen of trees.

It was a bigger place that it had looked from the road; he had obviously built on to the original structure. The old farm-yard had become a walled garden through which you walked to a main entrance flanked by carved stone urns with trailing plants growing in them. A pair of electrified coach lanterns lighted the approach to a heavy carved oak door. As my footsteps sounded on the flagstones of the garden, a dog inside the house began to bark. As I rang the bell, the barking got louder and angrier. After a moment I could hear the maid with the Midi accent telling the dog to be quiet.

She had one hand on the dog's collar when she opened the door. I was only partially reassured; she was a small woman and the animal was a large Airedale. It barked at me again. The maid clouted it absently.

" Monsieur?"

" I would like to speak with Monsieur Sanger."

" Is he expecting you?"

" No. But I think he will see me." I gave her one of the bureau cards.

" Wait, please."

She shut the door. I waited. After a minute or two she came back, this time without the dog. She gave me back the card.

" Monsieur Sanger regrets that it is impossible for him to see you."

" When will it be possible, Madame?"

" Monsieur Sanger does not wish to be concerned with journalists." She said this haltingly as if repeating it verbatim. " He regrets . . ."

She started to close the door.

" One moment, Madame. Please take this to him."

I wrote on the back of the card: " *To discuss Mr. Patrick Chase,*" and handed it back to her.

She hesitated, then closed the door again.

There was a longer wait this time, but when she re-opened the door she stood aside to let me in.

" For a little while only, please. Monsieur and Madame have arrangements for this evening, you understand."

" Of course."

There was a hallway with a staircase up to the bedrooms

and an archway into the living-room. Sliding glass doors separated the living-room from a broad terrace beyond.

As I entered, a woman in slacks and silk shirt came through the archway.

She was about thirty-five with a good figure and hair bleached almost white. She wore heavy gold bracelets on her wrists and carried a copy of *Réalités*. When I stood aside to let her pass, she glanced at me. The lines in her face were those of a person who smiles easily and attractively, but she wasn't smiling now. She was trying to look as if she were not in the least interested in why I was there.

I murmured: " Good evening, Madame."

She was almost past me by then. The tone of her answering " Monsieur " said that she had already forgotten me.

She went up the stairs. The dog, which had been following her, paused to sniff at me suspiciously and then padded after her.

" This way, Monsieur."

I followed the maid across the living-room—soft carpeting with an Aubusson covering part of it, comfortable furniture, a large Braque on one wall—to a book-lined alcove with logs burning in a carved stone fireplace. A man in an armchair put down a book, took off his glasses and rose to meet me.

Phillip Sanger, alias Patrick Chase, was a tall, slender, agreeable-looking man with an easy, pleasant smile. He was wearing flannel slacks and a cashmere sweater with a silk foulard scarf loosely knotted about his neck. His complexion was sallow but healthy, and his dark, crisp hair had no grey in it. The eyes were alert and expressive ; the mouth was both determined and amused.

He glanced at the card I had sent in and held out his hand.

" Monsieur Maas. I am glad to meet you, if a little puzzled. By the reason you give for the meeting, I mean. Sit down please." He spoke in French with a lilting upward inflection which had the effect of making each sentence sound like a question.

" Thank you. It is very kind of you to see me."

As I sat down, he went on: " Mougins is a long way from Paris. I am curious to learn why an important American magazine should believe that I might know anything of interest to its readers."

I said, in English: "Anything to do with Lucia Bernardi is news at the moment, Mr. Sanger."

He seemed not to have heard the girl's name. He smiled politely. "Ah, you speak English. Yet your name . . ."

"I'm a Netherlander, Mr. Sanger. Which would you prefer to speak, French or English?"

His smile faded a little. "I couldn't care less, Mr. Maas. French or English. Just as long as you'll tell me what we're supposed to be speaking *about*."

"Lucia Bernardi."

He managed to look mildly interested and puzzled at the same time. He was giving a convincing performance; if it *was* a performance. I was beginning to have doubts. The report that Patrick Chase and Phillip Sanger were the same man could have been a mistake.

"Lucia Bernardi?" he said. "Isn't that the woman the police were looking for? I seem to have read something about the case."

"I'm sure you have, Mr. Sanger. The story was in all the papers for several weeks."

He shrugged. "We live a quiet life here. In any case, I'm afraid I still don't see what this has to do with me."

"Lucia Bernardi met Colonel Arbil in Switzerland, at St. Moritz. At the time she was in the company of an American named Patrick Chase. I believe Patrick Chase is a friend of yours, Mr. Sanger. I would like to talk to Mr. Chase about her."

He looked at me a bit helplessly. "Well, yes, I suppose if he knew her well you would want to interview him, but I'm afraid you and your people have put yourselves to a lot of trouble for nothing. I do know a Patrick Chase, yes. He was concerned briefly in an Italian real estate deal in which I was involved for a time. It came to nothing in the end as a matter of fact. But Chase wasn't a friend exactly, scarcely an acquaintance. You must have been misinformed. I don't see how I can help you."

"You couldn't tell me how I might get in touch with him, Mr. Sanger?"

He shook his head regretfully. "He was acting as agent for an Italian hotel group. Perhaps if you were to write to the group . . ." He broke off. "What I don't understand is why you decided to come to *me*. Who gave you *my* name—and this address?"

His performance was still as convincing as ever, but I suddenly felt that the New York report might not have been a mistake after all. "Who gave you my name?" would have been a natural inquiry. The additional three words "—and this address?" were not quite natural if he was only Phillip Sanger. But if he was Patrick Chase as well he would be worried about his cover now. In that case, he would have to find out where the hole was, and how big it had become; and he would have to find out from me.

I looked apologetic. "I'm sorry, Mr. Sanger, you know we never divulge our sources of information."

"Ah yes, the so-called ethics of the profession." For a moment he looked anything but agreeable, then, as if to put away his annoyance, he suddenly stood up. "This has all been so surprising," he said, "that I forgot to ask you if you'd care for a drink. What'll it be, Mr. Maas—Scotch, gin, schnapps?" He was already moving towards a drink table.

"Scotch would be fine, thanks."

"Soda, water, ice?"

"Soda and ice, please."

I watched him as he made the drink. It seemed that there was to be only one, mine. All his movements were very neat and economical. His hands were never uncertain. Everything was well under control. I decided to press him a little.

"Thank you." I took the drink. "What sort of man is Patrick Chase, Mr. Sanger?"

"What does he look like do you mean?"

"Well, how would you describe him? I don't mean his physical appearance necessarily. The general impression."

"Oh, typical American businessman, I suppose."

"Plenty of money?"

"That's hard to say. He was interested in European investments, but mostly as an intermediary I would think."

"An operator?"

"Possibly."

"You're not an American citizen yourself, I believe, Mr. Sanger?"

"No. I was educated in America during the war." He

smiled. "I'm sure those sources of yours told you that. What was the real point of that question?"

"To check for accuracy, Mr. Sanger." I put the drink down. "You see, I was told that a very close connection existed between you and Patrick Chase. Now, you tell me that's untrue. Naturally I would like to know how much of the rest of my information about you is untrue."

The pressure seemed to be working; he went back to the drink table and poured a Campari-soda for himself. Then he turned and looked across the room at me.

"I don't have much time to waste," he said; "but if you'll tell me briefly what information you have, I'll be glad to tell you whether it's true or not."

I didn't answer immediately. He had to feel that by helping me his position would be made more secure than if he just kept his mouth shut, and I wasn't sure how to put that proposition to him.

I said: "I would like to feel that you were able to trust me first."

He came back to his chair but he didn't sit down again. He was watching me intently now.

"Trust you with what?"

"The truth as you see it, Mr. Sanger. Frankly, I think that the information I have might be very useful and important to you. In fact, I'm certain it would. But I have to be certain that I'm going to get some information from you in return."

He smiled again. "That rather sounds as if *you* have to trust *me*, doesn't it?"

"Not altogether. You see, the person I'm interested in is Lucia Bernardi. Not you, Mr. Sanger, not Patrick Chase. But if I can't get the story I want on Lucia Bernardi, I'll have to do the best I can with a story about all three of you."

He sat down. I was glad he did, because for a moment I had thought that he was going to throw his glass in my face. I couldn't really have blamed him if he had.

"That sounds a bit like blackmail," he said.

I picked up my drink again: I needed it. "I'm afraid that's how it's meant to sound. I'm sorry. I don't like this any more than you do, I assure . . ."

"Oh for God's sake!" he said angrily. "Not the sob-stuff,

too! Come on! I'm calling you. Let's have the information. And it had better be good, because if it isn't, I'm going to break your teeth!"

A different Mr. Sanger had appeared, one decidedly less courtly than the other. It was a comforting apparition.

"Very well," I said. "First, you wanted to know how I found this address. Six months ago you bought some property in Sète."

"What of it?"

"Correspondence about the purchase was reported when Patrick Chase's baggage was searched by a U.S. Treasury agent at the time. I don't know where the search was made. Maybe you do. The report was made with a copy to Interpol. It said that Sanger and Chase were the same man."

"Then why haven't I had you bastards on my neck before?"

"Because the St. Moritz police check on you was made long before the report had been filed. So they never connected Lucia Bernardi with Phillip Sanger. They only connected her with Patrick Chase."

He eyed me bitterly but said nothing.

"Of course," I went on, "sooner or later, when the Swiss start double-checking, your name is bound to come into it, and the police, as well as a lot of other people, will be invading your privacy. Unless, that is . . ." I paused.

"Unless what?" But he knew.

"Unless Lucia Bernardi is found. As soon as she is, they'll automatically lose interest in her former associates."

His response was ambiguous. He muttered "Shit," and went back to the drink table. He put some gin in the Campari-soda.

I stood up, so that I could watch his reaction, before I asked: "Have *you* any idea where she is?"

There was no reaction at all. He ignored the question and called across the living-room: "*Chérie, viens!*"

The woman in slacks came in from the hall, where she had evidently been standing to overhear our conversation.

"Shall I tell Marie that we will be three for dinner?" she asked.

"Yes, darling, you'd better do that," he said wearily.

As she turned away she looked back and smiled at me.

"You *can* stay to dinner, I hope, Monsieur Maas."

"Thank you. I shall be delighted."

She smiled again. The smile bothered me. It wasn't just polite. For some reason, she seemed genuinely pleased.

III

Phillip Sanger, alias Patrick Chase, had met Lucia Bernardi in Paris.

"I was working on a deal at the time," he said.

"What sort of deal?"

He sighed. "Look, Mr. Maas, it's Lucia you want to know about, isn't it? If you're going to ask irrelevant questions, we're all going to get bored. As you have already found out, I deal in real estate, buying properties, improving them, then selling or leasing them. That's my business, and there's nothing in the record that says different. Right?"

"Whatever you say. Were you using the Patrick Chase alias at the time?"

"No, I never did in France." He assumed his most candid and convincing manner. "Frankly, I use the Chase name only for taxation purposes on foreign deals. I want to make that clear. It is not an alias."

"*Un nom de guerre*," said Madame gently.

"That's right," he said. "You don't call a corporate set-up an alias, do you? No. Well, there you are."

I thought of reminding him that corporate set-ups did not usually involve the use of false American passports, but decided to let it go. After all, I was a guest in the house; a blackmailing guest admittedly, but still a guest. There was no reason why he should not be allowed to keep up some sort of front.

"So you met her in Paris. What was she doing?"

"Working in a shop. You know those places on the Champs Elysées and near the Madeleine where they sell perfumes at a discount to foreign tourists? One of those. I was in there with a German friend who was buying a lot of stuff to take home to his wife. That's when I spotted her. She interested me."

"She is very beautiful," Madame said drily. "You know, Mr. Maas, those pictures in the newspapers and magazines do not really do her justice. And she is intelligent also."

"You know her too, Madame?"

"Oh, I met her, yes! Phillip values my judgment in these matters. It is, after all, necessary for our business, but one could not expect him to use his wife in this way."

It was said quite calmly and sensibly and with a smile. You could not hear the bitterness, but you could feel it. Obviously, Madame Sanger had once been her husband's partner in crime. It was natural that she should be a little jealous of the various younger women who had been her business successors.

I glanced at Sanger. He was looking bland.

"You know how it is," he said casually.

I did, but I wanted to hear how he explained it. "No," I said, "I don't think I follow."

He made a deprecating gesture. "You're in a deal with a man. You want to sell, he wants to buy, or maybe the other way around." But mostly sell, I thought, mostly sell. "It's a game," he went on; "everybody with a *misère* hand of course. But you know something? If you can make the other guy think he's cheating you, you're in good shape. So you let him see something he'll want and try to steal."

"Such as your mistress?"

"Sure. Make him feel guilty or nervous, and he won't think too clearly about business." His eyes flickered in his wife's direction. "Only the girl's not for real, of course. She's just a . . . an element. It's psychological warfare," he concluded a trifle lamely.

His wife gave him a fond smile, and briskly rang the hand-bell for the maid to serve the coffee.

I went with him back into the living-room.

"When was it that you met Lucia?" I asked.

"Oh, let's see. About two years ago, maybe a bit less. She'd been working here in the South during the season, and hadn't been more than a month or so in Paris."

"Working in the scent-shop?"

"Yes. And I'll tell you what interested me most about her. Oh sure, she looked great, but she had something extra. It was the way she handled figures."

"Money, you mean?'

"In a way. You know how it is when they start writing out the bill in those shops? First they have to figure the discounts on pieces of scratch paper, then they have to convert the francs into dollars or whatever, then there's the tax and addition. It takes for ever usually. Well, with Lucia it didn't. She did it in her head, quicker than she could write. Real fast mental arithmetic."

"It didn't do her much good in business when she was in Antibes."

"I'll bet that was her partner's fault, not hers."

"Then what?"

"Adèle and I made friends with her, and we all had a little chat together."

"And there was a meeting of the minds."

"She's very quick. No nonsense. She liked the money."

"So off you went to St. Moritz."

"No, there was a deal in Munich first. We went on to St. Moritz from there."

"And found Colonel Arbil. He was the next sucker, eh?"

He stared at me in blank amazement. "Arbil a sucker? Whatever gave you that idea?"

"That's what the police thought. That's when they checked you out with Interpol. You knew they had you under surveillance, didn't you?"

He laughed. "The Swiss are always putting people under surveillance. It doesn't mean a thing."

"Then why did you skip to Italy?"

"Skip?" He sighed in exasperation. "I left. Look, do you want *me* to tell it or not?"

"Go ahead."

"What happened was this. Arbil was there for the bob-sledding, only he didn't do any. He took one look at Lucia and fell in a big way. We couldn't get him out of our hair. And then after a few days Lucia took the tumble, too, and didn't want him out. She wanted me out instead."

"So you went?"

"We talked it over. You know, Lucia's no tramp. She doesn't sleep around. She was just crazy about him. She offered to give me back her cut on the Munich deal, if I'd call it quits. I knew then there was no sense in trying to persuade her to stay in the partnership."

" So you took the money."

He shook his head. " She's a good kid, Lucia, but . . ." He broke off as if he had forgotten what he had been about to say.

His wife had come back into the room. She finished the sentence for him. " She would not be malicious, you understand, but it was better if she *had* to be discreet about our business, for her *own* good as well as ours."

" West German income taxes, that's what Adèle means," he explained firmly.

She smiled. " Of course, taxes. Everyone has to be discreet about income taxes, don't they?"

The maid came in with coffee. Sanger got out brandy glasses.

" When did you see Lucia last?" I asked him.

" The day I left St. Moritz."

His wife was handing me a cup of coffee. Her hand stopped for an instant, and she half turned her head as if she wanted to supplement his statement in some way. Then she seemed to change her mind. I took the coffee, thanked her and put it down on the small table beside me.

He was across the room pouring brandy. I lowered my voice so that he would have to strain his ears to hear. " You see, Madame, I am in a difficulty. I am under considerable pressure from our New York office to get a story on Lucia Bernardi. You heard your husband say that I was a blackmailer. You heard me admit it. I don't like the situation, but there is nothing I can do about it. I must have your husband's help."

" I am sure he will do what he can."

" Of course I will." He put a brandy down beside me.

I looked up at him. " Are you sure you don't know where she is, Mr. Sanger?"

" If I did, I'd tell you."

" Would you?"

" Why not?"

" Then, if you really don't know, how are you going to help me?"

He sat down opposite me and picked up his coffee. " Find her for you, of course."

" How will you know where to look?"

" I have a few ideas." He sipped his coffee and then put it down again. "I'll help you all I can," he said ; "I'll help you, because it's in my own interest to do so. But it's going to take time."

I let the last statement go. Obviously, he was going to play for time. If he did not know where she was, he could only try to string me along and hope for the best.

" Tell me about these ideas you have."

He did not answer me directly, but looked at his wife. " Honey, you remember when you first met Lucia and we took her to dinner at Fouquet's? Remember she talked about ski-ing and how crazy she was about it?"

His wife nodded. " Yes, I remember."

" Well, when I decided to go to St. Moritz we got to talking about it again. She was upset because she'd left all her ski things in her aunt's house in Menton. She wanted to go down there and get them. Naturally, I didn't want that, so I promised her she could have a new outfit in St. Moritz. She wasn't too happy about it. Said her own boots were better than anything she could buy new. While we were on the subject she told me that until she went to Paris she'd gone ski-ing every year since she was a kid. Her parents used to take her up to a place called Piera-Cava in the mountains above Nice. It was only a small village, she said, cheap and not at all fashionable, but even though the slopes weren't very good, she used to love it. It's in France near the Italian frontier by Sospel, about forty kilometres from Nice."

" You think she'd go there, where she'd be known?" I asked.

" Not to a hotel or *pension* or anything like that ; no, of course not."

" She had friends there?"

He grinned. " Not friends exactly. But she told me a story about the place that stuck in my mind. You know about that dike partner of hers, the one at Antibes?"

" Henriette Colin?"

" That's right—Henriette. Well, three years ago, before their business folded, Lucia took Henriette up to Piera-Cava for a week or so after Christmas. Henriette couldn't ski and hated everything. The heating went wrong in this cockeyed hotel they were staying at, and the management had to pass out hot bricks wrapped in newspaper so that the guests could warm their hands. Henriette wouldn't go out at all. She just sat wrapped in blankets and nursing a hot brick by a stove they'd lighted in the hotel bar. Lucia wanted her to go back down to Antibes, but she wouldn't go back alone. Lucia wanted to stay and ski? Okay, she could ski. Henriette would do the suffering. And then she found a friend."

He got up and poured me another brandy.

"Henriette found a friend?"

"That's right. An old lady who used to come into the bar for cigarettes. They got talking. Henriette found out about her from the hotel proprietor. The old lady was the widow of some big industrialist and stinking rich. She had a big chalet about a kilometre outside the village, and except for a married couple, her servants, who lived in, she lived by herself. Lonely, of course, and a bit peculiar, Henriette was told. The proprietor didn't say how peculiar, and Henriette wasn't put off. When the old lady told her how warm her house was and asked Henriette and Lucia if they wouldn't like to move in with her for the rest of their stay, Henriette couldn't wait. Lucia went along. Anything that would make Henriette less of a bore was all right with her. Besides, she liked the old lady and felt sorry for her. They would save on the hotel, too. That would count with Lucia. So they moved in." He paused.

"And the old lady turned out to be very peculiar, indeed, I suppose."

He nodded. "She was an ether-drinker."

"A what?"

"She drank ether. She was quite used to it. She could drink five hundred grammes a day when she was on a bender."

"You never told me this before, Phillip," said Madame Sanger. She was not reproachful, only interested.

"I'd forgotten it myself until I began to wonder where Lucia might have gone to hide out," he said.

"But why should she go there?"

"You haven't heard the rest of it. You see, the old girl wasn't on the stuff all the time. For a week or ten days she'd be all right. Then she'd have herself driven into Nice and come back with a big blue bottle. The spree would last for two or three days. You know, for those who just want to unwind and get stoned, and really don't care what the stuff tastes like, ether's not bad as a drink. It's quicker than liquor, it's less toxic than liquor, and there's almost no hangover. I'm speaking relatively. Of course, some people just throw up at the thought of it. It takes all kinds. When Henriette realised what she'd got into, she couldn't take it and went back to Antibes. Lucia stayed on."

"But why?" Madame was asking the questions now. I let her. They were my own anyway.

He thought for a moment. "Well, I think for one thing she was glad to get rid of Henriette. In fact, I wouldn't be surprised if that was the moment when their business really began to fold. Then, there was the ski-ing. And then . . . well, I don't think the old lady and her ether would worry Lucia too much. She wasn't scared of people. She wouldn't run away."

"She ran away from that villa in Zürich," I reminded him.

"Then she must have had very good reasons," he replied.

"You said there was a married couple living with the old lady. If she were there now they'd be bound to talk."

"That's the funny part," he said; "they wouldn't. Lucia told me that those two never said a word in the village about what went on with the old lady. The village knew, of course, because every now and then she'd come in loaded to the gills and smelling like an operating theatre. But the couple never gossiped. They weren't local people, you see." He shrugged. "Anyway, I think it's worth trying."

"I know how to reach Henriette Colin," I said. "I could get the address from her, I suppose."

He pursed his lips. "Bit risky for you, that, isn't it? You'd be putting the idea into her head. Supposing she told someone else. She might even tell the police. No, I think the best way is just to go there and make a few inquiries. It's late in the season there now. There'll only be the locals. It shouldn't be difficult. You could go to-morrow morning."

And be back in the evening, having wasted a day, I thought. It was an unreasonable reaction, I knew. I had requested his help, in no uncertain terms, and appeared to be getting it. But there was something about the "you" in his "you could go to-morrow morning" that I didn't quite like. I had an uncomfortable vision of myself driving all over Southern France finding remote villages, while he sat cosily by his log fire dreaming up the next day's wild-goose chase.

"You said you had a few ideas," I said. "What are the others?"

"She could be in a private sanatorium. Have you thought of that?"

"She couldn't be there without several people knowing it. That means a lot of connivance."

"There has been a suggestion going around that the police know where she is, but aren't saying."

"A couple of newspapers have made the suggestion. Have you any way of knowing if it's true?"

"If you mean am I in with the police here, the answer's no. Anyway, I still think that Piera-Cava's your best bet."

I put my brandy down. "*Our* best bet, Mr. Sanger," I said. "My deadline is Friday, eleven p.m. Eastern Standard Time. I already have enough from you to justify a follow-up piece on the missing bikini girl, and, if I don't get anything better, that's what I'll have to file. To-day's Tuesday. I suggest that we *both* go to Piera-Cava to-morrow. If, by any chance, Lucia Bernardi is there, she would be more likely to co-operate, I think, if you were on hand to explain the situation. I'm not concerned with putting the police on to her. I simply want her story of what happened in Zürich and why. Then she can disappear again if she wants to."

Madame Sanger leaned forward. "Do you really mean that, Monsieur Maas?"

"Of course. As far as I am aware she hasn't committed any crime—at least not in France or Switzerland. I just want the story. But if *I* told her that, she might not believe me. I think she'd be more likely to believe your husband."

"And if you don't find her in Piera-Cava?" she asked.

"Then I can't waste any more time. I'll have to go back to Paris."

Sanger laughed shortly. "And get to work spoiling our lives, I take it."

It was not a question. I said nothing.

He sighed. "Okay. I'll come with you. Ten o'clock?"

"I'll pick you up." I rose to leave, and noticed that Madame Sanger was smiling again. She had seemed pleased when I had said I would stay to dinner. Now she seemed pleased that I was going. I could scarcely blame her for that.

IV

When I got back to the inn, I called Sy at his apartment. He and his wife were reputed to give good parties, and, judging from the talk and laughter in the background, there was one in progress at that moment.

"Yes, Piet. How are you doing?" He sounded as if he had had quite a few drinks.

"I think I may have a lead."

"No kidding. Well, you see?" He was guardedly pleased.

"I said 'I think,' and I don't want to say anything more about it now. I'll probably know for sure by to-morrow night."

"Don't you want to tell me more than that?"

"I'd rather not. I'll tell you one thing. There might be *a* story. Whether or not there is also *the* story, I don't know yet."

"He isn't going to like just *a* story, I'm afraid."

"He may not even get that. I can't tell. Oh, there's one thing. Is it all right with you if I buy a camera?"

"To photograph a girl?"

"More likely a man. But I don't want to hire a local photographer down here."

"For God's sake no!" He paused. "Do you know how to use a camera, Piet? Properly, I mean."

"Well, you just point it and go *click*, don't you? I expect the man in the shop will show me how to load it."

Suddenly, he raised his voice. "Cut it out, dammit! I asked you a question."

"The answer is yes, and I don't like being shouted at. Now, do I buy a camera?"

"Okay, okay. But look—I have to know what's going on. I know you have to be careful on that phone, but you don't have to spell it out. What have you done? Have you located our man?"

"I'll know to-morrow."

"Then you don't really know yet if there might even be *a* story."

"I'll tell you to-morrow."

" My God, Piet, if you've got something and you foul it up because you're too bloody-minded to even discuss . . ."

I cut in before he could finish. " I've made some progress. We'll both know if there's anything worth discussing tomorrow. I can't make it any clearer than that. Good night."

I hung up and waited for him to call back. He didn't. As long as the thing smelled, even faintly, of failure and discredit, I would be left alone. That suited me.

I had bought some more sleeping pills before leaving Paris. I took three and was awake again in five hours.

It was still dark, and for a time I stayed in bed thinking about the Sangers and the Lucia Bernardi who had been crazy about Arbil. Then I got up and had another look through the photo-copy of the file on the story which I had brought with me.

The biographical material on Colonel Arbil was not particularly revealing.

He had been born in 1917, the son of a wool merchant, at Kirkuk in Southern Kurdistan, then a part of the Ottoman Empire. After World War I, it had become part of Iraq. In 1932, when the British mandate ended and Iraq became an independent state, he had been accepted by the army as a cadet. He had been commissioned in 1936 and later sent to England for specialised training in communications and intelligence work. In 1946, a captain by then, he had again been sent to England, this time to attend a course at the British Staff College. While in England, he had married (by civil ceremony) an Englishwoman. She had later divorced him on the grounds of desertion. In 1958, he had participated in the army *coup d'état* of Brigadier Kassim which had overthrown the government of King Faisal and established a republic in Iraq. Soon after, he had been appointed Director of Internal Security Services, a post embracing civil as well as military police powers. It had been in this capacity that he had attended the Geneva conference during which he had decided not to return to Iraq.

A researcher had done some work on the Kurdish nationalist movement, of which Colonel Arbil had been a supporter.

The Kurds, I learned, are an ancient people of mountain origin who inhabit a region stretching from Soviet Armenia, through the north-east corner of Iraq to Syria, and from Kermanshah in Iran to Erzurum in Turkey. They thus form minorities in five separate states. There are approximately four million of them, mostly of the Sunni, or orthodox, Moslem faith. The Kurdish part of Iraq includes the rich oil-fields of Kirkuk and Mosul.

In 1920, the Allied treaty of peace with Turkey, known as the Treaty of Sèvres, created an autonomous Kurdish state; but this treaty was never ratified, and was later replaced by the Treaty of Lausanne, which divided Kurdistan.

In 1927 a Kurdish independence movement, the Khoibun, came into being. In Iraq alone there have been five major Kurdish revolts. In 1946, a Soviet-sponsored independent Kurdish republic was set up at Mahabad in Iran. It lasted eleven months. Then the Iranian army succeeded in recapturing the area.

According to the researcher, Alexander the Great, Xenophon, Marco Polo and the Peace Treaty Commission of 1919 had all had dealings with the Kurds and all come to similar conclusions about them. In the Commission's words, the Kurds were " a fierce and predatory people, unsafe to trifle with." A modern expert on the Middle East had noted that " their tendency to shoot on sight at moving objects has kept outside interference in their affairs to a minimum." On the other hand, they had always been more than ready to interfere in the affairs of their neighbours. The periodic massacres of Armenians had nearly all been the work of Kurds.

Colonel Arbil had been a Kurd, and also Director of Internal Security Services, with police powers. The combination did not sound pleasant. I wondered how much Lucia Bernardi had really known about him.

Soon after nine o'clock I walked into the town and found a camera-shop which had a second-hand Rolleiflex for sale. I loaded it in the shop and put some extra rolls of film in my pocket. Then I went back to the inn, got the car and drove to La Sourisette.

I stopped half-way down the driveway and took a roll of pictures of the house. Then I reloaded the camera and went on down to the entrance.

I left the camera in the car when I went to the front door. The Airedale barked and the maid came with her hand on its collar as before. When she recognised me she asked me to come in. I told her to tell Monsieur Sanger that I was there and that I would wait outside in the car for him.

I did not have long to wait. He came out looking very " country-gentleman " in tweeds. I got two good shots of him before he even saw what I was doing. As he started to protest I got a close shot with the sun right in his eyes, and Madame Sanger in the background by the front door. I hoped that there was enough depth of focus to make it good for both of them, but I knew that I had him all right.

" What's the idea?" he demanded.

" Insurance," I said.

Madame retreated hastily into the house. I saw him toying with the idea of trying to take the camera from me and deciding against it. I knew that I didn't look impressive enough to stop him ; he had simply judged it wiser not to antagonise me at that stage.

He stared at my rented car. " You want me to go to Piera-Cava in that?"

" It runs."

" I have a Lancia in the garage. That would be more comfortable."

" We don't have far to go."

" As you please." He smiled patronisingly as I put the camera in the glove compartment and locked it. " Do I detect an element of distrust?" he asked.

" You do."

He suggested that we should by-pass Cannes and pick up the autoroute by Antibes. There was a silence after that until we reached Nice. Then he directed me through the back streets of the town on to the Sospel road.

The traffic was light. Above Escarène the road was covered with slushy snow which became firmer as we climbed. The car heater became necessary. At Piera-Cava, the road had been cleared by plough, but there was deep snow on the slopes and the trees were white. It was still winter there.

" There'll be ski-ers up here for Easter if the snow lasts," Sanger remarked.

Piera-Cava is a scattered collection of small hotels and *pensions* with alpine views. When we arrived it was nearly lunch-time. At Sanger's suggestion we stopped at one of the hotels which advertised a bar-restaurant.

The bar was warm but empty. In the restaurant, a waiter wearing an apron was setting a solitary table for six, presumably the staff. He agreed to bring us drinks and we went back to the bar.

"Do you want to ask the questions, or shall I?" Sanger said.

"You know the background better than I. Maybe you'd better do it."

"As you please."

The way he went about it was interesting. If I had been asking the questions I would have begun by inventing some laborious excuse for my curiosity. I had stayed in Piera-Cava the previous year; I had met a rich old lady with a big chalet and two servants who had been charming and hospitable, and now that I was thinking of returning for the Easter holiday I had completely forgotten her name, and so on.

Sanger's approach was no less devious but far more efficient. As soon as he heard the waiter coming in with the drinks he raised his voice slightly and began tapping the table in front of us.

"You, a layman, say that it is impossible, that the person would be poisoned. I, a doctor, tell you that such a person can become immune. Ether is less toxic than some alcohols. One may argue that a person who drinks ether is unusual, but she is not necessarily insane if she drinks four hundred grammes of ether. If she is used to it, she could drink as much as five hundred grammes with safety."

The waiter was standing over us with the drinks listening fascinated to every word. Sanger glanced up at him.

"Thank you, my friend."

The waiter served the drinks, Sanger turned to me again. "And she can go on doing it too. You don't believe me?" An idea seemed suddenly to occur to him. He looked up at the waiter. "Ah, I will prove it. Waiter, have you ever heard of a person drinking ether?"

The waiter grinned. "Yes, Doctor."

Sanger grinned back. "Yes, of course! What is her name, the widow, Madame . . .?" He snapped his fingers, trying to get the name off the tip of his tongue.

"Madame Lehman, Doctor."

"Yes, Madame Lehman. Five hundred grammes a day at times, isn't it? Tell my friend here."

The waiter looked at us both a little uncertainly. "Oh yes, that is what it used to be from time to time."

"Used to be?" said Sanger sharply.

"Madame Lehman died six months ago, Monsieur. She had a heart-attack."

There was a brief, strained silence; then Sanger became professional again. "I'm sorry to hear that," he said quietly. "Of course, I told her she had a cardiac condition when she consulted me last year. I had not expected the end so soon, however. What has happened to the chalet, and the servants?"

"Ah, Doctor, the servants went back to the north where they had come from. She left them a little something in her will, you understand. Her nephew, who inherited the rest, sold the chalet to a Belgian family."

For the waiter's benefit Sanger played his part unflinchingly to the end. He looked significantly at me, and tapped the table again. "But she died of a heart-attack, you see, my friend. Not from ether."

The waiter grinned and left us.

I swallowed half my drink. "I think we might do better for lunch if we went back down to Nice," I said. "That is, unless you want to eat here."

He shook his head.

V

We went to a restaurant where he was known, in the rue de France. He had been glum and silent on the drive down, but the *maître d'hôtel*'s warm greeting seemed to raise his spirits a trifle. When the food had been ordered he leaned back in his chair and gave me a small, reproachful smile.

"Want to talk some more about the sanatorium idea?" he said.

"Not unless it's more than just an idea."

"You're surely not serious about involving Adèle and me?"

"Perfectly serious."

"Pretty unfair, isn't it? What do you gain? A pat on the back maybe? A small bonus? Think what we have to lose for that."

"Only a little privacy and a local reputation to which you are not really entitled."

" *Only!* My God, man . . ." He broke off, and lowered his voice. " Look, Maas, I don't think you like this any more than I do. In fact, I know you don't. So why go on with it?"

" Did you ever give a sucker an even break, Mr. Sanger?"

He shook his head slowly. " It's no use, Maas, you're not the tough, rough type. And you are a European. That's not how you think."

" You seem very sure about me."

He looked surprised. " Naturally, I'm sure. Did you think I wouldn't be? I spent half the night on the phone to Paris, getting a run-down on you."

" I see. Invading *my* privacy?"

He shook his head again. " You don't have any. You have friends, people who are sorry about what happened to you, but you don't have privacy, not as I understand it. Four phone calls out, four phone calls back, that's all it needed."

I didn't like this ; I didn't like it at all ; but there was nothing I could say.

" Naturally," he went on, " I didn't get everything. I didn't have the time."

" I'm sorry."

He ignored the sarcasm.

" Of course," he said, " you had a difficult childhood— parents killed in the Rotterdam bombing, evacuation to England, war orphan and all that—but you weren't a very young child and you had better luck than some. There was that London business associate of your father's to take care of you. You were sent to a good school. And after the war you were able to claim your parents' estate. Not a lot of money perhaps, but quite a handy sum for a young man just going to college. What went wrong?"

" I'm sure that's a rhetorical question."

" Not really. Oh, I know how the money went, yes. It's the attempted suicide that puzzles me."

I said nothing. He took a sip of his Campari-soda and went on.

" I could understand that you would be depressed. The failure of the magazine would account for that. But it wasn't a disgraceful failure, I'm told. It had a considerable *succès d'estime* with people who count. It was even quoted on the floor of the United Nations. If you failed, it was because you refused to compromise the standards you had set yourself. Your capital was insufficient to support complete honesty. True, you were a part owner, but you must have known that experimental magazines are always highly speculative ventures. Besides, you are young and talented, and you have friends. Your reputation stood high even though you were bankrupt. Why should you try to destroy yourself?"

What could I answer? *"That's easy, Mr. Sanger. It wasn't just the magazine. I just came home early that day and found the woman who was living with me in my own bed with another man. I tried to kill him and found I couldn't. In fact, he knocked me cold. Three failures on the same day were too many. So I let myself in for a fourth."* It would not be an honest reply, but it would sound like one for a moment. But then the inevitable question would come: *" Surely many other men have suffered worse humiliations without trying to kill themselves? Why couldn't you?"* There were two courteous answers ; one, the gentler, couched in the aseptic language of psychiatry, the other in the language of the moralist. My own personal answer had to be: *" Go to hell."*

I said: "I don't think that's a matter I want to discuss with you, Mr. Sanger."

He nodded understandingly. "I once knew a man who tried to shoot himself. He was a little drunk, and it also happened that he didn't know anything about heavy revolvers—the way they kick, you know. As a result, he missed himself completely. It made him feel very silly, and he would never talk about it afterwards. There must have been an element of catharsis in the act, though, for he never tried again. He lived for another ten years and died in a plane crash."

The service of food interrupted him for a while, but when the waiters had gone he returned to the attack.

" Have you ever thought of starting up your magazine again?"

" Many times."

" But of course it would take quite a bit of capital."

" And still be highly speculative."

" Less so, surely, now. After all, you must have learned a lot of lessons from the first failure. You wouldn't make the same mistakes twice."

I was getting very tired of this. "I should stick to real estate, if I were you, Mr. Sanger," I said. "It's much safer than publishing."

But he was not to be put off. "You think so?" He chuckled. "Well, perhaps you're right. I must say I like bricks and mortar, and land even more. Tangible assets. But also one likes to speculate occasionally." He raised his eyes to meet mine. "And if at the same time one can avoid some unpleasant notoriety, that makes the venture additionally satisfying."

I was suddenly curious. "Do you realise how *much* money you're talking about?" I asked.

"I know the amount of capital you had to start with the first time. Costs have risen since then. Presumably you'd need more. Around thirty thousand dollars, I'd say."

I didn't answer for a moment. If he was serious, and at least it looked as if he was, he must be either a lot richer than I had supposed, or much more desperate. If it was desperation, then there had to be more at stake than his privacy and local reputation. It might be that he had depended too much on the protection of an alias, and that public exposure of Phillip Sanger as Patrick Chase could lead to a criminal conviction.

He was watching me intently. I could almost feel the tension in him. He was a cheat and a swindler, of course, and one is not supposed to waste compassion on crooks. All the same, I felt sorry for him. I always find it saddening when success, even ill-gotten financial success, turns to failure. The tolling of the bell, no doubt.

I sighed. "It's tempting, Mr. Sanger. I can't tell you how tempting. But you'd better understand the position. There's not much that I can do. I've already told my people in Paris that if I don't get *the* story on Lucia Bernardi there will be *a* story concerning her. So they know that a story exists. So . . ."

He broke in quickly. "Do they know what the story is, the details about me?"

"Not yet."

"Well, then . . ."

"Mr. Sanger, if I don't deliver, they'll guess what's happened and have someone else down here in a few hours.

They'll charter private planes, they'll tear the place apart to get the story. Even if I were prepared to try, I couldn't kill it all by myself, not now."

"Not if . . .?"

"You'd be wasting your money, Mr. Sanger. If it's any consolation to you, I'll tell you this. The fact that I file the story doesn't necessarily mean that it'll get into print. They may decide that, as the Arbil affair has dropped out of the news lately, there isn't enough meat in this new material to bring it back again. They may see it that way, they may not. I don't know."

He grasped at the straw. "Who will decide? Your people in Paris?"

I had a vision of him taking his thirty-thousand-dollar offer to Sy, and wondered if I knew enough about Sy to predict his reaction.

"No," I replied; "our people in New York."

He brooded for a moment; then his mouth took on a mulish look. "They'll have to watch themselves on the libel angle," he muttered.

"They always do, especially with the European edition."

"A French citizen in a French court could make things pretty rough for an American magazine."

"Because they said that you, Phillip Sanger, are also Patrick Chase? Oh, no. That's a matter of record with Interpol now. The explanation of *why* you are also Patrick Chase could be libellous; but if it is, they'll leave it out."

He was silent for a moment, then he pushed his plate away.

"Do you mind if we get back now?" he said. "Adèle will be worrying. I could call her, but they listen at the exchange." There was a pause. "Not that I've anything good to tell her," he went on heavily, "but she'll be waiting to know the worst." He looked me in the eyes again. "If it was just me I wouldn't care too much. It's her."

He may have been speaking the truth.

The drive back to Mougins was as silent as the rest of our journey had been that day. Once, I noticed him eyeing the glove compartment with the camera in it. I suppose he was wondering whether it would be worth his while to use force to destroy the photographs I had of him. Evidently, he decided that it wouldn't. When I stopped at the bottom of the driveway to La Sourisette, he got out and walked into the house without a word.

I watched him go, and sat there for a moment after he had disappeared. I would have liked his thirty thousand dollars. It was a pity, I thought, that there had been no way for me to take them.

I drove back to the inn.

He had been right about his wife's anxiety, but wrong about the nature of it.

She was sitting waiting for me at one of the tables in the garden of the inn. There was a drink in front of her.

She got up as I approached. She was wearing a dress instead of slacks. It made her look younger.

I started to utter some polite phrase, but she cut me short.

"I must speak to you, Monsieur."

"Of course, Madame. I'm afraid my room is not very big. We could go into the bar."

She glanced around at the garden. The *concierge* could see us from his window, but there was nobody there who could overhear us. "This will do," she said.

We sat down at her table. I thought that I had better get the thing over as quickly as I could.

"I'm sorry to have to tell you, Madame, that our journey to-day was completely unsuccessful," I began.

"Oh, I knew it would be." She tried, not quite successfully, to smile. "But my husband really thought that there was a chance she might be there. I could not tell him that she wasn't."

"You mean you knew that the old ether woman was dead?" I was being very stupid. The previous night she hadn't known the old woman had existed until Sanger had talked about her.

"I mean that I knew Lucia was not in Piera-Cava."

"Because you knew that she was somewhere else?"

"Yes."

"And your husband didn't?" The great reporter's razor-sharp mind was hacking its way through to the obvious.

She nodded. "Last night," she said, "I asked you a question. You said that you were not concerned with bringing Lucia forward for the police and others to take possession of her, that all you wanted was to interview her; that then she could be private again. I asked you if you really meant that. Do you still mean it?"

"Certainly. Do you know where Lucia is, Madame?"

She hesitated, then nodded. "Yes, I know. She came to me for help—to *me*, a person who scarcely knew her. I think perhaps she had liked and trusted me, even though I had only met her twice, and then only for a few hours."

"Where is she, Madame?"

She shook her head, but it was a movement of indecision rather than refusal. I waited. She sipped her drink and stared at a bowl of hyacinths on the next table.

I said: "Your husband told me last night that he had not seen her since he left St. Moritz. That wasn't true, was it?"

Her eyes returned to me. "No. My husband is too cautious sometimes. It would have made no difference if he had told you. We saw her in Zürich about three months ago. It was an accidental meeting in the foyer of our hotel. She had been shopping. Colonel Arbil was not with her. She lunched with us. It became obvious that she was troubled about something."

"Colonel Arbil?"

"In a way, but not in the sense of being unhappy. Of course, I know now that she was frightened. It was the time when he began to put burglar alarms in at the villa. She did not speak of that to us, but when my husband was out of the room taking a telephone call, she asked me if I thought that it would be difficult for Colonel Arbil to get a *permis de séjour* in France. I said I thought he should talk first to the French Consul-General in Berne. Then she asked if she could write to me in France. I gave her my address here."

"With your real name?"

"Only my maiden name. But my husband would not have liked even that, so I did not tell him." There was the near-smile again. "It did not seem important at the time. Now, perhaps, it can save us."

"Save you?"

"If Lucia had not known how to reach me, I could not have arranged for you to talk with her." She pressed her hands together. "That will save us, won't it, Monsieur Maas? You

will not have to tell anyone—your editor, the police, anyone
at all—about us?"

"If I can see Lucia Bernardi and talk to her, that's all I
want. As far as I am concerned, you and your husband will
be completely forgotten."

"Even if it means that you cannot show the world how
clever you have been to succeed where so many others have
failed?"

"I've not been clever, Madame. I've been lucky. If I say
nothing at all, though, it may *look* as if I have been clever. I
take it you don't want your husband to know either."

"I will tell him now. I had to be sure that I could rely
upon you first. Can I, Monsieur?"

I said, as gently as I could: "I think you will have to. My
guess is that she is living in one of the small houses you and
your husband own. Would it be at Roquebrune or Cagnes-
sur-Mer?"

She looked shaken. "I can't tell you that."

There was no sense in pressing her. If it became absolutely
necessary, I could reseach the archives in Nice for the houses
he owned, and find the right one by a process of elimination.

"It's not really important," I said. "You take care of the
leasing of these houses you and your husband own, I believe.
Is that the way you were able to take her in—just by renting
her a house?"

She nodded. "Some of them are empty at this time of
year."

"And she is willing to be interviewed?"

"She understands that I need your help."

"When can the interview take place?"

"To-night."

"Where?"

"She will telephone you as soon as she hears from me. She
will use my name, Adèle, in case the operators are listening."

"She understands that I will have to see her and identify
her, I hope. This just can't be done on the telephone, you
know."

"I thought that might be the case. Providing you will do
exactly as she asks, she will agree to meet with you." She rose
to her feet. "If you will wait here I will use the telephone
inside."

She was away five minutes. When she returned she picked up the sweater she had left lying on her chair, but did not sit down again.

"Adèle will call you in a few minutes," she said. "I must go home now and talk to my husband." She hesitated. "I will be interested to read your article, Monsieur."

"Your name won't be in it, Madame, I can assure you."

She shook her head. "I am glad to hear you say so again, but I did not mean that. I meant that perhaps Lucia will say more to you than she has to me."

"She hasn't told you anything?"

"Only that if she had nowhere to hide, she would be killed." She smiled as she held out her hand. "Yes, it must be hard to believe that I know no more than that, but she said it would be safer if I didn't know. Safer for me, she meant. The way she said it made me believe her."

As she left, the *concierge* came out to say that I was wanted on the telephone.

CHAPTER III

Her French had a faint Niçois accent. Her tone was peremptory.

"This is Adèle. I understand that you wish to give me private news of my brother."

"I wish to help you, yes. Where can we meet?"

"You have a car?"

"Yes."

"What kind?"

"A blue Simca."

"Do you know the Relais Fleuri on the Moyenne Corniche above Villefranche?"

"I can find it. A restaurant, is it?"

"Yes. Be there at ten o'clock to-night. When you arrive, go in and telephone eighty-two, fifty-one, sixty-nine."

"Whom do I ask for?"

"Adèle."

"Is that all?"

"Yes. I expect you to be alone. No camera, but bring the photographs you took this morning."

"I understand. Where do I . . .?"

But she had already hung up.

Brief, businesslike and wary. The restaurant she had designated would be almost exactly half-way between Cagnes-sur-Mer and Roquebrune. A reference to the telephone directory established that the prefix of the number she had given me referred to the Villefranche—Cap Ferrat area. That, too, told me nothing.

I had six hours in which to keep the appointment. I considered calling Sy, but decided to wait. My news was too good; he would take no more chances with me unless he had to. Six hours would give him time to fly Bob Parsons in to take over.

I suppose that if I had had the kind of newspaper training he valued so highly, I would, in the approved tradition, have put the magazine's interests before my own. As it was, I had no intention of doing so. Neither Sy nor Mr. Cust inspired me with any feelings of loyalty. If I succeeded, Cust would attribute the success, rightly in a way, to his own acumen. If I made a mess of things, he would have the pleasure of telling Sy to fire me. With nothing to gain and little that mattered to lose, I could please myself. I had become interested in the mystery of Lucia Bernardi. I wanted to know what lay behind it, and I wanted to hear the truth from her own lips.

I spent two hours re-reading the file, so that everything already known would be fresh in my mind, and jotted down some of the key questions. That done, I went down to the bar and had a drink. While I was there the *concierge* came in to say that there was a call for me from Paris. Sy was becoming impatient. I told the *concierge* to say that I was out, and left the inn immediately.

There had been a shower of rain earlier, and the road down into Cannes was slippery. I saw a car in front of me skid slightly on a bend, and was suddenly beset by anxieties. Supposing I couldn't get to the Relais Fleuri. Supposing I had an accident. Supposing the car, which had been running perfectly until then, suddenly broke down. Supposing I missed the sign on a one-way street and got arrested. So many things could go wrong.

C

I had meant to have a splendid dinner at La Bonne Auberge, call Sy from there afterwards, and then go on to keep the appointment. Now I decided to drive, slowly and very carefully, straight to Nice. If I got there safely, I could take my time over dinner, knowing that I was within a few minutes of the Relais Fleuri. If, on the other hand, I ran into trouble, there would be time left in which to deal with it.

It had not rained in Nice and the streets were dry. I had a drink in the Ruhl bar, waited until seven-thirty and then called Sy at his apartment.

He started to tell me that he'd been trying to call me for the past hour, but I cut him short.

"Look," I said. "I'm in Nice, and I've just spoken to her."

He let out a yelp of excitement. "Where did you find her? What did she look like? What did she say?"

"I haven't seen her yet, and so far she's said nothing usable. I have a meeting with her to-night around ten. Only me, no camera, cloak-and-dagger security arrangements, false names. The intermediary says she's frightened."

"Of what?"

"I'm hoping she'll tell me."

"When did you get the word?"

"A few minutes ago."

He swore in frustration. "What made her decide to play ball?"

"Moral blackmail, indirectly applied. But we don't use that part of the story. That's the deal I made with the intermediary."

"Mr. Chase?"

"No. Another person entirely. Unless it becomes necessary to apply further pressure—if the girl doesn't show up, I mean —I've forgotten the name already."

There was a pause. "Well, we can decide about that later," he said at last. "You say no camera. What about tape?"

"Nothing said about it."

"No witnesses. No photos. We ought to have something in the way of evidence in case there are denials later. You have a recorder with you?"

"No." Even if I had been taking the assignment seriously when I left Paris, I doubt if I would have thought of encumbering myself with a tape-recorder.

Sy managed to stifle his exasperation ; he wanted me to feel calm and confident. " Think you could pick one up locally?" he asked. " That small German battery-driven job would be best. You could slip it in your pocket."

" Record without telling her?"

" That's up to you. See how co-operative she is. Play it by ear. Are you all right for money?"

" Yes."

" Call me at the office later, eh? The moment you can."

" I will."

" And, Piet. Don't let her off the hook, will you? Make sure we know how to get on to her again. If the fuzz get excited we may have to produce her. Right?"

" All right." By the " fuzz " he meant the police.

" And, Piet . . ." He paused. He hated letting me go. He was wishing desperately that he had someone with his kind of know-how on the job. He was wishing that he were on it himself.

" Yes?"

" Make this good and you'll not only get a whopping bonus, you'll have wiped the old bastard's eye for good."

" If I'm going to buy a tape-recorder, I'll have to hurry, or the shops will all be shut."

" Yes, sure. Talk to you later. I'll be at the office with the night crew, waiting."

He was finally persuaded to hang up.

I went out and managed to find a hi-fi shop that sold miniature recorders. With it, the man sold me a microphone disguised as a wrist watch, and showed me how to thread the cord up my sleeve so that it could be plugged into the recorder in my breast pocket. He leered over the ingenuity of the contraption. I left wearing it, and feeling ridiculous.

My car was parked by the Ruhl. The idea of a splendid dinner no longer attracted me, so I left the car where it was and found a small restaurant in a nearby side-street.

At nine-thirty I was on the road up to the Moyenne Corniche. I arrived at the Relais Fleuri fifteen minutes early.

It was a small café-restaurant beside a diesel filling station. The same man probably owned both establishments. There were no houses near by. The restaurant had a *Routier* sign outside and plenty of parking space. It obviously catered mainly for truck-drivers using the Corniche.

I parked the car alongside a small van and went into the café area. A cheerful waitress brought me a coffee and a *fine*.

The time passed very slowly. At five to ten, I asked where the telephone was and paid for a *jeton*. The telephone was beside the lavatory so I killed another two minutes there before making the call.

A man's voice answered.

" I want to speak to Adèle, please," I said.

" Who?"

" Adèle."

" There is no Adèle here. You have the wrong number."

" What number is that?"

The number he gave me was the one I had.

" Adèle?"

" I told you. There is no Adèle here. You have the wrong number."

He hung up.

I got another *jeton* and tried again, with the same result.

It was maddening. I went back to my coffee. I was certain that I had made no mistake when I had written down the number. Either she had made a mistake, or she had failed to contact the man who had answered me in time to give him the message I was supposed to receive. I knew that there was a third possibility: that the whole thing was a put-up job designed to side-track me long enough for the Sangers to get clear away; but I wasn't yet prepared to entertain that. Besides, getting away from me would not really help the Sangers; I already had all I needed on them, including the photographs.

I decided to wait fifteen minutes and then try the number again. Another *fine* would have helped to pass the time, but in the state I was in then it would also have given me indigestion. I smoked two cigarettes and went back to the telephone.

I got the same man. This time he was angrily jocular, and offered to give me the address of a brothel. Perhaps I would find someone there named Adèle, he said, as he hung up yet again.

There seemed no point in my staying any longer. I paid for the coffee and *fine* and left.

I was so bemused by the disappointment that I did not notice until I had a hand on the door of my car that there was a woman sitting in the driving seat.

She was wearing a patterned silk scarf over her hair and a light raincoat. A pair of sun-glasses looked up at me as I opened the door.

" You were very patient, Monsieur," she said. " How many times did you call the number I gave you?"

" Three, Madame."

" You won't mind if I drive, I hope. I have to be certain that I am not taken anywhere I do not wish to go." She held out her hand. " May I have the key?"

I gave it to her.

" Thank you." She motioned me into the front passenger seat.

I went round and got in. As I did so I switched on the recorder in my pocket.

" May I ask where we are going?"

" There is a place where one can talk," she said. " I am sorry that you had to make the telephone calls, but I did not wish you to be expecting me, to be watching when I arrived."

" What was that number you gave me?"

" I don't know. It was the first that came into my head."

" You *are* Lucia Bernardi, I take it?"

She took off the sun-glasses and put them in her raincoat pocket. Then she turned and looked at me, smiling slightly.

" Of course," she said, " I am not wearing a bikini now, and the hair under my scarf belongs to one of the new American fashion wigs, but you should be able to recognise Lucia Bernardi from her photographs, I think."

I turned on the car lights, and the glow from the instrument panel touched her face.

Her eyes met mine.

" Are you satisfied, Monsieur?"

I nodded. Then, for the recorder's benefit, I said: " Yes, I am satisfied. Our friend was right. Your photographs do not really do you justice."

II

She drove east along the Corniche for about a kilometre and then turned right down a steep secondary road leading to Beaulieu and Villefranche. After a series of hairpin bends we came to a crossroad. She turned left, and then, almost immediately, swung the car off the road on to a small flat ledge under the hillside. It looked as if there had been a rockslide there at some time; the ledge must have been formed when the hill had been re-graded to avert another slide.

She stopped, but left the parking lights on and the engine running.

"I do not wish to stop here long," she said, and held her watch near the panel light so that she could see the time. "But first there must be an understanding, Monsieur Maas."

"Very well."

"Before I answer any questions, a certain matter must be clear. The photographs you took in Mougins to-day. I must have them, please."

They were in the glove compartment. I said: "I have already promised your friend Adèle that they will not be used."

"Of course. That is why I am here. But how do I know that you will keep your promise?"

"Because if I get the story I'm hoping for from you, Mademoiselle Bernardi, the photographs will be of no serious value."

"Adèle spoke to me again this evening. Her husband does not think that. He is very angry with her."

"He is mistaken about the photographs. In any case, don't you think it might be a good idea to trust me?"

"Trust a journalist?" She almost laughed.

"Many people do. Journalists can be very useful sometimes. Take your case. I don't know yet why you felt you had to hide yourself, but you must see now that you can't hide for ever. I found you. Others will find you, too; as long as they have an incentive to look, that is. By telling me the story you remove that incentive. Once the questions are answered, you are no longer news."

She looked at me shrewdly. "That sounds as if you have said it many times."

I smiled. " It has been said many times, though not by me, as it happens. There is some truth in it. Not much, but a little."

She was silent, thinking, trying to make up her mind. I made up my mind, instead.

I took the ignition key and opened the glove compartment. " All right," I said. " There are the photographs. You'd better take both rolls. One has shots of their house on it."

She gave me a quick look, then reached for the films and stuffed them into her raincoat pocket ; but she was still suspicious.

" How can I be certain that these *are* the photographs?"

" Unless you process them you can't be certain, but they *are* the photographs all the same. And there's something else," I went on, and showed her the microphone on my wrist. " This is a microphone and there's a recorder in my pocket. I'd like to record what you say, but if you don't want me to I won't. I'm not out to play tricks on you. In fact, I'd like to help you if I can. But until you tell me what the problem is all about, I can't. Now, you said you didn't want to stop here long. Where do we go next?"

She hesitated, then she locked the glove compartment again and re-started the engine.

" To a house," she said.

It was about a quarter of a mile farther down the road on which she had stopped. She turned into a narrow opening between two crumbling stone walls, and then we were on a roughly cobbled ramp leading down to a garage. The doors of the garage were padlocked. She stopped in front of them and took a flashlight from her pocket before she switched off the car headlights.

" It will be easier if you follow me," she said.

As I got out I could see the house below us, a small L-shaped building with a tiled roof. A flight of brick steps led down from the garage level to a paved patio half-enclosed by the two arms of the L. The unenclosed side looked out over the lights of Beaulieu and St. Jean-Cap Ferrat to the sea.

She led the way across the patio to the front door. She behaved as if she were familiar with the place, but I noticed that the key she used to open the door was not the only one in her bag, and that she chose it by looking at a label tied on with string. When she had the door open it was necessary for her to use the flashlight to find the light-switch.

Inside, there was a living-room with a brick fire-place at one end and a tiled dining table at the other. There were white walls, brightly coloured hessian curtains and easy chairs covered in the same material. In the summer it would be a cool, cheerful little room. Now it was chilly and had an unoccupied smell about it.

She switched on a single-bar electric fire and went to a cupboard by the dining table. She took out a bottle of brandy, two glasses and a corkscrew and put them on a table near the fire.

" Please open the bottle," she said.

As I did so, she took off her raincoat, and then her headscarf, and then the fashion wig. She was wearing slacks and a black wool sweater. She ran her hands through her hair to loosen it, then took the bottle from me and poured two very large drinks.

" I can stay for half an hour," she said briskly ; " then I must go." She picked up one of the drinks and sat down at the end of the sofa farthest from a light.

I took the photo-copy of the *Partout* article from my pocket and showed it to her.

" Have you read this?" I asked.

" Yes."

" What did you think of it?"

She thought a moment. " It made me feel sick," she said finally, and then added: " It made me laugh, too."

I switched on the recorder.

III

It is difficult for me now, to write objectively about Lucia ; but I will try. I still have a copy of the tape of that interview, with the truths, lies, half-truths and evasions all there in her own words.

" What was it in the *Partout* article that made you laugh?" my voice begins.

" It said that Ahmed had not engaged in any political activity while he had been in Switzerland."

" Ahmed being Colonel Arbil?"

" Yes."

" And he *had* engaged in political activity?"

" Oh yes, all the time, except for the last few weeks, before they killed him. Men came to the villa late at night. There were secret meetings when two or three at a time would be there. They would always come separately, though, and after the servants had gone to bed. It was all very discreet, you understand."

" What kind of men were they?"

" Mostly Iraqi Kurds. Members of the Militant Committee."

" What committee was that?"

" For the Autonomous Rights of the Kurdish People. It has its headquarters in Geneva. They are exiles working for the creation of an independent Kurdish state which would have the oil revenues of Kirkuk and Mosul."

" You say they were *mostly* Iraqi. What were the others?"

" There were two who were Syrian, I think. And there was an Englishman, or he may have been an American. He didn't speak their language. They spoke French with him, but he wasn't French. He had an accent like yours."

" Did he come often?"

" Two or three times."

" Do you know what they talked about? Were you ever at these meetings?"

" Oh no. They are strict Moslems, you understand. With them, women are not allowed in men's affairs. I had to stay out of the way."

" Did Colonel Arbil feel that way about women, too?"

" When they were there, yes."

" But at other times he would confide in you?"

" He would say things sometimes, yes."

" What kind of things?"

" He would tell me how the Kurdish people were tricked and cheated after the Treaty of Sèvres. He was a patriot."

" Is that why he was killed, do you think?"

" Naturally."

" By agents of the Iraqi Government?"

" Perhaps. Or agents of the oil company."

" Why the oil company?"

"Ahmed said they are afraid of Kurdish independence."

"They?"

"The Americans, the British, the Dutch, the French. They are all in it."

"You seriously believe that this international oil company organised a political assassination?"

"Why not? Big oil companies are like governments. They can do what they like. Besides, the men who did this were not Iraqis. I know. I heard them talking."

"What were they?"

"They spoke German to him, but they used another language between themselves, a language I did not know. It was not Arabic."

I changed the subject there. I wasn't yet ready to come to the night of the killing itself. There were two other points I wanted to clear up first.

"In the article," I go on, "it says that Colonel Arbil's income was believed to come from a family business in Iraq. Was that true?"

"I think so, yes. But he did not speak much of such matters to me. He had plenty of money. There was no reason to speak of it."

"Didn't it strike you as strange that an exile, a declared enemy of the Iraqi Government, should have no difficulty in getting money out of the country?"

"If it was family money . . ."

"In a country like Iraq there would still have to be a Government permit to transfer funds abroad."

"Perhaps it was sent secretly. Perhaps it was done with bribes. I do not know." There are frequent changes in her voice level during this. She had begun to walk up and down the room as I questioned her.

"All right. Now, a few months before he died Colonel Arbil received some sort of warning that his life was in danger, didn't he?"

"No."

"No?"

"He was warned that there might be an attempt to steal some important records that he had."

"What sort of records?"

"They concerned political activities."

"Who warned him?"

"I don't know."

"How was the warning given?"

"He received a telegram."

"Where from?"

"I don't know. He burned it."

"And it was after that that he installed the floodlights and the special locks and alarms. Couldn't he just as easily have put the records in a safe-deposit box? It would have been safer."

"He did not discuss such things with me." I remember the way she shrugged that off. "Why should he?"

"When you had lunch with Adèle in Zürich she thought you seemed worried. You asked her then about the possibility of Colonel Arbil's being given a *permis de séjour* for France. What had you in mind?"

"Only that it would be more agreeable for him, for us, to live in France."

"Not safer?"

"The lease on the villa had only a few months to run. He was undecided whether to renew it or not. He talked about a place in the South near the sea. In summer it would be better than Zürich, and in the winter the snow at Chamonix is as good or better than that at St. Moritz."

"Did he ever speak of returning to Iraq?"

"No."

"Not even if the Government there were to change? It often does."

"Its attitude towards the Kurdish people does not change."

"You said that there was no political activity on his part during the weeks immediately preceding the murder. Do you know why?"

"No."

"It wouldn't be that he had decided that it might be too dangerous just then to have any meetings at the villa?"

"I don't know."

"Did he go to any meetings elsewhere—at Geneva for example?"

"He may have done. I don't think so."

"Did he ever go out at night by himself?"

"Sometimes."

" During that last month?"

" I don't think so."

" How about the last week?"

" No. He had the *grippe*."

" All right. Now tell me what happened on the night he was killed."

This was what she had come prepared to tell. There is a slight pause while she collects herself; then she begins.

" As I said, Ahmed had had the *grippe*. It had affected his chest and the doctor had given him antibiotics to take. While he was sick I slept in another room at the end of the passage by one of the little towers."

A pause. The memory is painful. She goes on:

" Ahmed had been up most of that day, but he was still taking the antibiotics and he did not feel well. He went to bed early. I sat with him in his room for a time. Ernesto brought up the little television set. There was a Eurovision programme that Ahmed wanted to see. It was over at nine-thirty. Ahmed said he would sleep then. I gave him his pills to take and said good night. Then I went to my own room."

" Were the floodlights on outside?"

" Yes."

" Who locked the doors?"

" Ernesto. He had a key so that he could get in early in the morning. He locked them every night when he and Maria went to their cottage."

" Then what?"

" Because of Ahmed I had not been out of the villa for several days, and I had a headache. I thought that I, too, might be getting the *grippe*. I made a tisane for myself, took some aspirin and went to bed. It was early, but I went to sleep at once."

" What woke you?"

" Ahmed. He was crying out with pain."

" What did you do?"

" I got out of bed and started to go to him. Then I saw that the floodlights were out. There was one just outside that room on the corner of the villa. The lamp in it was very strong, and even with the curtains drawn the light showed through them into the room."

" Then?"

" I heard a man shouting angrily: '*Los! Los!*' and Ahmed cried out again. And then there was another voice saying something in German. I couldn't hear what that one said."

" So what did you do?"

" Nothing then." A slight pause, then defensively: " Is that bad? I was terrified. I was trying to think. I thought of the pistol that Ahmed had bought—he had shown me how to work it—but that was in a drawer by the bed in the room where he was. I went to the door of the room I was in. I didn't know how many men there were. I had heard two. But there could have been more. I didn't know if they knew where I was or if I was in the villa. There was no telephone in the room where I was. I thought that I might perhaps open the door quietly and get past the other room without their hearing me and get to the telephone downstairs. Then one of the men was shouting again: '*Wo ist? Wo ist?*' and suddenly Ahmed screamed."

She sobs and there is nothing on the tape for almost half a minute. At last she goes on quietly:

" He didn't cry out any more. I suppose he must have fainted then."

" What did you do?"

A pause. " I made the bed."

" You made the bed?" I sound incredulous, understandably perhaps.

" Yes. You see, I knew what they had come for and where it was. And I had realised by that time that, although the men might have expected to find me with Ahmed, when they *hadn't* found me there they assumed that he was alone that night. But once they started to look for what they had come for they would find me, and treat me as they had treated Ahmed. From that room I knew that I could get to a place where I could hide. But if they saw an unmade bed they would know I must be near the room, and keep on looking for the hiding place until they found it. So I quickly made the bed and tidied the room. I had been wearing after-ski clothes. The rest of my things were in the closet of the other room. There wasn't much to do, but it seemed to take a long time. I could hear the two men arguing about something. Then they stopped arguing and there were two shots fired."

" Only two?"

" Only two, then. For a moment I hoped that perhaps Ahmed had been able to get to the gun in the drawer and kill them. But then I heard men talking again and knew that they had shot Ahmed. They were coming out into the passage. I dared not wait any longer, so I hid."

" Where?"

" In the little tower."

" I didn't think those things were real. In the photograph they look like ornaments."

" They are. They are wood frames covered with zinc and painted to look like stone. But they have slit windows in them as if they were real towers and that gave the man who owns the villa an idea. In one of them he put a big loudspeaker and connected it with a phono below so that he could play records of a carillon. It was absurd, of course, but he did it. And to do it there had to be a way into the tower. So a hole was cut in the back of the clothes closet of the bedroom. It was covered with a small panel."

" I understand. So you crawled in there."

" Yes, and I took my after-ski in with me. I was glad later because it was very cold in the tower. There was just this space a metre or so wide, and the loudspeaker and the wind whistling through the wire mesh over the slits."

" How did you know about this way into there?"

" That was where Ahmed had hidden the suitcase with all his papers in it that these men wanted."

" He told you that he had hidden it there?"

A pause. She hesitates, then: " Yes."

" He trusted you completely."

" Yes."

" What were these papers?"

" Records."

" Records of what? His political activities?"

" Of many things."

" Had you read them?"

" They were written in Arabic."

" So you stayed there in the tower while they searched the house for the suitcase. Did they search the room you had been in?"

" Oh yes. I was very frightened. I had forgotten to hide the empty cup which had had the tisane in it. Luckily they did not notice it. After, they went back into Ahmed's room. That was when the third shot was fired. They must have found him still alive."

" This language that they spoke between themselves, how did it sound? Could it have been a Slav language?"

" Perhaps. I don't know."

" How long were you in the tower?"

" A long time. I don't know for certain. I could not hear them very well when they were downstairs and I did not hear them go. I was afraid to leave the tower in case they were still there."

" But eventually you did come out, and you found Colonel Arbil dead?"

" Yes."

" You said that when you first woke up and heard these men you thought of trying to get to the telephone downstairs. Who were you going to call? The police?"

" I suppose so."

" Then why didn't you call them now that you were able to do so?"

" Ahmed was dead, and I had the suitcase with all his records. There was nothing the police could do for him and much that they could do to hurt his associates, his friends. So I did what Ahmed would have wanted me to do. I took the suitcase and went where the police could not find me, and where those men could not find me. I had to go quickly. I was terrified that the men might come back to search the villa again. When I saw the lights of that truck on the road outside I thought that it must be a car with them in it. At the airport while I was waiting for the plane I hid in the *lavabo*. That was when I thought of going to Adèle and asking her to help me."

" So now you have the suitcase hidden away safely, I take it?"

" Yes."

" Then why are *you* still hiding?"

" I must. Don't you see?" Impatiently. " They know now that I was there in the villa that night. They know that I must have the records they came for. If they find me, they will treat me as they treated Ahmed."

"Then why not destroy the records and let me announce that you have done so?"

"They would not believe it. Besides, they would think that I had read them or made copies."

"All right. Send them to this committee in Geneva."

"How can I trust them now? It must have been one of them who betrayed Ahmed. It is obvious."

"Not to me."

"You do not understand."

"I'm trying very hard to do so. As far as I can see, it amounts to this. You are convinced that some mysterious agency—you're not really sure which one or what it represents —is after the suitcase you took from the villa, and will go to any lengths to get it. You don't really know what is in the records in the suitcase, but the enemy will assume that you do know. Your feelings of loyalty to Colonel Arbil prevent your just handing the whole thing over to the police and asking for their protection. Is that right?"

"Yes."

"You couldn't be imagining this danger, could you? Or the consequences to Colonel Arbil's friends if you come forward and let the police take over?"

"Ahmed's murder was not imaginary. I must do as I think best."

"It doesn't really make sense, though, does it? Unless, of course, there's a lot you haven't told me."

"I have told you all I can, Monsieur."

"Then what are you going to do now? Hide for the rest of your life?"

"I have other plans."

"To do what?"

"If I told you, they would be useless. I must go now."

"One more thing. How do I get in touch with you again?"

"There is no reason to."

"Do these plans of yours include moving from the place you're in now?"

"Perhaps."

"Will Adèle still know where to find you?"

"Yes. Finish your drink, please. I must go now."

"Very well."

That was the tape.

I V

She rinsed the glasses and put them away, and emptied the ashtray I had used, before we left. I tried to get her to say something more about her plans, but she wouldn't.

She drove back up to the Corniche. About half a kilometre from the Relais Fleuri, she pulled over to the side of the road and stopped. She kept her right hand on the ignition key as she turned to me.

" I would like you to walk back to the Relais from here, please."

" What happens to this car? It isn't my own, you know."

" I will leave it for you at the Relais. My own car is parked there. I would prefer that you do not take the number or try to follow me."

" Oh, I understand." I opened the door. " If you have any second thoughts and want to get in touch with me, Adèle will know where to find me. *Au revoir*, Madame, and thank you."

" Monsieur."

I got out and shut the door. She drove off. Ten minutes later I reached the Relais. It was in darkness. My car was outside. I drove down into Nice. I considered stopping there and calling Sy, then changed my mind. I would have to play the tape over the line to Paris and that would be awkward in a phone-booth. Besides, the roads were clear and dry. It wouldn't hurt Sy to wait another half an hour.

I was back in Mougins a little after midnight. The night *concierge* put the call through after a ten-minute delay. Sy was already on the line when I picked up the phone in my room.

" Did you see her?"

" Yes."

" Great! Where?"

" In an unoccupied house just outside Nice." I told him about the mechanics of the meeting and then went on: " I have a tape. Do you want to hear it?"

" Give me a moment to switch on. Okay, go ahead."

" The first part is in my car. Then we go to the house."

" Shoot."

I played back the tape with the miniature loudspeaker of the recorder clamped to the telephone. When it ended I switched off and said: " That's it."

Sy did not reply for a moment; I could hear him discussing it with someone else in the office, probably Ed Charles, the re-write man. I could not hear what they were saying. Then Sy came back.

" Piet?"

" Yes."

" How do you evaluate this? Is she on the level? What was your impression?"

" I think that her account of what happened in the villa at the time Arbil was murdered rings true."

" So do we. And?"

" As you may have gathered from the questions I asked, I found the rest of it hard to believe."

" *She* could believe it. Delayed shock and all that jazz. Neurotic young woman sees murderers under bed."

" I think that's how it was meant to sound."

" Could be. Okay, we'll analyse all that after it's transcribed. Now then, what about the background stuff? I take it that the Adèle mentioned on the tape is the intermediary. How did our man in Mougins get to her? What's the story there?"

" No story. I told you. I made a deal."

" Well, you can forget it now. Come on. We'll tape it."

" Sorry."

His tone sharpened. " Now look, Piet, have a bit of sense. You've licked a tough assignment, you've done a great job. Now we've got to milk it for all it's worth. So give."

" I've given. You told me to find the girl and interview her. That's what I've done."

A pause. Then he said: " Piet, two things. First, you had no authority to make a deal without checking with me first. You didn't check. Second, you got this story because you were given a damned good lead. If you think the Chief's going to let that story go on without a play by play account of how we beat *Paris Match* to it on their own home ground, you're crazy."

I thought as quickly as I could. " You told me to make certain that we could contact the girl again," I retorted. " If I break faith with the intermediary there'll be no more contacts."

He laughed shortly. "Think again, buddy boy. The intermediary won't know anything until she reads the magazine. That gives us four days to make further contacts and follow up. After that the whole world'll have the story and it won't matter a damn whether she thinks you're a son-of-a-bitch or not, because we won't need her any more. Now stop horsing around and let's have it."

"I'll think over what you say."

There was quite a long pause after that. Sy had put his hand over the phone mouthpiece so that I wouldn't hear what was being said. I could imagine it, though. When he came back his tone was carefully genial.

"Okay, Piet, you think about it. We have a few hours in hand, and we can warn New York now that the story's on its way. Meanwhile, I'll bet you could use some sleep, huh?"

"Yes."

"Well, I'll tell you what. We're going to need a big followup story on this, so I think we'll all have to pitch in and help. I'm going to hitch a ride down on one of the newspaper flights from Orly. You grab a couple or three hours' sleep and meet me at Nice airport at around seven. Okay?"

"Yes."

"Oh, and get me a room at your hotel, will you? No, wait. Make it two rooms. I'll probably pull Bob Parsons in from Rome, too. He should be able to make it almost as soon as I do. Meanwhile, you can dream about that bonus you're going to get. Right?"

"Oh yes, of course."

"See you at seven."

He hung up.

He had been right about one thing: I was tired. However, I had no intention of going to sleep.

I packed my bags and then went down and found the night concierge.

"I'm sorry," I told him, "but I have to leave for Paris immediately, within the hour. You'll have to find out how much that last telephone call cost and put it on my bill. I'll be going out again now for half an hour. I would like the bill ready for me when I get back."

He protested that the only person who could make out the bill was already in bed. However, twenty-five francs per-

suaded him that this was a business emergency calling for
extreme measures. I left him busy at the switchboard and
drove to La Sourisette.

I would liked to have telephoned first, but I was afraid the
concierge might remember the number later.

Except for the lanterns outside the front door, the place was
in darkness. The dog had heard the car, however, and had
begun to bark even before I rang the bell. After a bit the
maid opened the door, but with the chain on it.

Monsieur and Madame were asleep and could not be dis-
turbed. I argued ; the dog barked ; finally Sanger called down
the stairs.

" Who is it? What is it?"

" Maas. It is important that I see you now."

The maid and the dog were dismissed. After a moment or
two he took off the chain and opened the door. He was in
pyjamas and a silk dressing-gown.

" It is after one o'clock," he said plaintively. " Couldn't it
have waited until the morning?"

" No. This is important. I mean important to you, not to
me. May I come in?"

" Very well."

He led the way through into the rear living-room.

" Is your wife awake?" I asked.

" I doubt it. She has had a trying day," he added a trifle
sourly. " She took something to make her sleep."

" Then I think you'd better have some black coffee made
and waken her."

His eyes narrowed. " You got what you wanted. You spoke
with Lucia. She telephoned and told us. Now what is it?"

" Did she tell you that I gave her those photographs you
wanted?"

" Yes. What about it?"

" I tried to keep my side of the bargain I made with your
wife, but I'm afraid my editor isn't interested in bargains. He
wants the whole story, everything."

" So you've given it to him?"

" No. I refused."

" You did what?"

" I refused, and I came here to warn you. He's on the way
down by air from Paris. He'll be at Nice at seven. There's

another man on his way here from Rome. They'll come straight to Mougins. Now listen to me, Mr. Sanger "—he had started pacing up and down the room—" they don't know that I reached Lucia through your wife, and I purposely misled the editor when he questioned me on the point. But he knows your name and he knows about Patrick Chase. It only took me twenty minutes to find out where you lived here. When they arrive, they'll probably find it in ten."

"I can refuse to see them."

"They're not as easy as I am, Mr. Sanger. If you want to keep them out, you'll have to call the police in to do it. I came here to warn you to get away while you can."

His brain was working quickly and suspiciously now. "Why should you? What's the idea? What are you trying to pull now?"

"As far as you are concerned, I am merely keeping the promise I made to your wife. I'm supposed to be meeting the editor at Nice airport at seven. I won't be there. I won't be here either. They're making out my bill at the inn now. I'm going to move into some small hotel in Nice to-night."

"You mean you're double-crossing your paper? They'll fire you."

"I hope they do, but I doubt it. At least, they won't fire me immediately. Unless they can interview you personally, they can't print anything about you in connection with this story. So when they can't reach you, they'll try to find me. If they do, they'll appeal to my professional pride and good sense."

"Would they succeed?"

"I have no professional pride where they are concerned, and my ideas of good sense are different from theirs. I'll continue to protect you if I can. There's one condition."

He sighed. "I was afraid there would be."

"I must be able to keep in touch with Lucia Bernardi. And I must keep in touch direct."

"Oh, that." He seemed relieved. "Well, I'd better go and wake Adèle." He started to go, then hesitated. "I don't understand why you're doing this. A simple determination to keep a promise that I can understand. And, needless to say, I'm very grateful for it. But is it *really* simple? You're the man who couldn't be bought for thirty thousand dollars, yet you claim

to have no professional pride. You do this job you have as if
it were important to you, yet you say you hope to lose it.
What is it with you, Maas? Self-destruction still, or is there
a new kind of anger now?"

A good question. I wasn't sure how to answer it. " Perhaps
there is," I said. " We must have a long talk about it some-
time. Now, don't you think you ought to get moving?"

He shrugged. " Oh, sure." He went on up the stairs. " Help
yourself to a drink."

I poured myself a large whisky, and tried to think of the
precautions that ought to be taken. The maid, for example.
She would have to be told by Sanger to say that I had called
there once only; that would give the impression that I had
been given a lead by Sanger which had sent me elsewhere for
information. The maid would also have to be warned not to
say that Madame Sanger's Christian name was Adèle if she
were asked.

After a while, Sanger came down again, dressed. He was
carrying an attaché case which he proceeded to fill with papers
from a small wall-safe in the alcove. I told him about the
precautions I had been considering.

He nodded. " I've already gone into all that with Adèle,"
he said. " Marie is used to discretion when we are away. She
will say that you went on to Piera-Cava. As, of course, you
did. The waiter in that hotel might even remember you if
your people make inquiries there."

" What about my contact with Lucia?"

" Adèle will tell you about that." He thought for a moment.
" They'll try quite hard to locate you, won't they?"

" Probably. But I don't see how they could."

" That's a rented car you have, isn't it?"

" Yes."

" Do you know what I'd do in their place?"

" What?"

" I'd check with the big car rental agencies—there aren't
many—and I'd get the registration number of the car you're
driving. Then I'd go to the police and have you picked up on
some phoney charge—petty theft, maybe—and then, when they
had you, apologise, drop the charge, and say it was all a mistake. If you really don't want them on your neck, I'd get rid
of that car quick."

"Where will you go?" I asked.

He eyed me speculatively. "I think it would be better if you don't know that. Mixed motives can be funny things. You might decide to change your mind."

I had noticed that he had put two French passports with the papers in the attaché case. "Will you be leaving France?" I asked.

"Only if it becomes necessary. I don't think it will."

Adèle Sanger came through from the living-room. For someone roused from a drugged sleep to face an emergency, she looked remarkably composed.

"Marie is making coffee," she said, then turned to me. "I expect my husband has already thanked you for your consideration, Monsieur."

"There is no need for thanks. I'm sorry that you have to be inconvenienced in this way."

"The alternative would have been much worse." She became businesslike. "Now, I have spoken to Lucia and done what I can with her. She is not happy, of course. I could persuade her only to allow me to give you the telephone number of the house, not the address." She handed me a sheet from a telephone pad. "There it is. Also she says she may decide to go somewhere else. But in that case she will let you know first. She is very positive that she will do so. And I am to call her back to tell her where she will be able to find you."

"I don't know for certain yet."

Sanger reached up to one of the bookshelves and tossed me a *Guide Michelin*. "You said you were going to a hotel in Nice. You'd better decide which one."

"All right."

I had to think about money now. I had spent quite a lot of the expense money and it was unlikely that there would be many more salary cheques coming from *World Reporter*. I picked a cheap hotel from among those listed as not having restaurants, and gave Adèle Sanger the name of it.

She wrote it down. "Very well," she said. "You should be able to get a room there easily at this time of the year. If, by any chance, you can't, go to the next hotel on the *Michelin* list. If you have to move for any reason, also go to the next on the list. I will tell Lucia that that is the arrangement."

" I understand."

She sighed. " I suppose I will never know now why she was frightened."

" You'll soon know as much as I know, Madame. It will be in the magazine next week. They'll use that part of the story all right. As for her being frightened, I'm not so sure you're right about that."

" What *did* she tell you?"

" A little truth, Madame, but mostly lies, I think." I glanced at Sanger, who was shutting the safe. " You were asking about my motives. They're not really mixed. I have nothing to lose except a job I don't want and I have a lot of curiosity to satisfy. Isn't that enough?"

He looked amused. " I get the picture now. Maybe I'd put it a different way, though."

" Oh?"

" Lucia interests you and attracts you. So much so that you are prepared to cheat on your bosses to pursue the matter with her in your own way. That's your new kind of anger. Adèle knows what I'm talking about, don't you, honey? Why do you think we decided on Lucia for those trips to Munich and St. Moritz? She was the right kind of girl for what we needed. They're pretty hard to find, and she was one of the best. It's not just the way she looks. It's not just that she's a lady with a mind. She has a funny effect on men. They want to go to bed with her, only there's something about her that makes them uncertain. They're not sure if they're good enough to make it. Even the big lover-boys get that feeling. I've seen it happen. Look at Arbil. He behaved like a kid."

" Middle-aged men sometimes do," I remarked pointedly.

He said " Oops!" and grinned. He wasn't disconcerted, but he knew that I was.

I turned to his wife. " You said she was frightened, Madame. Would you describe her as a neurotic person who might possibly just imagine that she was in danger?"

" No. Most certainly no."

" Could she pretend to be frightened?"

" Why would she pretend with me?" She looked at her husband. " I shall go now and pack."

" You do that, honey." He held out his hand to me. " It's

been a damned nuisance knowing you, Maas. I hope we never see you again. Nothing personal, you understand."

"I understand."

His hand-shake was perfunctory and limp.

He was already calling up to his wife to make sure that she packed plenty of his underwear as I let myself out.

My bill was ready at the inn. Before I left, I made the room reservations for Sy and Bob Parsons and wrote a note to Sy to let him know the position as far as I was concerned.

Dear Sy,

I'm sorry, but it's still no story. I made a deal to get this tape, and I think I have to abide by the terms I accepted. Clearly, this is high treason and washes me up as far as World Reporter is concerned. I will turn in the rented car as soon as I can, and mail you an itemised expense sheet along with hotel bills, etc. The magazine may end up owing me some money, but we can sort that out later when the story's cold and you are back in Paris. Meanwhile, I am taking that unpaid vacation you mentioned.

By the way, what happens if, during the vacation, I turn up some more publishable material on the Arbil story? Do I let you have it, or do I just forget it? I can't remember what the contract says. I'll just have to play it by ear.

Regards,
P.M.

P.S. I enclose the original tape of the Bernardi interview for your file. So that you don't waste time unnecessarily, Sanger's villa here is called La Sourisette. Anyone will direct you to it. However, he is away at the moment. I have no idea when he will be back.

CHAPTER IV

The Hotel I had chosen in Nice was near the Gare Centrale, and the *concierge* was used to travellers arriving in the early hours of the morning. I signed in as " Pierre Mathis." I managed to get four hours' sleep without taking any pills.

The car rental people from whom I had rented the car in Marseille had a branch in Nice, and the first thing I did after breakfast was to return the Simca to them. I had the receipt for the deposit and that almost covered the extra mileage charge I had to pay. Next, I went back to the man who had sold me the tape-recorder, and sold it back to him at a discount. A nearby camera shop gave me a fair price for the Rolleiflex. I was ready now to rent a cheaper car from a smaller organisation. I found one eventually. They let me have a decrepit *quatre-chevaux* Renault. The man only glanced at my driving licence. When I gave my name as Pierre Mathis he wrote it down on the rental form without troubling to check my identity card.

I drove to the Hotel de Ville.

The prefix of Lucia's telephone number belonged to an area west of Nice, so I guessed that the house in which she was then staying was probably at or near Cagnes-sur-Mer. However, Adèle Sanger had said that Lucia has spoken of moving, and I wanted to be prepared for that eventuality. The agent in Sète had mentioned only Cagnes, Mougins and Roquebrune ; but the house in which I had interviewed her had been near Beaulieu. I had to assume that there might be Sanger properties in other areas along the coast.

My experience at Montpellier had familiarised me with the procedure for indexing and cross-indexing employed in *département* property registration archives, and I was able to call for the record volumes I needed and pay the required search fees without having to ask a lot of questions first. I was not the only person there. The bureau of archives was scarcely a hive of activity, but during the morning there was a steady stream of callers. Some were women. The senior

90

archiviste and his staff greeted many of them by name, and I concluded that they were mostly clerks from lawyers' and surveyors' offices and bank mortgage departments. Nearly all of them knew the routine well.

There was one man, however, who had to be shown, as I had had to be shown in Montpellier, how the records system worked. He was additionally hampered by speaking less than fluent French with a strong foreign accent. I was concentrating on my own inquiries and was only dimly aware of him at first, and, even then, only because he seemed to be having an argument with the *archiviste*. It was some time before I realised the nature of the misunderstanding that was taking place.

The record volumes could only be taken out one at a time, and each had to be returned, and recorded as having been returned, before it could be released again. Presumably, this was done so that the search-fee receipts could be more easily checked by the *département* auditors. The man had made out a list of volumes he wanted to consult, and he was having to wait far too long to get them: or so it seemed to him, The *archiviste*'s explanation for the delays was less lucid than it might have been because he was by now annoyed. The stranger's defective French was an additional complication. But, as I listened, I suddenly realised what had been happening. The list of volumes the other man had made out was exactly the same as my own list. The delays had been caused by the fact that I had started ahead of him.

It could have been a coincidence that the lists were the same, but I knew that it was an unlikely one. I decided that I had better take a look at the man before he managed to understand the situation and become interested in me.

The public counter of the registration archive was tilted like a long lectern, so that the bulky volumes could be referred to without straining the bindings, and divided up by thin partitions into a series of booths. Consequently, you could not see along the counter. However, across the room by the entrance there was a desk where you paid the search fees and received the request slips.

As soon as I had finished with the volume covering the La Turbie area (no property there in Sanger's name) I requested the volume for Eze and went back to the desk and bought some more fee slips. From there I could see into the booth where the other man was.

His back was towards me. All I could see was that he was tall and thin with a narrow head and wispy grey hair combed over a bald patch. He wore glasses and a dark grey suit. The suit didn't look French; it didn't look as if it had any particular nationality.

I returned to my own booth and waited for the Eze volume. It was nearly noon and the Hotel de Ville office would soon close for the two-hour lunch period. At the other end of the counter, the *archiviste* had at last succeeded in making himself understood and there was silence in the room. I wondered who the man could possibly be. If he had been a local man I would have concluded that he had been sent in hurriedly by Sy. As it was, the most likely explanation seemed to be that he was another foreign journalist who had somehow found the same road that I had taken.

As the assistant returned with the Eze volume and put it down in front of me, he looked inquiringly over my shoulder. I glanced round. The man was standing close behind me.

He smiled, exposing a set of long, yellow teeth in a lined, sallow face. The eyes behind the glasses were brown with large, loose pouches under them. The smile, though clearly meant to be affable, was spoilt by the teeth; they gave it a predatory look.

He said, in his very odd French: "Please excuse me, Monsieur. I am told that our respective researches are following similar or parallel courses. No doubt our destinations are totally different, but I wonder if, until our courses diverge, we might not usefully and, in the sense of saving time, profitably collaborate in our endeavours."

He showed his teeth again as he concluded, and raised his eyebrows questioningly.

He had taken me by surprise and I felt stupid. It seemed advisable, until I had had time to think, to look stupid as well. I stared at him blankly. The assistant behind the counter helped by staring, too.

Eventually, I shrugged. "Possibly."

Thin lips closed over the teeth. "Good. We have a basis for negotiation. We might continue over a glass of wine, if you agree."

It would do no harm, I decided, to find out who he was and what he wanted. I nodded. "Very well."

"My name is Skurleti."

"Mathis," I said.

He bowed. "Then shall we go, Monsieur Mathis?"

"All right." I collected all the notes I had made, and put them in an inside pocket.

We had to pass through a number of doorways to get out of the Hotel de Ville, and Skurleti proved to be one of those men, over-polite or fearful of attack, who will never go through a doorway ahead of the person he is with, even when it is obviously simpler for him to do so. Our progress to the street was an idiotic sort of "after-you-no-after-you" minuet that ended by making me feel that I was being escorted from the place under guard.

The Hotel de Ville is only a few yards from the Place Masséna and we went to the nearest corner café. When we were seated Skurleti ordered a vermouth-cassis, and then turned to me with another show of teeth.

"An exchange of credentials would perhaps be in order?" he asked.

"Perhaps it would."

He extracted a large crocodile-leather wallet from his pocket and handed me an engraved business card. It read:

Mr. Kostas Politis-Skurleti
Authorised Agent

Member International
Detective Association

Transmonde Information Agency,
Box 1065 Muski Road,
Cairo, U.A.R.

"You have perhaps heard of Transmonde," he said.

"I'm afraid not."

He looked surprised. "It is one of the largest and most reputable international inquiry agencies."

The waiter arrived with the drinks and I waited until he had gone before I replied: "I'm afraid I have no card to give you, but my work is largely confidential, too. I carry out credit research investigations for a financial organisation. If you don't mind, I would prefer not to give the name of it. In matters of credit, you understand, it is necessary to be discreet."

"I understand. We also have a department that undertakes such work—on an international scale, of course. My own work, however, is concerned more with negotiation. I refer to confidential negotiations in which, for various reasons, it may be desirable for the parties concerned to deal through intermediaries."

"I see."

"I will add further," he went on, "that at the moment I am seeking to establish a certain contact, and that I have an idea that the person whose credit you are investigating and the persons with whom I wish to establish contact might possibly be connected."

The smile was on again, but with a look of expectancy about it now, as if he had just told a funny story and was waiting for the laugh.

I looked as sceptical as I could. "Rather a remote possibility, don't you think?"

"The name is Phillip Sanger, Monsieur Mathis, and he has a number of properties along the coast. Am I not right? Yes, I can see I am. Then, come now! You have told me your purpose. There is no conflict of interest between us. Therefore, as colleagues in a sense, surely we can be frank with one another? I can get the information I want without great difficulty, of course, but it will take time, and time is an important factor for the clients in this case. To save time I am prepared to pay money."

"For Monsieur Sanger's home address?"

"Monsieur Sanger does not have one home address. He has many. I need them all, and at once."

"You say that there is no conflict of interest between us. How can I be sure of that? Who are these clients of yours, and what do they want?"

He raised protesting hands. "You cannot seriously expect me to tell you that. A group of business men urgently wish a negotiation. That is all I can say. But it has nothing to do with lending or borrowing money, that I can assure you."

He had said that he wanted to establish contact with "persons," in the plural; but he had only mentioned one name,

Sanger's. If he knew or suspected that Sanger was also Patrick Chase, there was nothing improbable about his story. I could well believe that there were a great many men who had urgent business with Phillip Sanger, alias Patrick Chase, and who might employ private detectives to find him. It was also likely that the recovery of money, rather than the lending or borrowing of it, would be the subject of the desired negotiations. But *did* Skurleti know? Or was the other person of whom he was thinking someone else? Adèle Sanger? Lucia Bernardi? Was Skurleti telling the truth about his mission, or had we both been lying?

I temporised.

" How much? "

" One thousand new francs," he answered promptly.

" There has been a lot of work involved, and it is not yet completed."

" I will give you a thousand for the incomplete list and a further five hundred when you have the rest of it."

I pretended to think about this. He took his wallet out again and began counting out one hundred-franc notes. I waved them away. " No, no. Please. I don't have the list. And in any case . . . "

" You have the list you made this morning," he broke in quickly. " That would be a beginning."

" I found nothing this morning. It was all unproductive. In any case, I must think the matter over carefully."

" Two thousand francs."

I hesitated, then shook my head. " I will let you know later."

" When? Time is important. Perhaps we can work together at the Hotel de Ville this afternoon."

" I am afraid I have some other business to attend to. I could meet you here again at four o'clock."

" With the list? "

I did not answer for a moment. Then I finished my drink, set the glass down firmly, as if I had arrived at a decision, and looked him straight in the eyes. " Two thousand five hundred," I said challengingly.

He smiled. That was the kind of talk he understood.

II

As soon as I got back to my hotel, I called the number Adèle Sanger had given me.

The ringing tone went on for nearly a minute before Lucia lifted the phone. She said nothing until I spoke.

"This is Maas."

"Yes?"

"It is important that I see you."

"You have already seen me."

"We have to talk again."

"About what?"

"I told you that if I could find you, others could find you, too. I think there is a possibility that that may already be happening."

"Another newspaper?"

"I can't be certain, but I don't think so. Someone representing a group possibly."

"How do you know this?"

"I'll tell you when I see you."

"You say a group," she said thoughtfully. "What nationality?"

"I don't know. But their representative is a Greek and he comes from Cairo."

There was a long silence, so long that, although I knew she hadn't hung up, I said at last: "Are you still there?"

"I was thinking." Then she went on briskly: "Very well, I will meet with you. The same arrangements as before. To-night at ten."

"No. It has to be within the next three hours. The sooner the better. I have to meet this man again at four. For your protection, I must know what to say to him. I suggest that I come to you."

"Impossible."

"It's not impossible at all. I know where you are, but not which house. Just give me the house number and I'll know which street to go to."

"You could be followed."

"I'll see that I'm not followed. What's the number?"

"Eight."

"Good. Now, I will have a different car, a grey Renault. Can you see the street easily?"

"Not the street immediately outside the house, but lower down the hill, yes."

"Well, I'll park down the hill."

"Outside Number Five would be best."

"All right. You watch for me. I'll be there in about an hour. Understood?"

"Understood. But . . ."

I hung up before she could change her mind, and got out the list of Sanger properties I had made that morning.

There were four houses in the Cagnes area on the list, only one with the street-number 8. Cagnes-sur-Mer is composed of three distinct villages: Haut-de-Cagnes, which is medieval, Bas-de-Cagnes, which is mostly eighteenth-century, and Cros-de-Cagnes, which is an unsightly modern beach-bungalow, apartment-building development sprawled across the coast road from Nice. The survey descriptions in the record books had not recognised these aesthetic distinctions; but, from what I had seen of the Sangers' taste in houses, and from the fact that their Cagnes properties all had street numbers rather than names, I guessed that they were in the older parts of Cagnes.

I now had to think about the possibility of my being followed. I didn't take it very seriously. Mr. Skurleti I had left sitting in the café. Sy and Bob Parsons would almost certainly be making some sort of effort to locate me, and I didn't underrate their ingenuity and persistence; but at that point they couldn't have had sufficient time. Still, I had promised to take precautions, so I did the best I could.

I walked over to the Gare Centrale and bought a railway box-lunch; then I went back to the car and drove out on the autoroute. I went through Cros-de-Cagnes without stopping. Just before the turn-off for Antibes the road is straight for a kilometre or so. I pulled into the solitary filling station there and asked the mechanic to fit a set of new plugs. While he did so, I ate the box-lunch and watched to see if any of the cars coming from the Nice direction stopped on the road. None did; there was nothing on that stretch of road to stop for, except the filling station. If I had been followed, the driver of the following car must have driven past and stopped farther along to wait for me. I finished my lunch, paid for

D

the new plugs, and then drove back the way I had come. I reached Bas-de-Cagnes just before two o'clock.

It was the rue Carponière I wanted, and I found it without much difficulty. It was a steep, crescent-shaped cul-de-sac off the road up to Haut-de-Cagnes. The eight houses there were mostly hidden by courtyard walls or behind iron railings screened by tall bushes. The Sangers' feeling for privacy must have warmed at the sight of them.

I parked outside Number 5 and walked up the narrow pavement to the end of the road. Number 8 had railings with big mimosas behind the bushes. Through the tops of the trees you could see parts of the tiled roof of the house and one upper-floor window. To one side there was a double gateway wide enough to admit a car. The railings of the gateway were backed by iron sheeting so that they could not be seen through. There was a bell-pull beside the gates. I pulled it and found that it no longer worked. I tried the handle of the gate. It was unlocked, so I went in.

The first thing I saw was a car, a black Citroën. It was parked under a canvas awning stretched over a metal frame. A path off to the right led to the front door. The house was a brick and stucco affair that looked as if it had been built in the mid-nineteenth century for some local professional man, a doctor or a lawyer. It was not pretentious, but there was nothing rustic about it. All it had needed from the Sangers, probably, had been modern plumbing and some paint. It had a comfortable air.

I shut the gate behind me and walked along the path between the trees. As I did so, the front door opened.

The moment I was inside she shut the door.

"Did anyone see you in the street outside?"

"I don't think so. Would it matter if they did see me? The neighbours must know there's someone living here."

"They think that I am a German Swiss and that I am recovering from an accident and plastic surgery to my face. It is understood that I do not wish to be seen by anyone. A man coming to the house might make them curious."

She started to lead the way towards the back of the house.

"What about the local tradespeople?" I asked.

"Oh, there is a woman that comes to clean. She has cataracts in her eyes and cannot see much anyway. She does the shopping for me. I promised to pay for her eyes to be done when the doctor says it is time for the operation."

"That was generous of you."

She shrugged. "It was Adèle's idea. She thought that it would help the woman to believe what she was told." She turned to face me. "Now, tell me what has happened."

She had led me into a room that I would not have expected from the appearance of the front of the house. Originally, it must have been a terrace. Now it was enclosed by thick walls with arched window embrasures, and had acquired a massive stone fire-place. On one wall there was a niche containing a near-life-size Madonna and Child. Another section of wall had been faced with Spanish tiles composing a large, fiercely-coloured portrayal of the martyrdom of Saint Sebastian. A crucifix, also in tile, adorned the wall opposite the fire-place. The furniture was noncommittally modern, and a log fire burned cheerfully in the grate, but the total effect was oppressive and disconcerting; it was as if one had blundered into a private chapel.

Lucia, in lime-green slacks and a suède jacket, had obviously become used to the décor. Her lips tightened impatiently when I stared around at it.

"Yes, yes, it is all very strange. Adèle has not yet been able to make changes here. Now then, please. I would like to know what has happened."

I told her about Skurleti.

She listened intently, then made me describe his appearance in detail.

I did so.

"Did you keep his card?"

"Yes." I gave it to her.

She studied it, back and front. "And he was only interested in Patrick?"

"In Phillip Sanger, you mean? Yes."

"He mentioned no other name?"

"No. But, then, neither did I when *I* was trying to find you. This could be a coincidence, I suppose, but I find that hard to believe. Don't you?"

"Yes." She looked at the card again. "It might be the Italians," she said thoughtfully.

"What Italians?"

She ignored my question and suddenly resumed her inquisitorial manner. " And what were *you* doing at the Hotel de Ville?" she asked sharply.

" Finding this address for one thing. Finding other Sanger addresses, too."

" Why?"

" Adèle Sanger said that you might move to another house. I wanted to be able to find you again quickly if you did."

" I said that I would let you know if I moved," she said defensively. " Besides, I gave you the interview you wanted."

" You gave me an interview, yes. But surely you don't think I believed all you told me?"

She considered me for a moment, then smiled. " That is not very polite."

" Oh, I'm sure you have excellent reasons for being careful what you say."

She smiled again. Her face was delightful when she smiled. " Yes," she said ; " particularly to you."

" Why particularly to me?"

A mocking expression came into her eyes, mocking and calculating ; then she chuckled. " You know, even Patrick believed it."

" Believed what?"

" That story about your keeping your promise to Adèle, about telling your paper to go to hell."

" I didn't tell them to go to hell. I just walked out on them."

" It is the same thing. You made a noble gesture." She rolled her eyes towards the Madonna and placed her hand over her heart. " The journalist who keeps faith."

" You don't believe in such gestures, I take it." I tried not to show my irritation.

" Oh yes, of course." The smile was scornful now.

" It happens to be true. Why should I invent a story like that?"

She pretended to take the question seriously. " Well, let us see. Adèle told me some things about you. She said that you were blond and handsome and very intelligent, but also serious and a little sad because of things, bad things, that had happened to you. She did not say that you were an imbecile."

" That was good of her."

"And especially she did not say that you were a sentimental imbecile."

"Though, of course, I might be that."

She went on as if I had not spoken, ticking off the items on her fingers. "There was a certain sincerity, she said, also probity. When Patrick offered you a lot of money to protect him you refused. You would not betray your paper then. How curious!"

"That was different."

"Naturally. That was in the daytime. You only betray your people at night." The smile vanished and her eyes hardened. "You were here for a story and you were determined to get it. You even told Patrick how soon you had to get it —before eleven, Friday night, New York time. To-day is Friday. That gives you over twelve hours still, doesn't it?"

Idiotically, I said: "Oh, I hadn't thought of that."

It must have sounded artless as well as dishonest. She laughed angrily.

"*I* am not an imbecile, Monsieur."

"I didn't think you were. I'm sorry, but, very stupidly, I hadn't realised how reasonable and logical it would be for you to distrust me. You think that I just pretended to help the Sangers so as to gain your confidence and make you talk more for the magazine's benefit. Is that right?"

"What else is there to think?"

"Phillip Sanger asked me the same sort of question, though in a different way."

"And what reply did you give?"

"I didn't have to give any. He supplied the answer as well as the question."

She was still looking at me warily, but I had aroused her curiosity. She shrugged. "Well?"

"Do you mind if I sit down?"

She motioned me to a chair, but did not sit down herself; she thought faster on her feet; I had noticed that at the first interview. "Well?" she repeated.

"He didn't think I was bluffing," I said. "What he wanted to know was what made me tick. 'What is it with you?' he asked. 'Self-destruction still, or is there a new kind of anger now?' Do you know why he referred to self-destruction?"

"No."

"One of those bad things Adèle mentioned was that I once tried to kill myself by taking a lot of sleeping pills."

I had her whole interest now. She walked over and looked down at me.

"Did you mean to fail, or was it an accident?" she asked.

That told me a lot about her. Most people simply want to know "Why? What made life so intolerable that you wanted to give it up?" Some, those who have read the textbooks, inquire shrewdly about self-hate. There are very few who know about the nadir of desolation themselves. They do not have to ask the wide-eyed questions, only the essential one: "Did you *really* try?"

"I didn't mean to fail," I said: "I was just taken to hospital an hour too soon."

"Have you ever tried again?"

"No. What Sanger meant, though, was that I might have turned to other means of self-destruction. It can become a habit, you know. People say: 'Just because a thing is bad for you, *that's* no reason for going on doing it.' But they are so wrong. It can be a reason, and a very sound one."

"Psychiatry!" She held her fingers to her nose as if at a bad smell. "What is the new kind of anger?"

"Sanger seemed to think that it must be you."

"Anger with me? Why?"

"Not anger *with* you, anger *for* you. The dragon-hater abandons all to rush to the aid of the beautiful damsel in distress."

"But that would be childish."

"It's Sanger's explanation, not mine. He also thinks that I am under the spell of your personal attractions."

She looked amused. "Oh yes, Patrick would always think that. He is a romantic." She became businesslike again. "So he told himself some fairy tales and believed them. I do not."

"All right," I said, "I'll give you a different answer. The reason I didn't take Sanger's money was that I couldn't have got away with it. As simple as that. The reason I told the magazine to go to hell, as you call it, is that I want to break a contract with them, I want to break a contract with them, I want them to fire me. So I've done something professionally unforgivable. I've walked off a job at the worst possible moment and in the worst possible way.

My being here now is nothing to do with *World Reporter* or any other magazine. I'm here because I'm interested in you and curious about your story, and also, to be frank, because I have nothing else to do at the moment. I daren't go back to Paris yet. When that interview appears on Monday I may even have the police looking for me too. I have to keep out of the way. You see how it is?"

She thought before she answered. " Why do you wish to break your contract?"

" Because I've been offered a better job, of course. Why else?"

The final lie convinced her. She smiled mockingly but not disapprovingly. " Just another son-of-a-bitch, eh?" She used the American phrase.

I smiled back at her. " That's right. And now let me ask you a question. If you really thought that I was bluffing and just trying to get you to talk some more, why did you allow Adèle Sanger to give me your telephone number?"

That amused her. " I was wondering when you would think to ask that," she said.

" Then I'm sure you have a good answer ready."

" Of course." She sat down ; no further quick thinking would be necessary for the present. " It was because I wanted to keep in touch with you after the interview was published. With Adèle going I could not keep in touch through her. So I let her give you the telephone number."

" And made her give you mine as well. Was that really because you thought of moving or was it in case I didn't call you?"

" I have told you."

" A few moments ago you were accusing me of trying to trick you into a further statement. Do I take it now that you do want to make further statements?"

" Perhaps. I will think about that." Her eyes met mine. She went on slowly and with rather obvious care: " Mainly, I was thinking that after the interview is published I may need some help in dealing with other people who may want to talk to me."

" Other reporters, you mean?"

" Oh yes. Other reporters, and "—she held up Skurleti's card—" people like this."

" I see."

" This one has come too early. What will you say to him?"

" What would you like me to say?"

" The money he offers is serious." She smiled slyly. " You could sell him the list he wants but with certain addresses left out—this house, and the one at Beaulieu perhaps."

" That will delay him certainly. What would you like me to do then?"

" You could arrange to give him some more addresses, after Monday."

" After the magazine with the interview appears. Right?"

" It would be interesting to know for certain whether it is Patrick he is really interested in, or me. Interesting for you, too," she added winningly.

I got to my feet. " I think it's time I was going."

" Won't you have a drink, a glass of port, perhaps, before you go?"

" No, thank you. I think I'd better be getting back to Nice."

She stood up, too. Her smile was a little strained now. She was afraid that she had made it too clear that she intended to use me, and insufficiently clear that I could hope that there would be compensations.

She put a hand on my arm.

" You will be careful, won't you?" she said anxiously.

" With Skurleti?"

" With yourself." Her eyes looked up into mine. " You are forgetting. We are both fugitives now."

" I suppose we are."

My tone was intentionally non-committal. She had to try again.

" So you must be careful. You must take precautions."

" I'm afraid I'd look pretty conspicuous in a fashion wig."

" I am being serious."

" So am I."

She shrugged, then turned and led the way through to the front of the house.

At the door she made a final effort.

" If you wish to telephone, it is better in the afternoon or evening. In the morning the woman is here to clean."

" I'll remember that."

" It is lonely here," she said ; " and now Adèle has gone it will be lonelier. Perhaps, if it is safe, you will come again to-morrow."

" I'd like to." I grinned at her. " Then I can tell you what I got out of Skurleti, and you can tell me all about these Italians he may be working for. How does that sound to you?"

She burst out laughing. Evidently, it sounded fine. There was, after all, nothing at all for her to worry about; she had me just where she wanted me.

III

When I arrived back in Nice I went first to the hotel and pre-pared the list of Sanger addresses.

It wasn't very long. I considered omitting La Sourisette as well as the two houses Lucia had suggested. Almost certainly, Sy would have someone—the stringer from Marseille perhaps —covering Sanger's own place by now. If Skurleti began nosing around, too, there could conceivably be a pooling of resources and information. It wouldn't take Sy a split second to guess who " Pierre Mathis " was. On the other hand un-less I omitted all the Mougins addresses, Skurleti would be certain to hear of La Sourisette when he began his inquiries there. But *could* I omit them? He had already made some inquiries and it was quite possible that he already knew about the Mougins properties. In fact, I had been checking them out that very morning while he had been having his argument with the *archiviste*. He had had time since then to make some sort of a list of his own. If I wanted him to trust my list— and me—I would have to take a chance on his encountering Sy.

I thought of a way of reducing the chance, though, and put an asterisk against La Sourisette.

Skurleti was already at the café when I got there. I was ten minutes late and he was looking at his watch. He nodded as I sat down and waited impassively while I attracted a waiter's attention and ordered a drink. When the waiter had gone, he leaned forward.

" You have the list?"

" Yes."

He drew an envelope from his pocket and pushed it across the table. " One thousand five hundred francs," he said.

" Two thousand five hundred was the price we agreed."

" For the whole list, when the search is completed, and if it is completed quickly."

" It cannot be completed until late Monday."

" Why not to-morrow?"

" The record office is closed Saturdays and Sundays. Didn't you see the notice?"

He looked annoyed. " Very well, then. Now, your list, please."

I glanced at the number of notes in the envelope, then handed him the list. There were fifteen addresses on it, including those at Sète. When he came to these he frowned and looked up at me.

" Sète?"

" In Hérault, the other side of Marseille. It would have taken you a long time to find out about those," I added complacently.

" Then what about the other *départements* along the coast—Bouches du Rhône, Var?"

" They have been checked. Nothing."

I could sense his dismay at the prospect of a time-consuming journey to Sète. To check all the properties on the list would take him at least three days. I thought it a good moment to be helpful.

" You will notice," I said, " that I have put a mark against this property, La Sourisette, in Mougins. That is Sanger's own property."

" But they are *all* his properties."

" I mean it is the villa in which he lives when he is in France. It is his home."

" Indeed?" The teeth showed.

" But I happen to know that he is not there at the moment. There is a servant who says that he is away. She does not know when they will return."

" They?"

" Monsieur and Madame Sanger."

" Ah!" The teeth showed again. " There is a Madame Sanger?"

" Naturally. He is married."

" Have you seen this Madame Sanger?"

" No. But the fact that he is married is noted in the credit dossier."

He tapped the table thoughtfully with the list. " Tell me something," he said. " How did you know that the Sangers were away from their home? Have you been trying to contact him, too?"

" Him? What for?" I smirked. " It was the servant I was interested in. Servants sometimes know more than there is in the dossier about what goes on. Does the subject drink too much, does he gamble, does he keep a mistress? They know."

His eyes sharpened. " And what did you find out about this particular subject?"

I hesitated. " About him? Not much. He is away a lot on business trips. Very careful of his health. Not much entertaining when he is home, and then only local married couples. Plays bridge. A serious type. On the other hand . . ." I hesitated again, and then shrugged.

" On the other hand?" He beamed encouragingly.

" Nothing but gossip. Of no interest to you."

" Everything interests me, Monsieur Mathis. I am like a sponge. I absorb everything." The teeth were fully exposed now.

" Oh, well . . . It was the wife I heard most about. You know it is she who deals with the rental of the properties, not the husband?"

" No, I did not know. That is very interesting. What else?"

" It seems that in one of the properties she has a friend, a special friend her husband does not know about."

He looked disappointed and sniffed disparagingly. " It is natural," he said. " With the husband away so much, there has to be something—a muscular young man from the beach, a gigolo from one of the big hotels. It is to be expected."

I shook my head and leered, I think convincingly. " No, this is different. It's not a young man. The servant has heard them speaking on the telephone. It's another woman!"

He became, suddenly, quite still. It was a difficult moment. He didn't take his eyes off me. I had to let my expectant grin deteriorate into the sheepish look of the man who realises that his joke has fallen flat.

At last, he nodded. " So?"

"That's what I was told." I swallowed my drink.

He was still watching me carefully. "How did the servant know that it was a woman? How did she know that it wasn't a man?"

"Because of the name—Lucille, Lucy, something like that I think it was."

"Lucia, perhaps?" he asked softly.

"Perhaps. Anyway, it wasn't a man."

There was another awkward silence. Then: "And the husband, Sanger, did *not* know?"

"Does the husband ever know in such cases?" I laughed inanely, and then made a lot of fuss getting the waiter to bring us more drinks. Although I had compounded the bait with some care, all I had really hoped for had been a cautious, but possibly suggestive nibble. I hadn't expected him to go for it hook, line and sinker. It was unnerving.

Fortunately, he had stopped staring at me. His face had a curious pinched look now, and he gazed into space, thinking. He was holding his empty glass and took no notice when the waiter tried to relieve him of it. Finally, however, he let the glass go and looked again at the list of addresses.

"Where do you live, Monsieur Mathis?" he asked suddenly.

"Here in Nice." I gave him the name of my hotel.

"That is your home?"

"Ah no. My home is in Lyon, but I do not see it except at the week-ends. In my job I have to travel a lot."

"I understand. Are you married?"

"Yes. Two kids, a boy and a girl."

"That is a pity."

"What?"

The teeth showed again, this time with gums. "I was hoping that I could persuade you to give up a few hours of your home and family this week-end," he said affably. "There would be money to be earned of course."

I pulled a long face. "Well, I don't know. My wife is expecting me to-night."

"You drive all that way?"

"No, I take the Blue Train. It's quicker and I can have a nap if I feel like it."

"The Blue Train stops at Marseille, doesn't it?"

"Yes, why?"

" And Sète is near Marseille."

" Not very. It's nearly two hundred kilometres beyond."

" Still, you could be there to-night if you wanted to."

" I suppose so."

" And after a few hours in Sète you could be at your home again to-morrow night?"

" Well, no doubt I could," I said doubtfully.

" For five hundred francs perhaps?"

" What do you want me to do? Find out if Sanger is staying in any of those houses of his?"

" Not exactly. I am interested in Sanger, naturally, as I told you. But what I want to know is who is living in each house. Number of persons, male or female, ages, names."

" That would take more than a few hours."

" To a man of your experience? Surely not. The *patrons* of the cafés and the *garagistes*, they always know these things."

It might have been Sy talking. I continued to look unwilling. " There would be expenses," I said; " hotel, meals, taxis, additional train fares."

" A hundred francs extra for expenses. You can pick up to-morrow evening's Blue Train at Marseille. While you are there, you can telephone me with the information at my hotel. I will be waiting. Is it understood?"

I gave in. " Oh, all right." I glanced at my watch. " I will have to telephone my wife. She won't like it. She'll think I've got a girl here."

" Not when you tell her about the five hundred francs."

" If I tell her about that she'll want to buy some new clothes."

On this cosy, domestic note the negotiations ended. He wrote down the name of his hotel and the telephone number on another one of his cards, and gave it to me.

As I got up to go, however, he put a detaining hand on my arm.

" One other thing."

" Yes?"

His eyes held mine for a moment before he went on: " I have explained that this is a very urgent and important matter. So you will be very thorough, I am sure. There will be no short-cuts, no slipshod work."

" Certainly not." I tried to look indignant at the suggestion.

" And no indiscretion either, I hope. Your inquiries should on no account alert the subjects."

" We do not alert persons whose credit we are investigating," I said huffily.

" Good, good. No offence intended. I shall hear from you to-morrow evening, then."

" Of course."

I went back to my hotel wondering whether or not to call Lucia and tell her what had happened. I finally decided not to do so. When I saw her the following day I wanted to be in a bargaining position. If I were going to satisfy her curiosity about Skurleti, she was going to have to do some satisfying of her own first.

On the other hand, I was going to have to move out of the hotel for forty-eight hours. Although Skurleti had seemed to accept me at my own valuation, he was obviously no fool. From his point of view, this had been a remarkably good day. Now that he had time to look back on it, he might begin to wonder if perhaps it hadn't been too good to be entirely true. He might start checking up on me. He had urged me to be thorough. It would, I thought, be a good idea if I took the admonition seriously.

I looked up the next hotel on the *Michelin* list and then telephoned Lucia.

She recognised my voice now.

" Have you seen him?" she asked immediately.

" Yes."

" And?"

" I'll tell you to-morrow. I just called up to say that I'm moving out of here."

" Why?"

" I'll tell you that to-morrow, too."

" Is anything wrong?"

" No. Just a precaution. You have the next number?"

" Yes. Did he . . ?"

" I have to go now. See you to-morrow."

I packed and went down to the desk. While I paid my bill, I explained that I was going to see my family in Lyon and would be back late Sunday night. I told them to give that message to anyone who called, and asked if I could have the same room when I returned. That was all right. I left the hotel, put the car in a nearby parking garage, and carried my bags to the station. I had just over an hour to wait for the train. I left the bags in the *consigne*, bought a return ticket for Cannes, and then went out and had a meal.

I was reclaiming my bags at the *consigne* when I saw Skurleti. He was standing by the magazine stand watching the platform where the Blue Train would come in. He was making no effort to conceal himself. He was looking about him like a man expecting to meet a friend.

I suppose I should have been pleased that I had foreseen the possibility of his checking up on me and taken the necessary precautions, but I wasn't. Instead, I had an unpleasant feeling in my stomach, and began wondering if the precautions had been adequate. There was that damning return ticket to Cannes in my pocket, for instance. Supposing he caught a glimpse of that. Supposing he asked me for my home telephone number in Lyon. What did I do then? Give him any old number and hope for the best, or just turn and run? I suddenly felt appallingly incompetent, and also weak at the knees. I was about to make the fatal character mistake of telling a porter to take my bags to the train instead of carrying them myself, when he saw me.

He came over at once.

" Ah, I was afraid that you were going to miss the train," he said breezily. " It is due at any moment."

" I know."

" I wanted one further word with you, and at your hotel they said you had left."

Check and double-check.

" I was having dinner. The prices they charge on the train . . ."

" I understand. It was just that in case I should not be at my hotel when you telephone from Marseille to-morrow, I have arranged with the operator at the hotel, a very charming woman, that she will take a long careful message, if you will dictate slowly."

Teeth gleamed in the station lights.

" Yes, of course." My stomach began to return to normal. If that was the best excuse he could think of for his presence at the station, I had been over-estimating him.

" Enjoy yourself," he said. The train was coming in now.

"I always try to."

"It is good to be young. We will talk again to-morrow."

"In the evening."

I scurried away along the platform, ostentatiously looking for the "Marseille only" section of the train.

He did not wait for the train to leave, at least not on the platform; but I had to assume that he could be waiting outside, so I went through with my original plan. When the train stopped at Cannes, I got out and took the next local back to Nice.

The temporary hotel I had to stay at was near the harbour and seemed to cater for transients using the Corsican *paquebots*. The night *concierge* was a punctilious type with thin lips and suspicious eyes. He made me show my identity card, and so I had to sign the police *fiche* with my own name. I didn't like doing it, but I had no choice. He would have been quite capable of calling the police and reporting the incident if, at that stage, I had changed my mind about staying and left.

It was then ten-thirty—four-thirty p.m. in New York. Sy and Bob Parsons had another six and a half hours to go before the deadline. I wondered what they were doing. One of them, Bob Parsons probably, would still be trying to find me and scouting for leads. The stringer from Marseille would be helping him. By this time, Sy would have a line open to the Paris office. I wondered whether he had already told New York about my defection, or, hoping for a break, was so far only reporting me as out of touch. Most likely, I decided, he had told them the truth. After all, I had been Mr. Cust's choice for the assignment, not his; they couldn't blame Sy. If you handed a psychopathic amateur an assignment which called for a tough-minded pro, he would tell them, you had to expect a few surprises. In any case, they had most of the story, the part that really counted; and they had the tape to substantiate it. It might be a bit inconvenient if I hadn't shown up, or been located, by the time the story broke, but they could handle that situation if and when it arose. They had a beat on the competition, and the more noise it made the better.

But not better for me.

There are occasions when a newspaper or magazine editor may refuse to name his sources of information on the grounds of press privilege ; but this would not be one of them. *World Reporter,* on this occasion, would be ready and eager to co-operate with other news media and the authorities. They would have to do so, not only in order to refute the inevitable suggestions that the story was a hoax, but also to explain why they could not produce the man who had interviewed Lucia Bernardi so that he could be interrogated by the police.

It would be interesting to see how Sy dealt with the problem. He couldn't very well claim that I was mentally unstable without discrediting both the story and the magazine. Probably, I thought, he would assume an attitude of manly, innocent frankness and say that he didn't really know what had happened ; that he had been expecting to meet me at Nice airport, and that I hadn't shown up. He certainly wouldn't mention the note I had written to him. He would say that when he found that I had left Mougins in a hurry, he had naturally assumed that there had been an unexpected development in the story and that I was busy following it up. Now he would be seriously concerned about me, and glad of any help the police and press could give in finding me. There was a picture of me on file in the office for use on press cards. That would be made available. It wasn't a bad likeness. There were a number of people in Nice who would recognise it instantly.

The European edition of *World Reporter* is printed in Frankfurt and distributed in bulk by air. It was more than possible that some news agency man there would pick up the story before the magazine was actually published ; on Sunday night possibly, when the air freight people began to handle the distribution. In that case, the French morning newspapers would carry the bare bones of the story in some of their Monday editions, and the evening papers would have time to elaborate. By Monday afternoon, at the latest, I would be news.

As Lucia had said, we were both fugitives now. By Monday, I would have to find a hiding place as good as hers.

I could only think of one.

CHAPTER V

It was just before ten o'clock, and I was drinking my second cup of coffee.

I had planned to stay in my room for most of the morning, and then, on my way to pick up the car, buy a hat. Skurleti, I was sure, would be out working on his list of houses ; and, as I had given him two addresses in Cagnes, there was a possibility that his visit to Cagnes might coincide with my appointment with Lucia. If he should happen to catch a glimpse of me driving by, a hat, I thought, would make me harder to recognise. Sun-glasses would also be worn, but only, I had cleverly decided, if the morning overcast cleared and the sun came out.

The last hat of any kind I had worn had been an English school cap. I was wondering vaguely what sort of hat to buy —felt or straw, good or inexpensive, light-coloured or dark— when the telephone rang.

The sound made me jump. The only person who knew I was there was Lucia, and I hadn't been expecting her to call. Moreover, she didn't know that I had to register in my own name. She would ask for Pierre Mathis, and then realise . . .

I snatched up the phone and said " Hello."

" Monsieur Maas?" It was the hotel operator. " There is a call for . . ." She broke off and then said apologetically: " I am sorry, the person did not wait."

" What person?"

" There was no name."

" A man or a woman?"

" A man, Monsieur."

" What sort of voice? Was he French?"

" Oh yes. A Marseillais, perhaps."

" Did he ask to speak to me?"

" He asked if you were staying in the hotel. I did not know, so I looked at the list. When I saw your name, I said that I would call your room, but he did not wait. If he calls back . . ."

" Yes, of course. Thank you."

114

Obviously, the stringer from Marseille had been given the job of telephoning all the hotels. Now he had found the one they wanted and had hung up at once so as not to alert me.

I had to get out, and get out quickly. If they were still at Mougins I had time enough. If they had already moved into Nice, things were going to be difficult.

I hadn't shaved or even brushed my teeth. I scrambled into the clothes I had been wearing the night before, threw the rest of my things into the suitcase, and went downstairs. It can't have taken me more than five or six minutes. It took me another five to get the bill made out and paid.

There was no hope of getting a taxi quickly outside the hotel. I scuttled across the road and along the Quai Papacino. I felt horribly exposed. There was a ferry steamer tied up there with a large notice on the stern: ATTENTION AUX HELICES. It seemed an appropriate injunction at that moment. When I came to a side-street with a one-way-only sign, I immediately turned down it. I was going away from the harbour area now, and they couldn't use that street to approach it by car. In the Place Garibaldi I picked up a taxi and was driven to the first hotel I had used, the one near the station.

Luckily, they had a room for me. I mumbled something about a change of plans. A moment later I was registered again as Pierre Mathis.

As soon as I had bathed and changed, I went down and asked the way to the nearest men's shop. It was in a cheap department store, and there wasn't a wide selection of hats. They were short on sizes, too. I took the first one they produced which fitted me, a coarse grey felt with a wide brim and a deep black band. The salesman said that it had *ton*, and was the only one of its kind they had left; he was obviously eager to be rid of the thing. It gave me a seedy, hangdog look which I pretended to admire. He barely managed to conceal his contempt for my folly.

From the store, I went to the garage, picked up the car and drove, heavily hatted, to Antibes. There was time to kill before I went to see Lucia, but I preferred to kill it outside Nice. Besides, I had to decide how I was going to manage the interview; I had to think carefully about it, without having to look over my shoulder while I did so.

A bottle of wine and a good lunch seemed to simplify the

matter. Lucia wanted information, and I had some to give her.
Lucia wanted to use me, and I might be willing to be used.
But first there would have to be some plain speaking. I knew
enough by then to suspect that her reluctance to be inter-
viewed by me had only been pretended. She had fooled Adèle
Sanger completely. I had no intention of being fooled myself.
I wanted the truth.

After lunch I drove through St. Paul to Vence, and entered
Cagnes by the back road. By taking that roundabout route I
could get to the Rue Carponière without going through the
centre of the town. I parked outside Number 5, as before,
and walked up to Number 8.

The front door was open and she was waiting for me. She
stared at the hat as I took it off.

"Why are you wearing that? You look ridiculous in it.
When you got out of the car I hardly recognised you."

"That was the idea."

"That I should not recognise you?"

"That other people shouldn't."

"Why? What has happened?"

"Quite a lot."

She waited for me to go on. When I didn't, she shrugged
slightly and went through to the terrace room. I followed.

"You were very mysterious on the telephone," she said.
"What did you find out about this Skurleti? What does he
want?"

"To see you."

"How do you know? Did he tell you that?"

I sat down without replying and lighted a cigarette.

She stared at me impatiently. "Well?"

"Do you mind if I call you Lucia? It would make it easier
to talk."

"As you wish. It is my name."

"Then, Lucia, before I tell you anything more, you are
going to have to tell me some things. That was our understanding yesterday. Remember?"

"Perhaps. So much was said."

"Yesterday, you made a reference to 'the Italians.' I think
you meant me to think that it had slipped out accidentally.
But I don't think it was accidental. I think you were putting
ideas into my head."

She looked amused. "What ideas?"

"That you were not nearly as scared and helpless as Adèle Sanger had led me to believe. That you were not at the mercy of a situation, but in charge of it."

"Why should I want to do that?"

"It was an intriguing way of breaking the news."

"I don't understand you." She was no longer looking amused. "What news?"

"That the interview you gave me is really a carefully written advertisement for something you have to sell."

"You are saying this, not me."

"But it's true, isn't it? You have something to sell—a suit-case full of records, perhaps. But first you have to let the prospective buyers know that it is for sale. At the same time you have to be very careful not to let them know too much, or they might try to take it without paying, as those two men tried in Switzerland. So you waited to be found by someone who would publicise the fact that the sale was on. That turned out to be me. On Monday the news will be in *World Reporter*. By Tuesday the buyers will be gathering in Nice or near by. All you need now is a go-between, someone who will establish communication with the buyers, take the bids and conclude the deal. I think that also turns out to be me, doesn't it?"

She stared for a moment, then flopped back in a chair and burst out laughing. I waited. At last, she got to her feet again, still giggling weakly, and went to a drink cabinet.

"Now this time," she said, "you really must have a drink. Do I call you Pierre or Piet?"

"Pierre will do. And, yes, I'll have a drink. That is, if you will stop beating about the bush and talk sensibly. If you won't, I'm leaving, and you'll have to find somebody else to deal with Monsieur Skurleti."

She spread out her hands, wide-eyed in wonder. "But, of course, I will be serious. It was only that I was afraid that if I spoke too freely you would not accept the situation—that you would feel that I had humiliated you, and perhaps go back to your editor, or even to the police."

"Well," I said sourly, "you can speak freely now. What were you going to do if I hadn't come along?"

She brought me a bottle of brandy and a glass. "I was not

sure. I had become more and more nervous waiting. I tried to think of some other way of arranging it, not using a newspaper, but the other ways would have been too dangerous. I have to be very careful, you understand. If you had not come, I would, I think, have telephoned to the man in Nice who works for *Paris Match*." She paused. " I never thought of an American paper. That was stupid of me."

" You could have gone to Sanger."

" Patrick?" She made a face. " Ah, no! I know Patrick too well. He would have done things his way. There would have been very complicated manoeuvres. In the end, all I would have had would have been a small tip, while he would have bought some more houses." She sat down and sipped at her port. " It is interesting about this Skurleti," she went on ; " interesting that he should try to find me through Patrick, as you did. What happened when you talked to him?"

" I'll tell you later," I said. " First, I want to hear from you."

She hesitated. " You haven't told me yet if you will help me."

" You haven't told me yet what you want done."

" But you know. You guessed."

" With the help of some broad hints from you, yes, I did. But if you are asking me to take the risks involved in making this deal for you, I want to know more."

She bit her lip. " I did not say that there were risks."

" If there were no risks you wouldn't need a go-between, Lucia. You'd make the deal yourself."

" A woman could not negotiate with men like these. They would only listen to another man."

" The way they listened to Colonel Arbil?"

" You don't understand." She was getting a trifle pink.

" No, I don't. So, until you tell me exactly what I'd be getting into, I can't decide whether I'll help you or not."

" How do I know that you are serious, that you are not just trying to satisfy your curiosity?"

" You'll have to take a chance on that, I'm afraid. Or call the man at *Paris Match*. Maybe he'd be easier."

She eyed me coldly for a moment, then shrugged.

" That's better," I said. " Now, what was in the suitcase?"

" I told you. Ahmed's records."

" Records of what?'

" Of the Committee's secret activities."

" You told me that when you took them and left the villa, you were doing what Colonel Arbil would have wanted you to do. Would he have wanted you to sell them?"

She looked down at her glass. I thought for a moment that she was going to start lying again; however, when at last she did answer, I realised that it was not a lie she had been trying to evolve, but a way of explaining a relationship.

" You must understand about Ahmed and me," she said carefully. " I liked him very much indeed. It is hard for a woman not to like very much an attractive, rich and intelligent older man who adores her and yet who does not lose his good sense and dignity by insisting that she adore him in return. You understand?"

" Sanger said you were crazy about him."

She dismissed that impatiently. " Of course, I told Patrick that I was. It saved argument. My being in love would mean to him that I had become emotionally unreliable and therefore useless to him."

" I see." I wondered if it had been Sanger's respect for her rapid mental arithmetic that had prevented his appreciating her ability to calculate in other ways.

" So," she went on, " I was happy with Ahmed. He made me laugh, he made me feel like a woman, and he was generous. There was no misunderstanding between us. It was understood that one day he would return to his own people, and a high post in the Government ; perhaps, eventually, the highest. A French Catholic wife would have been unthinkable, even a wife who had changed her religion. The Kurds are very strict, you know."

" So I believe."

She brushed her hair away from her forehead, and her eyes met mine. " You know a lot about me, I think."

It was a plain statement ; there was nothing arch about the way she made it.

" I know what I've read. I know what the Sangers told me."

" And what you have seen for yourself, too."

" I have learned some things, yes."

" Perhaps, then, you have already guessed that money is a serious matter with me."

"It is with most people, I think, especially with most French people."

"I don't mean taking care of the sous. I mean that I am very afraid of not having money. When I was a child my father lost his business. It was just after the war. Although I was very small, I always remembered how frightened they were, he and my mother."

"But your father built up another business."

"It was never the same. My parents both came from working-class families. They had climbed a long way, and that meant much to them. They were always afraid of sliding back. When I went to live with my aunt in Menton, I understood why. It was she who made me learn to work with my hands. That was her idea of a good life—to be able to work for a few francs an hour and end by marrying a grocery salesman." She paused. "I suppose you think that I am a snob."

"Some grocery salesmen live very well, I imagine. But I understand what you mean. It must have been a bad shock when the business in Antibes failed."

She nodded. "It taught me a lesson. A small business is no good any more unless there is plenty of capital behind it, the means to grow. Ahmed and I talked about it many times. Although he was an army officer, he was very clever about money. His brothers are all in business, you know." A far-away look came into her eyes. "One is the concessionaire in Iraq for a big American automobile manufacturer. His profits are enormous. Cars, trucks, bulldozers, tractors—he gets a percentage on every one that is sold in the country."

She looked perfectly beautiful as she said it, as if she had been describing some exquisitely moving work of art. Then she caught my eye and shrugged. "Of course, there are big overhead expenses, too."

I smiled and she looked at me warily. She was not sure whether I was laughing at her or with her. I said: "Lucia, I don't think that you are afraid of not having enough money. I think you are afraid of not having a lot."

She made an impatient gesture. "It is the same thing. Ahmed understood. That is what I wished to explain. He said that when he went back to his people he would leave me some capital to use. It was his idea. We planned together what I could do with it."

"How much capital?"

The faraway look returned to her eyes. "Oh, half a million francs or so. Perhaps more." Her tone was almost indifferent.

That was the moment at which my motives really became mixed.

"And the money was to come from what was in the suit-case?" I asked.

"Yes."

"How?"

"That was also what I wished to explain, but you keep interrupting me."

"I'm sorry."

She poured some more port into her glass and composed herself. "Ahmed never had any difficulty about money," she said. "You asked me about this before. When he became a refugee in Switzerland, there was an understanding with those in Baghdad. Some were still his friends, of course, and some were his enemies, but they all knew Ahmed very well. He was greatly respected, even by his enemies. Besides, he had been in charge of intelligence. When he had left for the Geneva conference, he had known that there might be trouble while he was away, so he had taken certain dossiers with him."

"Dossiers that could be embarrassing to his enemies, I take it."

"And to his friends. It was simply a precaution. In Iraq, friends can easily become enemies, and enemies become friends. That is how he explained it to me. Ahmed was always very practical. So there were no difficulties when he wanted money in Switzerland. His brothers and the family businesses were protected, and they were permitted to send money to him. Everything could be arranged."

"Where are the dossiers now?"

"Oh, I have them." She waved the subject aside. "But they are not the important thing. It is what happened between Ahmed and the Kurdish Committee that matters. Ahmed was a patriot, you know."

"So you said before."

"But not a stupid patriot."

"I'm sure of that."

"For a long time, while he was in Zürich, he worked with the Committee. He was a man of experience and reputation, a high official, a military man and greatly respected in the army. He was a person of consequence, you understand."

"Yes."

"At first, the Committee did not wholly trust him. He told me that there were a few members who believed that his exile in Switzerland was not real, but a trick of the Baghdad Government to place a spy in the movement. As time went by, though, and he became more influential, they came to trust him, and took him more into their confidence. And then, about a year ago it was, some things happened which made him begin to distrust *them*."

"What kind of things?"

"Do you know anything about the Kurdish nationalist movement?"

"The Treaty of Sèvres and all that?"

"Yes, all the disappointments. Ahmed said there had been too many and that the Committee had become sick. He said that when men like that—exiles with a sense of injustice and a cause to fight for—have to wait too long for satisfaction, a change takes place in them. Some lose heart, and they no longer matter ; but others become desperate and ready to grasp at any means to power, even if it betrays the principles to which they are dedicated. 'Let us be practical,' they say. 'Let us get the power first, and we can reshape our policies afterwards.' Such men, Ahmed said, are either corrupt, or they are self-deceivers. In any case, they are dangerous and must be stopped."

"So he decided to stop them."

"Yes. You know after the collapse of the Kurdish Republic of Mahabad in nineteen forty-six, it had always been the policy of the Committtee to reject Russian support of the movement. The Russians had failed them once, they felt, and would fail them again. They realised, too, that a Kurdish state linked to the Russians would never be acceptable to the West. At least, most of them realised it. As Ahmed became closer to the Committee he began to see that there were several members who, while pretending to accept the official policy, spoke of it in private as if it were a joke. At first, he

took this to be no more than a normal expression of bitterness
and frustration. But he was interested in the men concerned
and allowed it to be thought that he might share their views.
Finally, he was approached by one of them who proposed a
secret meeting—secret, that is, from the Committee leaders.
It was held at the villa. By the end of that evening he knew
that the Committee had been completely betrayed and was
being used merely as a cover for a conspiracy with the Russians."

"What sort of conspiracy?"

"Simultaneous armed uprisings in the Kurdish areas of
Turkey, Syria and Iraq. But prepared very carefully in advance. Militant groups to be organised and trained in the use
of modern weapons. Arms caches to be established. Secrecy
and discipline to be maintained by special terrorist groups.
There is a lot more to it. It has a code name, *Dagh*. It is a
Turkish word that means 'mountaineer.' You know, the
Kurds are also called 'Mountain Turks.' Ahmed said that
Dagh was a clever, long-range plan, and that it had been
worked out with the strengths and weaknesses of the Kurds
in mind. He thought that it would be very likely to succeed."

"What did he do?"

"Naturally, he joined the conspiracy."

"Naturally? I thought he disapproved of it."

"He did. But how else was he to make himself valuable?
He was 'in place,' as they say. For over two months he was
at all the *Dagh* secret meetings, listening to what was said,
finding out everything he could—names, places, chains of
command, financial arrangements, communications, everything."

"These were the meetings you spoke of before— those held
at the villa?"

"Yes, but there were others, in Lausanne and Basle. That
was before he had the warning, of course, the warning that
he was suspect. After that, he went to no more meetings. It
would have been too dangerous."

"Then the *Dagh* people must have realised that he had
been warned."

"Not immediately. He told them that he had been interrogated by the Swiss federal police and that he thought that he
might be under surveillance. That made it reasonable for him

to stay away from them, and they from him. But he knew that the situation could not last. Sooner or later they would understand and try to kill him. He believed, though, that they could not succeed."

"You really don't know who warned him?"

"No. But the warning came from Baghdad. Somebody there had talked too much. They had been careless."

I was getting confused. "They?"

"His old government friends in Baghdad. Naturally, he was in touch with them again by then. He had already let them know a little about *Dagh* and what he was doing about it." She smiled knowingly.

I thought I understood. "Oh, I see. You mean he had decided to use this *Dagh* thing to buy his way back into favour?"

"*Buy* his way?" She looked affronted at the suggestion. "Certainly not. He was going to sell."

"But surely . . ."

"Where would be the sense in giving Baghdad the information for nothing?" she demanded. "Obtained free, it would at once be suspect. They knew that he was quite comfortable in Switzerland, that he did not *have* to return. Immediately they would ask themselves: 'Why? Why is this Kurd suddenly so kind to us? What game is he trying to play now?' But if they had to pay a lot of money they would take a different view. His motives would be understandable. That is how these people think."

"And they did agree to pay?"

"Yes. It was all arranged. A man was going to come from Baghdad to examine samples of the intelligence reports Ahmed had prepared and negotiate the purchase. Ahmed made only one condition—that the man who came would be a person he could trust. They were to send a former army colleague of his, Brigadier Farisi. He was to have arrived the day after Ahmed was killed. I was to be the go-between."

She looked at me expectantly. I poured myself another brandy, and made the obvious comment. "I take it, then, that Brigadier Farisi is the buyer you're waiting for?"

She nodded. "One of them. As soon as he reads about me in your magazine he will know that I wish to contact him."

"Who is Skurleti acting for?"

"The Italian consortium I think. In fact, I am almost sure."
She made a business of lighting a cigarette as she went on.
"Ahmed thought of it this way. Baghdad had been warned
about the *Dagh* operation. He had agreed to sell them all the
intelligence reports and other documents he held concerning it.
He had behaved as a responsible person and a patriot should."

She paused to let that sink well in.

"On the other hand," I prompted.

"Yes. On the other hand, the Baghdad people might not
be the only ones who would be interested in a sight of copies
of the reports."

"Sell them twice, in fact."

"It could do no harm. Ahmed found out during one of the
Dagh meetings that a new Italian oil consortium is extremely
interested in any possibility of a political change in the Mosul-
Kirkuk area. You see, it could perhaps lead to a revocation
of the present fifty-fifty oil concessions and the granting of new
concessions on the seventy-five-twenty-five plan. One Italian
company has already made such a deal in Iran. Now the other
oil countries want it, too. The American and British concessions are safe in Iraq as long as the situation there is stable.
But if it is going to become unstable this Italian consortium
means to be in there first. So they, too, would like to know
in advance about *Dagh*— what its chances are and who the
new leaders would be with whom they would have to do
business."

"From the fact that Skurleti is already on the job, I take it
that Colonel Arbil had let the consortium know that he was
open to a deal."

"Oh yes. They knew."

"So there are two buyers in the market. But what about
the people who murdered your friend? If they can read,
they'll be around, too, I should imagine."

Her face tightened. "Yes, they will be here. *Dagh* is clearly
compromised, but they must try to save themselves now, and
their organisation, too, if they can. That means destroying the
reports. They may have others to help them now, Russkis
perhaps. That is why I have had to be so careful. At first, I
thought of trying to contact Brigadier Farisi through the Iraqi
Embassy in Paris, but I know Ahmed would not have thought
that a good risk to take. Baghdad had been indiscreet once.

They could be indiscreet again. You see? I was terrified, but I had to be careful."

"Yes, I see." And I did see. She had been terrified; but not too terrified to keep her head and hide and wait and, ultimately, to find a way of getting her capital out of the Arbil investment. Hitherto, I had been fascinated by her. I had not yet come to the point of liking her; but that was the point at which I began to respect her.

" And *we* must be careful," she added. " That is, if you will help me."

She looked at me anxiously, ready to persuade; but I had already made up my mind.

" All right," I said. " But I think I had better make it clear to you now that I am a deeply neurotic moral and physical coward."

She laughed. " You told your boss to go to hell."

" I am very brave on paper."

" You are droll." She looked at me appraisingly. " I think I like you."

" You'll change your mind. We haven't discussed my fee yet."

" Oh that." She thought for a moment, then seemed to reach a bold decision. " You see, now," she said, " that it is only a matter of some telephone calls. I think that if you were to receive five per cent that would be satisfactory."

" Not to me."

" Twenty-five thousand new francs!" she said indignantly. " It is a fortune!"

" For a few telephone calls, possibly. Not for what I would have to do, Lucia. The reports have to be sampled. That means two meetings. Then the remainder of the reports have to be handed over in exchange for the cash. That means two more meetings. Four meetings in all. Four chances of being killed by the Committee."

She waved that away. " Oh, you exaggerate. I have said that it is necessary to be careful. If you are careful how will they know of the meetings?"

" In their place, I know what I would do."

" What?"

" Wait for the buyers to arrive and then see whom they contact."

"How can they identify the buyers?"

"Skurleti might not be too easy for them, but they'd certainly know about Brigadier Farisi. I think that we have to be more than careful about arranging these meetings. I think we have to be clever, too. Even so, they will be highly dangerous for the parties concerned. I don't blame you for employing a go-between," I concluded amiably, "but I'm afraid you are going to have to pay him properly."

She drank some more port. "And how much do you think is properly?"

"Thirty thousand dollars."

She stared aghast. "Thirty thousand . . . but that is a hundred and fifty thousand francs!"

"About that, yes. It's the capital I need. If you want my help, that's what it's going to cost."

She stood up quickly. "You are insane!"

"I would be insane to do it for less. I'm probably insane anyway, but if I could lay my hands on that amount of money I'm prepared to take risks. A sort of all-or-nothing arrangement you might say."

"I will give you fifty thousand francs."

"Call the *Paris Match* man."

"Seventy-five thousand."

"One hundred and fifty thousand, or I don't do it."

"*Salaud!*"

I waited while she called me a few more names. When she began to tire, I broke in. "Lucia, it has to be a hundred and fifty. I told you. There's no point in my taking the risk for less. But I promise you this. I'll make the very best bargains I can for you. You may still have your half million free and clear. If we're lucky and can get a Turkish bidder going against the Iraqis it might even be more."

"You are worse than Patrick."

"You said he would only leave you a tip."

"That is all you are leaving me," she retorted bitterly.

"Nonsense."

She threw up her hands wearily and sat down again. "You are a blackmailer."

"That is what Sanger called me, too. But I was very helpful to him all the same."

"You called it capital. You are a journalist. What do you need capital for?"

"For the same reason that you do—to retrieve a failure. As a matter of fact it was Sanger who worked out the amount for me."

She drew in a deep breath and let it out again. "Very well," she said.

"You agree? One hundred and fifty thousand?"

"Yes, yes, I agree. Tell me about Skurleti."

I told her.

She wanted to know every detail of the conversation I had had. My having been seen off by Skurleti at the station amused her. She was impressed by his readiness to pay so generously for my services. "He has been given a *carte blanche*," she commented approvingly.

"As far as expenses are concerned, perhaps," I said. "How much are you expecting to get from him?"

"I will ask for two hundred thousand francs and expect to receive at least half that. He must be told that there are other interested persons."

"If you are only selling him copies, that won't impress him. You could still sell to someone else."

"He won't know that they are copies. Ahmed made them himself in his own writing."

"What about Brigadier Farisi? How do we contact him? Always supposing that he's the one they send to Nice."

"He will be the one. There is no doubt of that. And Ahmed said he was no fool. I know what he will do here to make it easy for us."

"What?"

"In Zürich I was going to contact him at the Hotel Schweizerhof. There is no such hotel here, but there are several with Swiss names—the Helvétique, the Suisse, the Frank-Zürich, and others. I think he will choose one of those. You have only to telephone them. It is not difficult to find someone who stays in a hotel."

"I'm well aware of that." I told her about my hotel adventure that morning.

She was delighted. "You see? It will be easy to find him."

"It will be even easier to find me. By Monday my picture

may be in the papers. I ought to get out of that hotel by to-morrow night."

"Where will you go?"

"I was hoping that you would have some suggestions."

She thought for a moment. "There is a room here," she said at length; "but there is also the woman who comes in the morning. She would think it strange that while I am recovering from plastic surgery I take a lover."

"What about the house above Beaulieu, the one you took me to for the interview? Do you still have the key for that?"

"Yes. But you would have to be very careful there. It is supposed to be empty and there are occupied houses near it."

"Is there any food there?"

"Adèle left some cans of soup in case I had to move suddenly. But you had better buy some more things to-day before the shops close. There is no linen for the beds, but there is some here you can have. I will give you the key to the garage, too, so that you can put your car away out of sight."

"No, I'll have to get rid of the car before Monday. If I'm in the papers that rental garage man could recognise me. He'd worry about his car then and notify the police. You'll have to drive me there, I'm afraid."

"Not in the daylight."

"As far as I'm concerned," I said, "the later the better. I'm not much looking forward to my own cooking." I stood up. "I think it's time I telephoned Skurleti."

"Ah yes. The telephone is over there."

She listened on the extension in her bedroom while I made the call.

"Monsieur Skurleti? This is Mathis in Marseille."

"Have you been to Sète?"

"Yes. The houses are all empty."

"All of them? Are you sure?"

"Quite sure. No one could be living in them."

"Why not?"

"They are being rebuilt."

"All three?"

"All three. They are uninhabitable."

There was a pause. "Very well," he said at last. "I will see you Monday at the Hotel de Ville."

E

" I may be delayed, but I will see you there or speak to you at your hotel. Good-bye."

I hung up.

Lucia was smiling as she returned from the bedroom. " What an accent," she said. " But I suppose he can read and speak Arabic. That must be why he was chosen." She looked at her watch. " You had better go now and do your shopping."

As we went through to the front of the house, I said: " There is one thing we still haven't discussed. What happens after?"

" After?"

" Let us suppose that Skurleti is willing to pay, that Brigadier Farisi arrives and is also willing to pay, that somehow we manage to avoid getting murdered by the Committee . . ."

She cut in sharply. " You should not make jokes about that."

" I wasn't making jokes. But all right, we'll leave murder out of it. Supposing that everything goes according to plan, and that we are able to collect this money—what then? Do you continue to hide?"

" Only until the *Dagh* people know that the reports are in Baghdad, and they will know that soon enough. After that they will no longer be interested in me."

" But the police will be."

She gestured vaguely. " Oh, I will let them find me then. I will tell them what I told you for the magazine. I will have a lawyer and he will give them the rest of Ahmed's papers. I will be the silly, hysterical woman. They have nothing against me."

" They'll have plenty against me," I reminded her. " Failure to give information about a person wanted for questioning can be an offence if they decide to make something of it."

" Ah yes." She thought for a moment, then her face brightened. " Of course. You shall take me to the police. You will be the one who persuades me to surrender. It is you who gives them Ahmed's other papers."

" But who says nothing about the sale of the *Dagh* reports, of course."

" Oh no. They would not like that, I think."

" You realise that without the information in those reports

the Swiss police have no chance at all of ever catching the
men who tortured and killed your friend?"

She shrugged. " They have no chance now anyway. Besides,
Ahmed would not care. To send those men to prison would
not bring him back to life. For him the important thing
would be that the reports go where he wanted them to go.
And he would want me to have the money."

" Yes, of course."

She thought she detected a note of criticism. Her mouth
tightened. " I wept many times for Ahmed," she said quietly ;
" but that is over now and I will not pretend to things I no
longer feel. Especially I will not pretend with you. Since we
are business colleagues, we can do without hypocrisy and
pretence. I said I liked you, but I do *not* like you when you
put on a high collar." She meant when I became priggish.

I smiled. " I apologise. The collar shall be thrown away
at once."

" Good. What time will you arrive to-morrow?"

" At about this time, I think. I can transfer my bags and
the food supplies to your car. Then I'll take the Renault back
and return it to the rental place. You can pick me up in
Nice later when it's dark."

She approved that arrangement.

I put on the hat and left. I didn't have to worry now about
Skurleti being in the Cagnes area, so I drove straight back
to Nice along the autoroute. There is a big chain-store grocery in the rue Gambetta. I bought eggs, sardines in oil, can-
ned vegetables and fruits, some of the least perishable kinds
of *charcuterie* and a few bottles of wine. I had to make two
trips to get it all into the car. From there I drove to the
garage near the station and parked the car. There was rain
in the air, so I walked across to the hotel to pick up a coat.

I was thinking that if I were going to be holed up by myself
in the house at Beaulieu for several days, I ought to lay in a
store of books as well as food, and possibly get a small radio
as well. As I went through the revolving door into the hotel
lobby, I was adding cigarettes to my shopping list for the
next hour.

I saw Bob Parsons before he saw me. He was at the *concierge*'s desk showing him a photograph. The *concierge* looked

up automatically at the sound of the door. For an instant the hat prevented his recognising me; but only for an instant. He let out an exclamation and Bob Parsons looked round.

As I turned and blundered out through the door again, I heard Bob Parsons shouting after me.

"Piet! Hey, Piet, you damn' fool! Wait a minute!"

Then I was in the street again. There was a screech of brakes and tyres as I darted across in front of a moving car. The driver yelled something at me. I heard Bob Parsons' voice again faintly calling my name.

I didn't look back. I ran.

11

Luckily, the rain in the air had become a steady drizzle by now. A running man on a dry street attracts attention and may interest the police; but a running man with his collar turned up against the rain calls for no explanation. I ran until I was exhausted.

There is a big café at the end of the rue Rossini. I went in there and telephoned Lucia. Luckily I had written down her number on the back of the press permit I carried in my pocket.

I told her what had happened. She didn't ask stupid questions or waste time deploring the situation.

"Where are you now?" she asked.

I gave the address of the café and waited while she wrote it down. Then I went on: "The car, with the food in it, is in a parking garage near the hotel. I don't think I ought to go back there on foot. I think that you'd better wait for a while, until it's dark, then pick me up here and drive me to the garage. As soon as I can get rid of the rental car, I'll have to go to Beaulieu."

"What about your clothes?"

"I can use the next hour to buy what I need to tide me over."

"Very well. But I can't come into the café. There will be too much light there. You will have to watch for my car."

"The Citroën? All right. An hour from now?"

"Yes."

I went first to a pharmacy and bought the essentials: razor, toothbrush, and so on. I tried to buy some sleeping pills as well, but the woman would not let me have them without a prescription. Then I found my way back to the department store from which the hat had come. They were on the point of closing. I bought some socks and underwear, three nylon shirts, a plastic raincoat and a small plastic suitcase. On the way out, I added a hideous clock-radio to the collection. There was no time to find a bookshop. Back at the café, while I was waiting for Lucia, I bought some cigarettes.

It was raining heavily by then and it soon became impossible to see through the glass screens enclosing the terrace of the café. I moved out and stood in the doorway of an office building next door. Lucia arrived a minute or two later. I dumped the suitcase on the back seat and got in beside her.

"Where is the garage?" she asked.

I told her.

"Wouldn't it be better to leave the car there?" she asked. "I know a food store that stays open late. You could buy some more supplies there."

"No, I don't think so. I want to get that car back to the owner. It is rented in the name of Mathis, and Bob Parsons knows that means me now. It would only create more trouble with the police if the car I had rented were reported missing. I'd rather turn it in while I can."

"Yes, that is sensible."

I directed her to the parking garage. She stopped at the entrance. When I drove the Renault out she followed me. Just short of the rental garage, I stopped and transferred the cartons of food to the Citroën. She waited there while I returned the car and recovered my deposit. A few minutes later we were on the Moyenne Corniche going east.

We didn't talk much. I asked her if the telephone in the Beaulieu house was connected, and she said that it was. Apparently, Adèle Sanger always left everything ready for immediate use in her houses; she had found it more practical to do so.

Lucia had brought linen and bath towels with her, and some bread. As soon as she had opened up the house, I began carrying things down from the car. The rain and the darkness and the steps made it a slow business. By the time I had finished she had a fire started.

" In a little while," she said, " I will make us something to eat, an omelette perhaps."

My surprise was too obvious to go unnoticed. She raised her eyebrows. " Did you think that I would at once leave you in this mess and go straight back to Cagnes?"

That had been precisely what I had thought she would do. " I was thinking of someone noticing the car outside," I said.

" Who could see it there at night?" She did not wait for a reply. " Now," she went on, " we will see where you will sleep. There is a large bedroom immediately above, which Adèle told me to use if I came here. The windows on this side are not directly visible to the neighbours. With the curtains drawn nobody could see any lights from there. But we must make sure of the curtains up there first. I should have brought a flash-light."

I produced matches and we groped our way upstairs. I held a lighted match shielded in the doorway while she went into the bedroom and drew the curtains. Then she turned a lamp on to reveal a large double bed and an expanse of yellow and white striped cretonne. A narrow arched doorway led to a bathroom. Lucia looked around critically. There was a nine-teenth-century pine *armoire* in one corner. She went to it and began to pull out blankets and pillows.

" Not bad," she said. " Adèle's houses are expensive to rent, but she gives value for money."

" Nobody is likely to come here, I suppose?"

" Not for a month at least. Some of her houses are occupied all the year, but with most it is for the summer only, May to September. Will you be comfortable here?"

" I'm sure I will."

" It is not very warm now, but if you bring up the electric heater from below, it will air the blankets. Then we can have a drink. You must need one. The bed can be made later."

Lucia the domestic woman was something of a surprise. Her whole manner, even the way she moved, was suddenly and subtly different. In five minutes she had charted the unfamiliar kitchen arrangements and made herself at home there. She clucked a little over my food purchases—I had neglected to buy butter among other things, so the omelette was out—but she was not unduly concerned. Somehow she managed to produce a delicious egg-dish with the aid of a can of tomato paste and some chopped slices of garlic sausage. We had bread and a bottle of red wine with it on a low coffee-table beside the fire.

I had expected her to want to go on talking about our plans for the week to come, but I had been mistaken. Planning authority, it seemed, had been delegated to me; her concern, thenceforward, would be with supplies, tactical support and the state of my morale. She had gathered some facts about my personal life from Adèle Sanger; now she wanted to know about my friends—their occupations, ages, marital status, where they lived, how much they earned, what they said, what they thought. When I mentioned a woman I knew well who wrote for a fashion magazine, her interest sharpened and her questions became circumspect. Is this the one he goes to bed with? she was wondering. When she realised that it couldn't be, she became more direct.

" What about when everyone is looking for you next week?" she asked. " Won't your friends worry about you?"

" I expect so. It can't be helped."

" But your particular friend."

" My mistress, do you mean?"

" Ah, you have not told me about her."

" Because she doesn't exist."

" You don't have *anyone* like that?" The incredulity in her voice would have been flattering if I hadn't been wondering how best to get off the subject.

" Not at present, no."

" From choice?"

" Partly, I suppose."

Her eyebrows rose mockingly. " Ah, I see. You are one of those who are very difficult to please." She smiled. " What was the last one like?"

I drank some wine. " I've almost forgotten," I said. " The man in the hospital said that I would forget entirely after a while."

Her smile had faded. " What happened? Did she die?"

" As far as I know she is still very much alive. In that hospital *I* was the patient."

" And you do not wish to speak about her."

" Or even think about her if I can help it."

There was a pause, then she nodded. " I see. She was part of a bad time."

" Yes."

Mercifully, she didn't pursue it any further. She finished the wine in her glass and began to clear the table. I started to help her, but she stopped me.

" No. I do it quicker by myself. You finish the wine. I will make some coffee."

A minute or so later I heard her leave the kitchen and go upstairs to make the bed. I stayed where I was. I was very tired, and talking about Madeleine had made me horribly depressed.

There is, I know, something that happens to my face at those times. She saw it the moment she came back into the room with the coffee. When I took the tray from her, she went to the cupboard and got out the bottle of brandy which I had opened for her on the night of the interview.

" Do you think you will be able to sleep well here?" she asked. " Myself, I find that for some reason a strange house is not the same as a hotel in that way. Even a house like this is very personal."

" I dare say the brandy will help."

She sat down and poured the coffee. " When Adèle took me in," she said, " I was having, as you may well imagine, something of a *crise de nerfs*. She got some sedative pills for me from her doctor. There are a few left. I know that they are not the same as sleeping pills, but I could bring them to-morrow if you like."

" Do you know what they are?"

" Luminal, I think. Something like that."

" Thank you. I'd like to have them."

" If I had had any sense," she said briskly, " I would have put them in my bag to-night."

That made me smile. " You're not used to dealing with emotional cripples," I said.

She flushed angrily. " If you can smile when you describe yourself in that way one must assume either that you don't really believe it, or that you enjoy humiliating yourself. In any case, it is not attractive."

" It wasn't meant to be. I was simply stating the situation.

I smiled because you were trying to behave as if your forgetting to bring Luminal with you was as ordinary a thing as my forgetting to buy butter. It isn't, is it?"

She considered the proposition, then shrugged. " You said that you are a coward, now you say that you are an emotional cripple. You remember only bad times and say only bad things of yourself. Why? Because you are stupid? You don't appear to be. Perhaps, though, you think that because a person is afraid of many things that makes him a coward. Perhaps because you think always of the injuries you have received, you believe that you are for ever a cripple." She had been looking into the fire, but now she raised her head and looked straight at me. " But do you expect me to play this game with you? To me you look like a man. You may not be happy, but that is your affair. I do not wish to behave towards you with any kind of ' as if.' I do not wish to ' behave ' with you at all. In particular, I do not intend to behave as if you were a cripple. I have always disliked deformity."

" Then you'll have no trouble, I'm sure, in denying its existence. After all," I added reasonably, " ours is purely a business arrangement."

" Exactly." She stood up. " I think I will go now. Is there anything else I can bring to-morrow, apart from the things we have discussed?"

" If I think of something, I'll telephone."

She put on her coat and wig and head-scarf. I switched the light off before opening the front door. She went without another word.

Our mutual dislike was almost complete.

CHAPTER VI

A man, X, arrives at a hotel and takes a room. A second man, Y, is in a house on the outskirts of the same town. X wishes to meet with Y, and Y wishes to meet with X. However, they must meet without exposing X and Y (especially Y) to the hostile attentions of a third party, Z.

Question: Describe convincingly (1) the circumstances under which the desired meeting may safely take place, and (2)

how those circumstances are to be contrived. Give precise
details. If necessary, illustrate with diagrams, sketch-maps,
etc. Good luck may *not* be used as a factor in providing a
solution.

I spent most of Sunday on the problem.

The answers to the first part of the question were fairly
obvious. Assuming, as I had to assume, that Brigadier Farisi
would be known to the Committee agents and placed under
close surveillance, that surveillance would have to be evaded
effectively before a meeting could take place. Farisi must not
be able to lead them to me. Furthermore, because of the peculiar relationships between me, the police and the newspapers
which would obtain during the period under discussion, the
meetings would have to be at night and in a place which
Farisi could reach without being seen and identified. Ideally,
both Farisi and I ought, for an hour or so, to become invisible.

For part two, I could find no satisfactory answers at all. I
had seen films in which the problem of evading surveillance
had been solved by jumping into or out of moving trains and
buses, or dodging through large buildings with multiple exits ;
but I had to assume that the men sent in by the Committee
to find and destroy the reports would be experienced as well
as determined. Any crude and obvious attempt at evasion
would notify them that we were on the defensive, and, more
dangerous still, that a deal was impending. What I had to do
was to evolve a foolproof plan for the meetings which could
be explained to Farisi simply and concisely over the phone,
and which would call for no public behaviour on his part
that might arouse suspicion.

By the late afternoon I had reached the conclusion that the
task was virtually impossible, unless an element of risk was
accepted. It was relatively simple to think of ways of remov-
ing Farisi temporarily from direct visual surveillance while he
was out of his hotel. He could disappear into a doctor's
waiting-room, or a café toilet, or he could pay a visit to the
nearest brothel ; there were all sorts of possibilities. The real
difficulty was in effecting a rendezvous with him without, in
the process of doing so, exposing myself.

I telephoned Lucia. She was formally polite.

" Did you sleep well? " she asked.

" Well enough, thank you."

" Is the house warm? I should have told you, there is fire-wood in the staircase cupboard."

" I found it. What I'm calling about is this. Have you a good map of the area? Or any sort of guide-book?"

" Adèle left a map in the car, I think. Why?"

" I'll explain later. But it's important."

" Very well. I will be there as soon as I can."

When she arrived she had a carton of supplies, including a casserole of chicken, which she had prepared earlier, and two bottles of white burgundy. She put the casserole in the oven and asked me to open one of the bottles of burgundy.

" Yesterday we had too much alcohol," she said. " I talked unwisely."

" You said what you thought."

" That is often unwise."

" Did you bring the map?"

She had it in her coat pocket. It was a combination map and street-guide of the *environs de Nice* with a multiplicity of folds, and lists of street names which could only be read with the help of a magnifying glass. I opened it out on the floor and examined it gloomily.

" Why do you need it?"

I explained to her the problems with which I had been wrestling.

She seemed pleased with this evidence that I was adopting a businesslike attitude. She sat down on the floor beside me and listened intently.

" There is one thing," she said when I had finished. " We do not have to worry in the case of Skurleti. He is already here. We may be able to conclude the business with him before the Committee people have time to make it difficult."

" I thought your idea was to let him think that he had com-petitors so that he would pay more. We can't hurry things too much without weakening our position. I can call him to-morrow and break the good news to him. I could even arrange the first meeting with him for to-morrow night. But it will be Tuesday night at the earliest before we can expect to complete the sale. He'll have to consult the group he's working for. He'll have to get the cash. I take it we want cash?"

" Oh yes. French or Swiss francs, or dollars. That does not matter to me. But it must be cash."

"I might be able to arrange something with him at the first meeting that would make the second meeting absolutely safe. If he were to clear out of Nice immediately, for example, the Committee couldn't hope to pick him up. But that won't work with Brigadier Farisi. They could be waiting for him at the airport."

"Perhaps they will not be so quick and clever."

"I'd prefer to assume that they will. If Farisi has to fly all the way from Iraq, they'll have a twelve-hour head start."

"If he is at the Iraqi Embassy in Ankara it would not be so long. That was where he was coming from before."

"We can't take any risks, no matter where he's coming from," I said. "You can buy *World Reporter* in Geneva on Monday morning. The Committee could have people in Nice by to-morrow night. We have to have a plan worked out for the Farisi meetings that will be safe for all of us. There has to be a building somewhere in Nice that he can enter without arousing suspicion or being followed inside, and which I can enter without being seen by anybody, inside or out. It's as simple, and as difficult, as that."

She was silent, thinking. After a minute or two, she got up and went into the kitchen to see that the casserole was all right. When she came back she said: "The Prophylaxy Clinic."

"What's that?"

"I remember my father used to go there sometimes. When he had trouble with his liver the doctor used to send him there for colonic irrigation. It used to amuse him."

"The irrigation?"

She laughed. "The clinic. There were various treatments given there for men of a certain age, you understand, and some of them were for embarrassing gland conditions. A man would not like to advertise that he went there and he would not like to meet there anyone he knew if he could help it. So it was arranged as discreetly as possible. One entered through a pharmacy and went upstairs to the clinic. When one left, one descended by a different stairway to the courtyard of an apartment building round the corner."

"How long ago was this?"

"Nine years perhaps."

"Is the clinic still there?"

"We can find out." She reached for the telephone directory and looked up the name. "Yes, it is there." She glanced at the date on the directory. "At least, it was there two years ago. We could telephone in the morning."

"You say there was a courtyard at the back. Was it a closed courtyard or could one drive a car in?"

"You could drive in. There was a *porte cochère*."

"How late did the clinic stay open? Do you remember?"

"No. But the pharmacy would stay open until eight-thirty. I expect the clinic did, too. That would be late enough."

I thought for a moment. "It might do for the first meeting," I said at length. "If I could park the car in the courtyard, he could go in through the pharmacy, come down to the car and then return the way he came. That's if they haven't changed things."

"We could drive there later this evening and see. It won't be open, but perhaps you could see enough."

"Yes, we'd better do that." I thought again. "There's only one thing I don't much like. An Iraqi arrives in Nice. The first thing he does is pay a visit to a clinic which gives colonic irrigations and treats old gentlemen for prostate troubles. Wouldn't it look a bit suspicious?"

"Suspicious for him to enter a pharmicist's shop? It is a big shop and sells soap and other things as well as drugs. And how long is he there? Ten minutes at the most."

"You may be right. But for the second meeting we'll have to think of something else."

She frowned suddenly. "There is one thing I have remembered."

"What?"

"Ahmed told me that Brigadier Farisi does not speak French. Oh, a few words perhaps, but no more."

"What about English?"

"Oh yes. That is the second language in Iraq."

"Well, I speak English."

"I was thinking of when he went into the clinic. He would have to say something, make an appointment for the following day possibly."

"I could tell him what to say, I suppose."

"Or perhaps he will bring someone with him who can speak."

" I don't want to deal with more than one man. At least, not more than one at a time. Especially at the second meeting. They might decide just to take the reports and forget to hand over the money."

" You don't have a revolver?"

" No."

" Well, there is one in the car I am using. It belongs to Adèle. You can borrow that."

Carrying a loaded revolver in one's car is an old French custom. I have always thought it an absurd custom, but it didn't seem a good moment to mention the fact.

" All right," I said ; " but I still think it wiser to deal with only one man at a time. That's not *only* cowardice," I added meaningly. " It's greed and good sense, too."

She chuckled ; she didn't mind the talk of cowardice when there was a mild joke to flavour it. She poured me some more wine ; she was at ease with me again.

" There's another thing we haven't discussed," I went on : " the reports themselves. Where are they, and what do we do about extracting samples?"

" Ah yes. That I must tell you about. There will be no difficulty. Ahmed had already picked out certain pages from the reports to show these people what they would be buying. But he said that it was necessary to be cautious. They may see and read those pages once, but *only* once. And they must take no notes. What they could memorise from a single reading would not matter much, Ahmed said. But that must be all."

" How many pages are there?"

" Six. I will bring them to-morrow night."

" And the reports themselves? I take it that they are still in the suitcase."

" Yes." Her face had stiffened.

I grinned. " It's awkward, isn't it, Lucia? If everything goes according to plan, the dreadful moment is soon going to arrive when you have to trust me with everything—the reports *and* the money."

She flushed slightly and got to her feet. " I think that to-night it will be better if we eat properly at the dinner table," she said, and went towards the kitchen.

As she passed the sofa she stopped. Her bag was lying

there. She picked it up and took out a small glass pill-container which she placed with unnecessary firmness on the coffee-table.

She gave me a brief glance.

"The Luminal," she said.

II

The clinic was in a quarter of the city criss-crossed by streets named after composers—Gounod, Verdi, Berlioz, Glazunov. It was well away from the main tourist hotel areas. The pharmacy was, as Lucia had said, a large establishment. Moreover, its big display windows were so filled with advertising cut-outs and crêpe-paper dressing that it was impossible to see much of the interior of this shop from the street.

Lucia turned the corner and stopped the car just beyond the apartment house entrance. I got out and went through the *porte cochère* into the courtyard. There was a television set blaring in the *concierge*'s room. No one saw me go through.

There were two cars parked in the courtyard and space for two more, with a notice saying that the place was private. I did not have to look far for the rear door to the clinic; it was in the corner to the left. Fastened to the wall beside it was a small engraved plaque bearing the name of the clinic and the information that this entrance was for the use of professional personnel only.

I went back to the car and got in beside Lucia.

"It looks as if they're still in business," I said. "There's only one thing that bothers me. None of these hotels that you think he may go to is anywhere near here. Why should he come all this way just to go to a pharmacy? There would be several nearer the hotel. Why should he come to this quarter?"

She thought a moment. "To go to a cinema?"

"Is there one near here?"

"I will show you."

She turned the car and drove past the pharmacy again to the nearest main street, the Avenue Respighi. There was a Lux cinema on the corner.

I made a note of the address.

"I have been thinking," she said, as we headed back towards Beaulieu; " it would be better if he had a doctor's prescription to take to the pharmacy. If he really is under surveillance, that is."

" How do you mean?"

" As you said, this Iraqi gentleman arrives from the Middle East. Very well. The time is different. He hopes to sleep. He asks at the hotel for a doctor who will give him a prescription for pills. If the surveillance is efficient, that will be reported. He gets the prescription. All is well. He decides to go to a cinema to pass an hour or two before dinner. As he leaves the cinema he remembers the prescription. He takes it to the nearest pharmacy and waits. They are busy at the time. No one will be surprised if he waits twenty minutes or more. No one will ask why he is inside so long or what he is doing. Delay is to be expected. What do you think?"

" I think you are very much better at planning this sort of thing than I am."

She suspected irony or sarcasm, and became angry. " Why must you be so unpleasant? I am serious."

" So am I. I think it's a very good idea. The first meeting will be the more important, because it will decide the price. The easier and more relaxed we can make it, the better."

There was a short silence. Then she said: " I have been thinking about to-morrow."

" I have, too."

" About the magazines and the newspapers and the radio?"

" Yes. How do you get the papers?"

" The woman brings *Nice Matin*, and sometimes, if she thinks of it, one of the Paris papers."

" No evening paper?"

" No. She has gone by midday. We will have to listen to the radio news and wait until the evening for the papers. I will stop at the station on the way here. There is not too much light there. Anyway, the risk must be taken." She glanced down at the instrument panel. " There is one thing we must do to-night."

" What is that?"

" Get the car filled up. Adèle left me two *bidons* for emergencies but it is better to keep those. To-night is will be safe for you to go to a garage. There is one by the Michelin depot in the Rue Arson."

She stopped the car near the intersection of the Rue Bona-
parte and the Rue Arson, and got out. I drove to the garage
and had the tank filled while she walked on briskly towards
the traffic circle at the foot of the hill leading up to the
Corniche. I picked her up again five minutes later and drove
back to the house.

When I got out she moved over into the driving seat and
took something like an old polishing rag from the door
pocket.

"You had better have this now," she said.

"What is it?"

"The revolver."

I took it and the greasy cloth in which it was wrapped, and
shut the car door.

She smiled up at me. "Sleep well, Pierre."

"You'll telephone me if there's anything in the *Nice
Matin*?"

"Of course. As soon as the woman's left."

I watched her back up the track again to the road, waited
until the sound of the car died away and then walked down
to the empty house.

The fire was almost out. I put another log on and used the
bellows until it began to burn. Then I unwrapped the revolver. It was fully loaded.

I did my military service in the Netherlands. As I was a
university graduate, I spent most of the time attached to an
army education unit teaching languages. During my basic
training I had been instructed in the mysteries of stripping,
cleaning and firing the Armalite A.R.10 rifle ; but there my
knowledge of firearms ended. As far as I was concerned,
pistols and revolvers were for officers, policemen and criminals.

I examined the revolver gingerly, looking for the safety
catch. There was none. After a while, I managed to find the
cylinder release catch and unload the thing. This enabled me
to make, without danger to myself or to the furniture, the
momentous discovery that when one pulled the trigger, the
cylinder rotated and the hammer rose and fell.

The fire was burning brightly again ; but, unaccountably,
I still felt cold. I stopped playing with the revolver and put
it away, reloaded, in a drawer. I had begun to think of to-
morrow.

The Luminal was where she had left it, on the coffee-table. There were six 15 mg. tablets in the container. I took three, and went to bed.

III

I awoke soon after dawn. From the bedroom window I could see the Pointe St. Hospice on Cap Ferrat. There was a strong breeze blowing from the south, and the dark sea outside the bay was flecked with white. There was no early morning haze; it was already brilliantly clear. Far below, on the short loop of coast road that I could see, a white delivery van went by. I could almost read the lettering on the side of it. I had an absurd feeling of uneasiness. On such a day, I thought, nothing could be hidden. If the sky had been overcast, of course, I would have found anxiety in that, too. Rain or shine, it was going to be a bad day anyway.

I went downstairs, made some coffee and switched on the radio. Radio Monaco was delivering a mineral water commercial—"*L'eau qui fait Pfshit! . . . Pfshit! . . . Pfshit!*" I tried, with no success, to find a station with a news broadcast on, and turned back in the end to Monaco, which had the strongest local signal.

I toasted the remains of the bread Lucia had brought the previous night and ate that with the coffee. Then I bathed and dressed.

The news came on at nine o'clock. At the opening session of the international conference on tariffs, the French delegate was expected to oppose the election of a permanent chairman. A Belgian airliner with sixty-four persons on board was reported overdue on a flight to Brazzaville. Another communications satellite was to be launched that morning from Cape Kennedy. The second hatchet murder in the space of a week had taken place in the St. Georges quarter of Marseille. An insurance commission investigating the cause of traffic accidents had reportedly described Route Nationale 7 as the most dangerous road in Europe. The trial of a man and his wife on a charge of embezzling their daughter's trust fund was due to begin at Lyon.

Then the announcer went on: "*There is also to-day an*

echo of the mysterious Arbil affair. Listeners will remember that a beautiful young Niçoise, Mademoiselle Lucia Bernardi, was sought for questioning by the police in connection with the assassination of her lover in Zürich. Hitherto, the police have been unable to trace her. Now, this morning, comes an American news agency report that last week an American journalist succeeded in finding and interviewing Mademoiselle Bernardi at a house in the vicinity of Nice. She is said to have given a complete account of the events surrounding the assassination. No further details are yet available, but a police official in the office of the Commissaire Central stated an hour ago that they are aware of the report, that it is being investigated, and that a statement may be issued later this morning. We hope to include this statement in our midday news report."

He went on to give the week-end sports results.

It was more or less what I had expected, with the exception of the agency report. I had forgotten that there were news-stands in New York where you could buy *World Reporter* on Sunday night. I didn't much like the allusions to the police. The picture of an American journalist succeeding where the French police had failed was not going to endear the " American " in question to the Commissaire Central. Nor, when the " future details " arrived, would the situation improve. I won-dered where Sy Logan was and how soon the police and the French and Swiss reporters would start questioning him. If he was back in Paris, they would perhaps be on the job already.

I tried again to find another news broadcast ; again without success. There was nothing for it now but to wait. I looked through the books in the living-room. They were an assort-ment of the kind you would expect to find on the shelves of a furnished rental house in that part of the world: an old, in-complete encyclopaedia, books of colonial reminiscences, some unreadable French and Italian novels, religious books for children, a leather-bound, fourteen-volume edition of the works of Victor Hugo set in six-point type, and a curious little manual compiled to assist parents in naming their child-ren, *Un Nom pour le Bébé.* I looked up the name of Lucia.

It was, I learned, either a feminine derivative of the Latin *lucius,* meaning light, or a diminutive of Lucretia. The latter, the manual admitted candidly, was now little used because of

" unfortunate historic associations." See also Lucie and
Lucrèce, it advised.

For a while, to pass the time, I tried counting my chickens
before they were hatched. I began to organise the rebirth of
Ethos as a monthly magazine. As I had told Lucia, it had
been the too-ambitious fortnightly conception which had been
at the root of the trouble. With production costs the way they
were you couldn't operate on a shoestring. On the other hand,
a monthly would be an economically viable proposition. I
would need only a third of the staff. The new format I had in
mind carried the prospect of a serious advertising revenue.
And this time I would make certain of a more effective and
profitable distribution arrangement.

After ten minutes of this sort of day-dreaming, I realised
that the return to reality might become painful if I went any
further. I turned on the radio once more and listened to light
music recordings interspersed with commercials.

Noon came eventually, and I soon wished that it hadn't.

The announcer began with an item about the conference on
tariffs in Geneva, and then went on:

" *There have been sensational developments to-day in the
already sensational Arbil affair. In our nine o'clock news
broadcast this morning we reported that Lucia Bernardi, the
beautiful young Niçoise for whom French and Swiss police
have been searching for months in connection with the assassination of her Iraqi lover, Colonel Arbil, in Zürich, was said to
have been found and interviewed, in a house near Nice, by a
journalist working for an American magazine. This report
has now been confirmed. The interview was published to-day
in the American news magazine* World Reporter. *In it Mademoiselle Bernardi, who is quoted extensively, describes the
events of the night of the assassination and the way in which
she was able to escape sharing the fate of her lover. She also
says that she succeeded in saving the secret papers belonging
to him for which the assassins had been searching on the night
of the murder.*

" *There was a disposition in some quarters earlier to-day to
regard the interview as a* roman policier *thought up by someone posing as Lucia Bernardi in order to gain publicity, and
perhaps some money, too. But reports from Zürich have
eliminated that possibility. According to the head of the*

*Zürich criminal police, Commissioner Mülder, the interview
reveals knowledge of unpublished details and facts about the
scene and the manner of the crime which leaves no doubt that
the person interviewed was indeed Lucia Bernardi.*

" *As was to be expected, local police authorities immediately
wished to know more about this interview, and about Mademoiselle Bernardi, the missing witness they have been seeking.
The obvious person to tell them was the journalist who conducted the interview.*

" *But now mystery piles upon mystery. At the Paris office
of* World Reporter *this morning, a spokesman for the magazine said that they had no information as to the present whereabouts of their employee. They say that he telephoned the
interview to them last Thursday night, and then said that he
was going to take a few days' vacation. All attempts to get
in touch with him since then have failed.*

" *According to the police the journalist's name is Piet Maas,
a citizen of the Netherlands living in France, who also uses
the name Pierre Mathis. He is aged thirty-four. His height
is given as one hundred and eighty-one centimetres. He has
blond hair, grey-blue eyes, a high forehead and a clear complexion. He is also described as slim and having a certain
elegance in his appearance. The police are anxious to secure
his co-operation in their investigations, and request that any
person knowing of his whereabouts inform them of the fact.
Monsieur Maas is believed to be in the Nice area.*"

The announcer concluded on a note of pawky jocularity:

" *An American colleague of Monsieur Maas, now in Nice,
described him to-day as being a 'screwball'—an American
slang expression meaning that a person is eccentric or unpre-
dictable. Bearing in mind also Monsieur Maas' elegance and
the undoubted charms of Mademoiselle Bernardi, this will
perhaps, in some minds, account satisfactorily for his sudden
decision to take a holiday. The mystery may now possess, in
the best tradition of Hollywood, an added element of comedy.
We hope to report more fully on our six o'clock news despatch.*

" *In Lyon this morning . . .*" I switched off.

Almost immediately the telephone rang. It was Lucia. She
was bubbling with amusement.

"You heard Radio Monaco?"

"Yes."

" And you are not laughing?"

" I'm not exactly bursting my sides, no. Was there anything in *Nice Matin*?"

" Nothing. But it will certainly be in the evening papers, and on television, with your picture perhaps."

" No doubt it will."

" Ah, I see. You do not like publicity."

" No."

" Now you know what it was like for me."

" Not quite. In my picture I'm not wearing a bikini."

" But you have a certain elegance. They said so."

" It doesn't show in the picture they'll use." I changed the subject firmly. " Aren't there any other local radio stations that give news broadcasts?"

" Oh yes. Wait, I have a newspaper here."

I wrote down the times and frequencies she read out to me. It was then agreed that she would telephone me again after the five o'clock news broadcast from Nice.

I went back to the radio.

By two o'clock the police had issued a fuller description of me and repeated the description of Lucia which had been issued after the murder of Arbil. In an accompanying statement they affirmed that Lucia was wanted only for the purpose of questioning with a view to her making a deposition. They didn't say exactly what they wanted me for, but mentioned, ominously, that a foreigner resident in France, especially a foreigner holding press credentials, had special obligations where French law enforcement agencies were concerned —obligations that he would be both incorrect and unwise to ignore.

By three o'clock one station had information about my career, including my connection with *Ethos*. They were confused about that, however, and described it as a magazine devoted to ethology, the scientific study of animal behaviour.

By four o'clock *World Reporter* had found it necessary to issue a further statement emphasising the fact that they were co-operating with the authorities to the best of their ability, that my non-availability had in no way been devised by them to hinder the work of other news media, that they had no knowledge of the whereabouts of Lucia Bernardi other than that contained in their published account of the interview, and that they had voluntarily turned over the complete tape-recording of the interview to a representative of the Préfecture of Police in Paris.

Obviously, Sy had been closely questioned by the Préfecture. I wondered how he had accounted for my being sent to find Lucia in the first place, and if he had told the police about the Sanger-Chase tip-off. New York would probably have instructed him about that. Under the circumstances, I thought that they would most likely have decided that it would be too dangerous to tell the whole truth. I hoped so. I would know more when I saw how the story had been handled in the magazine.

By five o'clock a news agency had dredged up the fact that I had been a " war orphan." I knew then that it wouldn't be long before they got to the mental hospital and the shock treatments.

When Lucia called this time, she was rather more subdued.

" They are not agreeable, these things they are saying about you."

" So far they haven't said anything that's untrue."

" All the same . . ."

" They have to say something. It's their job." I paused. " How soon can you be over here this evening?"

" It cannot be very early. I have to go to the station first. Towards eight o'clock."

" I think it's time I called Skurleti. The sooner I arrange a meeting with him, the safer it will be. We talked about that."

" Yes."

" If you bring the samples with you, I could arrange a meeting with him for nine o'clock."

" Very well. Where will you meet him?"

" The place I first met you might be good, I think."

" It is near, yes," she said slowly. In my mind's eye I could see the indecision on her face. She was having to accept the fact that, for all practical purposes, this was the moment when she had finally to delegate her authority as a principal and trust to my judgment.

" What will you say?" she asked.

" That depends on what he has to say first."

" You will let me know as soon as you have spoken?"

" Of course. I'll call him now."

"Good luck to us both, Pierre." There was a tremor in her voice as she said it. She didn't wait for a reply.

I smoked a cigarette and thought carefully about the things I should *not* say, before I lifted the telephone again and dialled the number of Skurleti's hotel.

He answered the moment the operator rang his room; but there was a guarded note in his voice at first.

"Yes?"

"I promised to telephone you to-day, Monsieur."

"Ah yes." The relief was audible. "I have been waiting for your call. Has it been correctly reported that you speak English?"

"Yes."

"Then for convenience let us speak in that language." His English accent was as dreadful as his French, but in English his syntax was better.

"By all means."

"I have been most interested to-day in what I have read in a magazine."

"I had an idea that you might be."

"It seems a pity that we could not have discussed the matter on Friday. It would have saved time and been easier and less dangerous for both of us."

"I'm glad you are aware of the danger."

"Oh yes. I assume that you didn't trouble to go to Sète after all."

"I had already been there."

"I see. Then the reason for the delay was tactical. The lady is interested only in the highest bidder."

"Exactly."

"And how much am I to be asked to pay for the introduction?"

"There will be no introduction, Mr. Skurleti. I am the lady's sole agent in the matter."

"Fully authorised, I hope."

"Yes."

"And with credentials to prove that you are?"

"Certainly."

"What is your proposal?"

"First that you take immediate steps to avoid the possible danger you mentioned."

"Ah." He sounded pleased. "I believe that our thoughts may be running along similar lines."

"I suggest that you move out of Nice at once, to Villefranche perhaps, or St. Jean."

"You will be glad to know that I had anticipated your suggestion. My bag is already packed. I was only waiting here for your call. But I think a little farther away might be safer. Antibes possibly."

"Which hotel?"

"I have a reservation in the name of Kostas at the Motel Côte d'Azur. But I think we need not wait until I am there to make arrangements for a private meeting."

"Have you a car?"

"Yes."

"What kind?"

"A Ford Taunus."

"There is a café called the Relais Fleuri on the Moyenne Corniche above Villefranche. If you will be there, alone, at nine o'clock to-night, and wait in the car park, I will join you there."

"With your credentials?"

"With the credentials. There is one more thing, Mr. Skurleti." I paused.

"Yes."

"There is no point at all in our meeting unless we are seriously to talk business."

"Naturally."

"And unless we are to talk it in the same language."

The metaphor eluded him for a moment. He started to say that he didn't understand, and then stopped. "Ah, you are referring to the financial aspect."

"Yes. The price will be in the region of two hundred thousand new francs."

There was a silence before he replied. "Until I can be certain what is being offered for sale it is useless to discuss the question of price. But I will tell you now that I have no authorisation to negotiate such a large sum."

"Then I think you should obtain the authorisation. If necessary we can postpone the meeting. Now that we have re-established contact there is no immediate urgency. Shall I telephone you again to-morrow?"

"I would prefer to let our arrangement for to-night stand. Is there a telephone number where I can reach you?"

"No, there isn't, I'm afraid. If we meet to-night I shall expect you to make up your mind whether or not your principals would wish to buy and, if necessary, agree the price. As you are the first interested party to arrive, you have an advantage at present. If you are prepared to discard the advantage, that is your affair, of course. I am certain of one thing. The price will not go down, but it may very well increase."

He grunted. "So will the danger—the danger for you, I mean."

"That is why you are being given this early opportunity. The lady and I are both aware of the dangers. However, if necessary, we are prepared to accept them in order to get our price. You should be in no doubt about that, Mr. Skurleti."

There was a pause. "Very well," he said finally, "I will meet you to-night. Under the circumstances, however, I must ask you to make the time a little later. If I am to consult with my principals, that means telephone calls."

"How much later?"

"An extra half-hour should be sufficient."

"Very well. Nine-thirty."

I hung up, went to the drink cabinet and poured myself a stiff brandy. Then I telephoned Lucia and told her briefly what had been said.

Her reaction was characteristic.

"He did not object to the price?"

"No, but he will. You can be certain of that."

"But he did not seem surprised?"

"He didn't say he was surprised, he didn't say he wasn't. He was non-committal. He wants the meeting."

"Perhaps we have asked too little."

"We may also have asked for too much. We'll know later."

"I will be with you as soon as I can."

I nursed the brandy and listened to another news broadcast. Most of it was a rehash of the earlier bulletins; but the news reading was followed by a commentary. The commentator was a bitter man whose function seemed to be to discredit the news which had just been reported. After doubting the "shallow and foolish accounts" of the French *démarche* at the Geneva conference, he turned to the latest developments in the

Arbil affair. "*In Switzerland, a Kurdish exile is tortured and killed,*" he grated angrily; "*in France, the young Frenchwoman who fled his house crouches in terror waiting for the same assassins to find and torture and kill her, too. Here in Nice, a responsible and respected journalist has the courage to write the story of her plight, and he disappears!*" The voice dripped with contempt as it went on. "*And what do our gallant police do? They announce that they have some questions to ask. What do our colleagues of the press do? They make little jokes. We do not find such jokes amusing. Monsieur Maas found Mademoiselle Bernardi when the police had failed. Monsieur Maas has shown himself more astute than his supercilious colleagues. We hope devoutly that he, and the woman he is doubtless protecting, are found and brought to safety before they, too, are tortured and killed. Perhaps the police can be persuaded to forget their injured dignity for the time being and do their duty—if they know it.*"

His heart was in the right place, of course; but he made me very uneasy, and in more ways than one.

Lucia arrived somewhat flustered, just after eight. She had had trouble buying *World Reporter*. At the station newsstand they had sold out. There had been a run on the magazine. She had not dared to go into a lighted shop. Eventually, she had found a copy at a kiosk on the Avenue de la Victoire. She left me to read it while she made preparations for dinner.

Sy Logan, or someone in New York, or both, had handled the story ingeniously. After a brief recapitulation of the events in Zürich and the unavailing search for Lucia, it went on:

"*Last week, a staffer from the Paris bureau of* World Reporter, *then in the South of France on another assignment, called to say that he had accidentally come across a possible lead to the whereabouts of Lucia Bernardi. Should he follow it up?*

"*Suspecting a hoax,* World Reporter *was understandably cautious, but instructed him to find out more. On Thursday night, in a house near Nice, he taped an interview with a woman who claimed that she was Lucia Bernardi, but who refused to be photographed or to allow an independent witness to be present. Here's how the interview went.*"

There followed a version of the interview, edited and con-

densed with the usual *World Reporter* expertise, to occupy
two columns. There was also a picture of Lucia in her bikini.
The caption said: " LUCIA BERNARDI—*Is She or Isn't She?*"

The piece concluded on a waggish note: "*If the Dark
Lady of the Interview is Lucia Bernardi, the Swiss police have
food for thought; if she isn't, then France may have a new
mystery writer.*"

In other words, *World Reporter* had played it as safely and
lightly as they possibly could under the circumstances.

Nice Soir had quoted extensively from the piece and em-
phasised those parts of the interview which the Zürich police
had pointed to as circumstantial. There was the expected
picture of me. I was under a black caption: " MAINTENANT
C'EST ' CHERCHEZ L'HOMME '."

I didn't read what they had to say about me.

Lucia had returned from the kitchen and poured herself a
drink.

" You've read it?" I asked.

She nodded. " I stopped on the Corniche and used the
flash-light. I'm sorry, but I couldn't wait to see what they had
said about the reports."

" I think they've said enough for the purpose."

" Oh yes. Farisi will understand."

" And the Committee."

" Yes, the Committee, too."

I went to the drawer in which I had put the revolver and got
it out. " I suppose I had better take this with me to-night."

" If you think so, yes. But you said Skurleti had moved out
of Nice. The Committee will not have found him so soon."

" I wasn't thinking of the Committee. I was thinking of
Skurleti himself. Supposing he decides that there is a cheaper
way of getting what he wants. I'll be there alone. What is
there to stop him from planting a bunch of thugs there in
advance? There are plenty of nice quiet places they could take
me to. They'd soon soften me up."

She was looking at me curiously now. " Is that what you
think may happen?"

" When I am thinking reasonably, no. I don't think that
would be Skurleti's way of doing things. He's too much the
business man, the negotiator."

" Well, then . . ."

" I could be wrong. His ideas of reason may be different from mine." I tried putting the revolver in my hip pocket. It stuck out absurdly.

She laughed. For some reason I laughed, too, though I didn't at all feel like laughing. She went to her coat, produced a large envelope, folded in two, from the pocket, and gave it to me. " That will make him reasonable," she said.

I put the gun down and opened the envelope.

Inside were two legal-size, manila filing folders, each with some sheets of paper inside. There were three lines of Arabic script on the outside of each folder. They appeared to be identical.

The sheets inside were covered with Arabic script, all very small and neatly done in green ink. Pencilled in the corners were combinations of numerals. They were the only things I could read. I asked her what they meant.

" They are the report and section numbers to which the pages belong," she said.

" Do you know what any of the rest of it means?"

" No. But Skurleti will, and he will like what he reads. The pages were chosen very carefully for their interest. Those are the two sets I spoke of."

" I see." I put one folder away in the drawer and returned the other to the envelope.

She sipped her drink and watched me.

Although I had put the revolver down, I was still very much aware of it. It had been well cleaned before it had been wrapped in the cloth, and the gun-oil used had a pungent, acrid smell rather like that of a disinfectant. My right hand smelled of it, too. I picked the gun up again and put it in one of the side pockets of my plastic raincoat. The envelope I put into the other pocket. Then I went and washed my hands.

When I came down again Lucia was in the kitchen stirring a pot of soup.

She said: " My father told me that in the war some people became very hungry when they were nervous or afraid, and that others were not hungry. I am the not-very-hungry type. All I shall eat will be a cup of soup. What about you?"

" The same, please."

She looked at me significantly. " He also said that you

could always tell the ones who would run away first when things became dangerous. They could eat nothing at all."

IV

I left at nine o'clock. It was only a few minutes' drive to the Relais Fleuri, but I wanted to be there well before the appointed time in case Skurleti was early.

Lucia had explained to me where I should leave the car; there was a space behind the diesel filling station which could not be seen from the Relais parking area. It had been there that she had left her car on the night of the interview.

There was a quarter moon, but it cast deep shadows; I did not feel too exposed there. I did feel very much alone. I could hear voices and an occasional snatch of laughter from inside the Relais. There was a man there with a bad cough, too; but the place looked warm and friendly. As I waited, I kept wishing that I could go inside and be served coffee by the cheerful waitress who had served me five nights earlier.

The Relais was busier than when I had been there before, because, I supposed, it was the beginning of the week. There were three huge trailer trucks parked there. One, that I could see clearly, had the word " RHÔNE " painted in tall letters on its sides. The sides of the other two were plain, shiny, and anonymous—stainless steel, or aluminium. I began to wonder about them. They could be Trojan horses, large rooms full of men who would erupt from the doors at the back the moment I showed my face.

At nine-twenty, four men came out of the Relais calling good nights over their shoulders. They climbed into the cabs of the two trucks. Diesels chuffed, vacuum-brakes hissed, and the Trojan horses were driven away.

Four minutes later an Esso tanker pulled in. That made me a bit uneasy. I didn't think that the oil companies made filling station pump deliveries at night; but I didn't know for certain. If the station lights were going to be switched on I would have to get out in a hurry. It wasn't until the driver had descended, stretched, yawned and made his way into the Relais that I saw that, while I had been watching the tanker, the Taunus had arrived. Its headlights went out.

I waited a moment or two and listened to make sure that there were no other cars approaching on the road; then I got out of the Citroën, quietly closed the door and walked across the yard of the filling station towards the Taunus. It seemed a long way, and I had to keep one hand clamped to my side to keep the revolver still, but I forced myself not to hurry.

I approached the Taunus from the rear in order to make sure that the driver was Skurleti and that there was no one with him. He heard my footsteps and turned his head. I opened the rear door and got in behind him.

He threw me his toothy smile and said: " Good evening."

" Good evening, Mr. Skurleti."

" It is a great pleasure to see you again."

" The pleasure is mutual. Shall we get down to business?"

" Here?"

" No. Here we merely discuss how the business is to be conducted. Under the circumstances I feel that you won't mind if I determine the procedure."

" I am sure that it will not be unreasonable."

" Not in the least. First, I must tell you that I am armed."

" For a friendly business discussion?" He had twisted around on the front seat so that he could see my face. The light from the Relais sign gave him a lopsided look.

" You're not armed yourself, Mr. Skurleti?"

" Certainly not." He seemed irritated at the suggestion. " I have to do a great deal of travelling, and weapons can be a great inconvenience with customs authorities. In any case, we of the Transmonde Agency act only for serious business interests. It is our policy to avoid violence."

" I'm delighted to hear it. What I propose now is that you drive for about half a kilometre in the direction of Nice. There is a place there where you can stop. You may then examine the credentials we spoke about. After that we can talk. Agreed?"

" Agreed."

He was a painstaking but unskilful driver; I was glad that I didn't have to go far with him. The place I had chosen for the meeting was a small re-entrant in the hillside which was used by the road maintenance gangs as a dump for broken concrete and ballast. I had noticed it two nights earlier. Skurleti surveyed it approvingly, then switched off the lights.

" If a passing policeman were curious to know why we had stopped here," he said, " one could always say that it was for a call of nature. You could retreat behind that pile of stones over there. Yes?"

" I'll bear it in mind,"I said ; " but I hope we won't be here long. The next stage in the procedure is that I give you several documents to read."

" That of course, I expected. I came prepared." He produced a massive flash-light from the glove compartment and a small magnifying glass from his pocket.

" There are certain conditions attached to your reading these documents," I said.

" Conditions?" The lips closed sharply over the teeth.

" They must be read through only once and no notes must be taken, and they must be returned."

He thought before he answered. " That is not entirely acceptable. I must be permitted to make a thorough examination of at least one of the documents."

" What for?"

"Am I correct in assuming that these documents purport to have been Colonel Arbil's property written by him personally?"

" Yes, that's right."

" And they are the original documents?"

" Certainly."

" Good. My principals would, of course, be interested in nothing less. However, it is my business to make certain that they receive nothing less." He raised a hand in protest. " No reflection on your personal good faith, Mr. Maas. You appear to me to be most businesslike. But you, after all, are not a principal. We are both agents protecting principals. Is not that so?"

" I suppose it is."

" I have here "—he patted his breast—" a specimen of Colonel Arbil's script. What I must be given, what I must insist on being given, I am afraid, is the opportunity to make a comparison between the specimen and the documents."

I pretended to think it over before I nodded. " All right. That makes sense."

He beamed. " You see! Our negotiation makes progress."

"With a concession from me, yes. But it won't continue to progress that way."

The teeth still gleamed. "You are an interesting young man, Mr. Maas," he said; "very interesting. It is a pleasure to work with you."

"You're very kind. But I hope we understand one another. You may examine for the purpose of comparing the script with the specimen you have. Then you read once. You take no notes. You return the documents to me immediately after you have read."

"Agreed."

I gave him the envelope and watched him go to work. He took the specimen from his crocodile-leather wallet, put it on the seat beside him and switched on the flash-light.

The specimen looked as if it were a letter. It was written on hotel stationery, I thought, though I couldn't read the name of the hotel. The ink was green as on the pages I had given him. He took the folder from the envelope, glanced at the script on the outside, then opened it carefully and placed the specimen letter beside the first page.

He had propped the flash-light on the edge of the seat cushion. Now, as he bent forward, it rolled down.

"Perhaps it would be easier if I hold the light for you," I said.

"Yes, yes. I am obliged."

He handed me the flash-light and I directed the beam downwards with my arm resting on the back of the passenger seat. He went to work with the magnifying glass. For a minute or two there was a dead silence. The first page seemed to satisfy him. As he checked through the others, he began to talk.

"Very nice. Yes, very nice. You know, Mr. Maas, with the Arabic script there is much less room for deception when documents are questioned than with western writing. As Schneickert taught us, the old calligraphic method of comparing outer shapes is quite unreliable. But with the Arabic script it would never occur to one to employ it. The writer's personal signature is in every symbol. This, I am pleased to tell you, is undoubtedly written by Colonel Arbil."

"Then, since you are satisfied on that score, perhaps the reading could begin."

F

I moved the light away to emphasise the point.

" Ah, yes." He put the specimen and the magnifying glass back into his pocket, gathered up the papers and began to read.

I had decided to give him no more than two minutes a page but he made no attempt to linger over them. It took him about five minutes to go through them all. Then he put the papers back into the folder and closed it.

For about another minute he was silent, thinking.

Finally, I said: " Well, Mr. Skurleti?"

He turned to face me. " Do you know what is contained in those papers, Mr. Maas?"

" No. I know, of course, that they are pages taken at random from various reports written by Colonel Arbil. I also know, in general, the subject of the reports. That's as far as it goes, however. I can't read Arabic."

" Have the reports been translated?"

" Not as far as I'm aware."

" Or photographed?"

" I wouldn't think so. As you know, I imagine, these reports were written by Colonel Arbil for delivery to the Iraqi Government. They were not delivered. Since the Colonel's death they have been in Miss Bernardi's hands. She has been in hiding. I can assure you that she has no way of photographing documents."

" Phillip Sanger could have had them photographed."

" Phillip Sanger doesn't know of their existence."

" She did not tell him?" He sounded incredulous.

I grinned. " If she had, Phillip Sanger would be talking to you now instead of me. Miss Bernardi was afraid that Sanger's services might be too expensive. She knew him, and she didn't trust him."

" Ah, I see." He pinched one of his eyebrows and then twisted it as if he were operating a switch. " Well now, Mr Maas, I think we might take our negotiation further."

" Yes?"

He returned the file to the envelope and handed it back to me.

" The documents are now returned as you requested."

" Thank you."

He showed teeth for a moment. " It is, I realise, the custom of many persons when bargaining to belittle the value of the thing they wish to purchase. At Transmonde we do not believe in such old-fashioned methods. If the reports are complete and as you represent them, they would have a considerable interest for my principals and they would be prepared to pay a substantial price for them. All this can be admitted. The question is, how substantial should the price be?"

"I told you that over the telephone."

"Yes, you did. However, my principals thought the sum you mentioned quite excessive."

"Then, I'm afraid . . ."

His hand flew up to stop me. "No, please. Wait. Let us discuss these questions. First, the question of the other possible interested parties to whom you referred. Obviously one of those in your mind would be the Iraqi Government."

"Obviously."

"They would not pay half what you ask."

"I think you're wrong. I'm fairly certain they'd pay more. If it were up to me alone, I'd wait and see. However, Miss Bernardi feels differently. She's tired of all the uncertainty. She'd like to take the money and get out as soon as she can. But she's not tired enough to settle for just anything. If you won't pay the price and if the Iraqis won't, then perhaps the Turks will."

He grinned, and I knew that I had made a mistake. "Now here, Mr. Maas, *you* are wrong," he said. "The Turks would not bid against the Iraqis. Why should they? The oil is in Iraq. The problem is in Iraq. The Turks would receive all the information they needed from the Iraqis for nothing. If you had mentioned the Committee I might say ' perhaps.' They could be buyers, if they had money, or if they could persuade their Russian friends to lend it to them. But I think you have too much sense to deal with them from your position of weakness. You must be secret. Therefore you are vulnerable. They might speak to you of money, but you would never receive it. A knife in the stomach would be their method of payment. With me, on the other hand, everything is civilised. We are men of probity."

"Brigadier Farisi, the Iraqi Government representative, is a man of probity, too."

The name took the smile from his lips. He fingered the

steering-wheel. "I see. You are well informed. But he cann[ot] have arrived yet."

"He will."

"Then you are not in communication yet?"

"Not yet."

He pinched his eyebrow again. "I see no reason why w[e] should not continue to negotiate, Mr. Maas," he said at las[t].

"Neither do I—as long as you're prepared to make an offe[r] now."

"You said in the region of two hundred thousand, M[r] Maas. What does 'in the region' mean? That the sum is [a] negotiable asking price, I presume."

I suddenly felt confident. I shook my head. "Oh no. Wha[t] I meant was simply this. If the price is to be paid in Frenc[h] francs, then that is the amount required. If the price is to b[e] paid in hard currency—American dollars or Swiss francs, le[t] us say—I can accept the equivalent of one hundred an[d] seventy-five thousand francs. The money is to be paid in cas[h] of course, and the transaction completed by to-morrow night."

He sighed, then threw up his hands. "I am not authorise[d] to make such a choice," he said; "and it may be impossibl[e] to arrange for the transfer of such an amount of dollars o[r] Swiss francs by to-morrow. There are formalities here fo[r] such foreign currency transfers. I must consult with m[y] principals."

"Can you consult with them to-night?"

"Yes."

"By the time you get back to Antibes it will be ten-forty[-] five. If I telephone you at eleven-thirty will you have a[n] answer?"

"I can hope to have one."

He started the engine and switched on the light.

"Just a moment." I opened the door. "My car is back there at the café. I can walk. It's no distance."

He said nothing as I got out.

I watched him drive away towards Nice. When he was ou[t] of sight, I turned and started to walk back.

V

Lucia had heard the car stop at the foot of the ramp and was waiting for me in the darkness of the patio.

"Pierre?"

"Yes."

"Are you all right?"

"Yes."

Suddenly she put her arms out, and for a moment we embraced. Then we went into the house. She didn't ask about money or anything else. Instead, she went and poured me a drink, and then stood watching me.

I swallowed most of the drink and got rid of the hat, the raincoat, the revolver and the envelope. Then I went over to the fire. It must have been maddening for her, but some sort of a reaction had set in and I couldn't seem to think of a place to begin.

Finally, I said: "We'll know in an hour."

"Whether they will buy?"

"How much they will pay. Two hundred thousand French francs or the equivalent of a hundred and seventy-five thousand in American dollars or Swiss francs. One or the other. Delivery to-morrow night."

She stared at me and then sat down abruptly. I went and refilled my own glass and I poured one for her, too. Then I began to tell her how the meeting had gone.

When I had finished, she still seemed dazed.

"They must want . . ." she began, but didn't complete the sentence.

I completed it for her. "Yes, they must want it very badly. Even for an oil consortium that's a lot of money to pay for information. There's one thing, though. He was very insistent that it had to be the only copy, that it hadn't been photographed. I assured him that it hadn't."

"Did he believe you?"

"I think so. As I was telling the truth about the photographing, I was probably convincing enough. In any case, he more or less has to believe me. Even if he's not absolutely certain, there's nothing he can do about it."

There I was wrong.

The telephone number of the Travelodge Motel Côte d'Azur at Antibes was in the book. I put the call through at exactly eleven-thirty. The night *concierge* said that Monsieur Kostas was already talking on the telephone. I waited five minutes and called again. This time I was put through to him.

" Monsieur Kostas?"

" Ah yes." He recognised my voice. " The decision is to pay the money in French francs. The other method would not be convenient."

" Two hundred thousand then."

" Yes. What arrangements do you wish for concluding the business?"

" I'll let you know to-morrow. Supposing I telephone you at six o'clock."

" In the evening?"

" Yes."

" That will be convenient. There is one important matter." He paused.

" Yes?"

" I was authorised to tell you that my principals have information that three representatives of the Committee left Geneva by air this afternoon. Their destination was Nice."

" I see. Thank you."

" It is not only a gesture of goodwill. My principals are concerned that we—you and I—take every precaution possible to see that our business is concluded safely. May I offer you some advice?"

" Go ahead."

" The arrangements for our meeting used to-night were simple and worked well. They would work well again. Modify them if you wish, but do not feel that you have to change them to protect yourself from trickery on my part. We are serious people, not gangsters. Do you understand?"

" Perfectly. Thank you. I'll call to-morrow at six."

We had been speaking in English, which Lucia didn't understand very well. Even so, she had kept her head against mine trying to get the sense of the conversation.

" What is it? Will they pay?" she asked breathlessly as I hung up.

" Yes. The two hundred thousand."

She flung her arms round my neck and kissed me.

I kissed her back.

After a while she said: "What else was he saying?"

"Oh, that was just about the meeting to-morrow. I'm to all him at six."

She didn't ask any more questions. Quite suddenly, we had both lost interest in Mr. Skurleti, and even, I think, in the two hundred thousand francs. Our bodies were beginning to discover a more immediate interest.

An hour or so later, in the large double bed, I felt her leave me. When I opened my eyes I saw that she was putting her clothes on.

I started to get up, but she stopped me.

"No. You have nothing to wear. You will get cold. I shall be all right. I will telephone you when the woman has gone to-morrow."

Vous had become *tu*.

In spite of her protests, I draped a blanket round my shoulders and went downstairs with her. I hated the idea of her driving back to Cagnes alone, but there was nothing I could do about it.

She seemed touched by my concern. Then she put her hands up to my face and smiled.

"You have proved enough for one night, *chéri*," she said.

CHAPTER VII

The news from Radio Monaco went well with my breakfast. It reported that I had been seen the previous evening in St. Raphaël driving a Simca Etoile in company with a woman answering the description of Lucia Bernardi.

After breakfast I thought about the meeting with Skurleti that would come later that day.

He had invited me to trust him; and I did, up to a point, but only up to a point. The prospect of taking that long walk back to the Relais to pick up the Citroën, with two hundred thousand francs on me, was not appealing. If I used and let him see the Citroën, on the other hand, and left him later to do the walking, he would certainly get the car's registration number. Even though our business would, presumably, be

concluded after the meeting, and even though he would have
no further interest in Lucia and me, I didn't like the idea of
his knowing more about us than he needed to know. Some
thing might go wrong.

And then I had what I thought was an inspiration. He had
said that the previous arrangements had been " simple and
worked well." Well, there was a way of making them even
simpler and providing myself with additional insurance at
the same time. It would mean obscuring the registration
numbers on the Citroën for a time, but not while the car
was on the road.

I took the keys which Lucia had left with me, walked quietly
up to the garage, and undid the padlock.

There was the usual accumulation of junk inside: a broken
umbrella, an old inner tube, cans of dried-up paint. What I
was looking for was some grease, the dark, sticky kind. My
idea was that it could be smeared over the numbers, and later
quite easily, wiped off.

There was no grease. Instead, though, I found a pair of
discarded Triptyque de Tourisme registration plates. Their
validity had expired the year before, but they were good
enough for Skurleti. Even if he noticed that they were out of
date, the knowledge would not help him.

There was a length of wire there, too, of the kind used for
staking plants. I took the TT plates and the wire back to the
house.

Lucia telephoned at twelve-fifteen.

" You slept well?"

" Yes."

" Without Luminal?"

" Yes. And you?"

She chuckled. " I am still in bed. Would you like to hear
what the paper says?"

" Is it interesting?"

" It says that you are a man of mystery."

" That means they have nothing new. About this evening
How big is the package you will be bringing?"

" There are fifty more pages like the ones you have, all
fastened together in order. We have only to put the pages you
have back in their places and everything will be complete.
will bring the other copy at the same time."

" Good. I think that this afternoon I might start calling the hotels. Our second customer has had time to get here by now."

" I have been looking in the *bottin*. There are a great many hotels with Swiss names. I made a list yesterday. We could divide it between us to save time."

She gave me a list of eighteen names and numbers, which included several *pensions*. I decided to leave the *pensions* until the last. It seemed to me that Brigadier Farisi would most likely choose a hotel from one of those listed in the popular guide-books, *Michelin* or *Europa Touring* for example, and that, even if his choice were going to be dictated by a name, his standard of living would remain constant. The Hotel Schweizerhof in Zürich was unlikely to be succeeded by the Pension Edelweiss in Nice.

Lucia was doubtful, but agreed that we should concentrate on the hotels first.

At three o'clock in the afternoon we compared notes. Neither of us had anything to report. Lucia had begun to lose confidence in her Swiss name idea.

" It's too early for us to know yet," I said. " He won't have made a reservation in advance. He'll just arrive. We'll have to be patient and keep on trying."

" All the same, I may have been wrong. Perhaps his mind has worked another way. I must think."

I didn't tell her that I had begun to do some thinking of another kind. She had been so certain that Farisi would respond to the publication of the interview in the way she had predicted, that I had automatically accepted her view of the situation. Now I was beginning to have doubts. True, Skurleti had also seemed to expect Farisi to arrive in Nice. But supposing they had both been wrong; supposing that the Iraqi Government had decided to deal with the problem in a different way, on a higher level, through diplomatic channels with the French Government, say, or by getting Cairo to talk to the Russians.

I went on making the telephone calls, but my heart was no longer in it. I was wondering how soon I should begin to share my doubts with Lucia; perhaps to-morrow, when she had Skurleti's money in her hands and could afford to be more philosophical.

Forty minutes later she called me again.

"He's here," she said. She was breathless with excitement.

I had presence of mind enough not to ask who she meant, and changed my question to "Where?"

"I must tell you. I thought again how he might think. Schweizerhof means a castle or big house in Switzerland. So I looked for a hotel name that might have the same association here in Nice. I found the Hotel Windsor. There is a Windsor Castle in England, isn't there? So I called the Hotel Windsor."

"And he is there?"

"No. I was very disappointed, so I thought again."

"And? The suspense is killing me."

She laughed. "I thought that perhaps he might have a literal mind. The name of the hotel in Zürich is the Grand Hotel Schweizerhof. What Grand Hotels have we here?"

"The Ruhl? The Negresco?"

"No. One says the Hotel Ruhl, the Hotel Negresco. There is only one Grand Hotel in Nice, the Grand Hotel de la Paix. It is interesting, I think, that the word 'grand' should mean so much to him. He is there."

"Did you speak to him?"

"Of course not. I cut off as soon as they put me through. You'll let me know what he says?"

"Immediately. You are a remarkable woman."

"I agree."

The man who answered my call to Farisi sounded both angry and suspicious. He spoke accurate, strongly accented French in a high sing-song voice.

"Monsieur Farisi is not available at the moment. Who is calling him?"

"It would not be advisable to give names over the telephone. Monsieur Farisi is in Nice, I believe, to discuss a business matter with the friend of a former colleague of his. I am speaking on her behalf."

"I can give a message to Monsieur Farisi."

"I would sooner speak to him myself."

"That is not possible."

"When will it be possible? I will call again."

"Monsieur Farisi does not speak French."

"I can speak English as well as he can."

"One moment." There was a dead silence ; he had covered the telephone with his hand. The voice came back again. "Do you wish to arrange for an appointment for Monsieur Farisi to see the lady?"

"No, I don't. I am representing the lady."

"One moment." There was another inaudible consultation before he came back again. "Can you come to the hotel this evening?"

I began to lose patience. "No, I can't."

"Why not? If, as you say, you represent the person concerned . . ."

I did not wait for him to finish. "How long is it since you arrived in Nice to-day?" I asked.

"Why do you wish to know?"

"Get a local newspaper, this morning's will do. Read it carefully and then you'll understand. I'll call Brigadier Farisi again in half an hour."

"Who is speaking?"

I didn't answer. I called Lucia. My report did not seem to surprise her. "If they had to send an interpreter, they might have sent one with some sense," I complained.

"They are military men," she said resignedly ; "they have to shout and stamp their feet."

There was less shouting and stamping of feet when I called back.

"You say you speak English?" demanded the interpreter.

"Yes."

"One moment."

Brigadier Farisi's tone did not exude goodwill, but he spoke quietly and to the point. I had to explain again that he would not be dealing directly with Lucia, but through me as an intermediary ; but once he had accepted that, things went better. He even seemed relieved.

"Very well. I understand. Now we can be practical," he said. "I gather that there is danger of your attracting the attention of the police. The simplest plan seems, therefore, to be that I should come to you. If you will tell me where, I will leave immediately."

"I'm afraid it's not at all as simple as that, Brigadier. If you arrived here to-day, and I think you did, it is almost certain that you are now under surveillance yourself."

" By the police? But why? "

" No, not by the police. By the Committee, the people interested in Operation *Dagh*."

" I find that hard to believe. How would they find me? "

" I found you with very little trouble. They would have even less. They probably picked you up at the airport. Anyway, we have to assume that they did."

" They could not act so quickly." He sounded contemptuous.

" You think not? I have reliable information that three members of the Committee left Geneva for Nice yesterday afternoon. That would give them plenty of time. They know all about you. In Zürich they got to your friend before you did. They will try to do the same sort of thing here."

" You say they left yesterday. How could you get such information? "

At least he was no fool.

I said: " I had it from the representative of an Italian oil consortium who is as interested as you are in gaining possession of the material on Operation *Dagh*. He also arrived yesterday."

" And you have spoken with him? "

" Yes. You see, Brigadier, things are moving quite rapidly."

He swore ; at least it sounded as if he did ; perhaps he only called upon Allah.

In English he said: " You refused to discuss the matter with him, of course? "

" On the contrary, we discussed the matter at some length. He has made a substantial cash offer."

" This material is the property of my government," he snapped, " and I am here to claim it. If necessary I shall approach the French authorities."

" In that case, Brigadier, you will never see it. It will be in Italy by to-morrow." He made an angry noise. " Moreover," I went on, " it is *not* the property of your government. It was the property of your friend in Switzerland. Your government was going to buy it from him. It has now passed into other hands. Your government can still buy if it wishes. Come now, Brigadier, that is surely why you are here, isn't it? To buy? "

He drew a deep breath. " I have authority to pay compensation to the person you represent," he said stiffly. "Such compensation would be for the inconvenience and hardship and expense which this person has suffered in preserving the material from certain enemies of the State."

"Quite so. But I must tell you that the inconvenience, hardship and expense have all been considerable. In addition, the person has been, and still is, in considerable danger. Obviously, the compensation has to be substantial."

There was a pause before he said: "How substantial?"

"The initial offer from the Italians has been two hundred and fifty thousand."

"Italian lire?"

"French new francs."

He had a muttered conference with the interpreter to find out how much that was in Iraqi dinars. It was nearly eighteen thousand he discovered.

As he reached the figure, there were sounds of derision. I went on quickly: "Of course, that is merely an initial offer. My belief is that they would gladly pay twice that amount."

"Nonsense! It is not worth that to them."

"My impression is different. However, I am meeting with their representative this evening. We shall decide after that whether or not to accept their offer."

"To-night?"

"Every hour we delay now is more dangerous. If things become too dangerous we shall have to go to the police. We shall have to go to the police anyway in the end, but the lady would sooner dispose of the material first, taking whatever she can get for it. Otherwise, the material will simply be confiscated by the French authorities. I imagine their own oil people would be interested."

"But I am prepared to see you to-night. I have already said so." He was getting worried now.

"Brigadier, I have no intention of being killed, and I don't suppose you wish to die either. Any meeting between us must be carefully planned. It will still be dangerous. Unless there is a real purpose to it, I'm not going to take the risk. Why should I?"

"I have said that I am willing to pay."

"But the Italians will pay more."

"I will pay twenty-five thousand dinars. Wait a minute."

He worked it out for my benefit. " That is about three hundred and fifty thousand francs at fourteen francs to the dinar."

" I am certain that the Italians will pay more. All I can suggest, Brigadier, is a possible compromise."

" Compromise?" He said the word as if he had been offered a long drink of quinine.

" I must admit to you frankly that the lady would prefer that you had the material."

" Ah!"

" For reasons of sentiment, you understand. Because your mutual friend was a patriot and because she would like to avenge his death. That we can understand."

" Yes, there are compensations other than money, other satisfactions."

He sounded as if he would have liked to pursue that line of thought. It was time to get back to business.

" So," I said, " we will postpone the decision for a few more hours. After I have met with the Italian representative this evening, I will telephone you and report the state of negotiations. If you decide then that you wish to intervene, we can arrange to meet to-morrow."

" By ' intervene,' you mean . . .?"

" To increase your offer, naturally."

" I see." He was thinking fast. He had to make sure that he would not lose touch with me. " Very well. I am prepared to increase our offer now to thirty thousand dinars."

" That's very tempting, Brigadier, but I think that I must keep faith with the Italians. I must at least hear what they have to say."

" As long as it is understood that you do nothing final before we have had a further discussion. That is most important."

" I will be in touch with you again this evening."

" At what time?"

" Eight o'clock, or a little after."

" What is the name of this Italian agent?"

" I don't think it would be proper for me to tell you that, Brigadier."

" Very well." He breathed deeply again. " I shall expect to hear from you."

" You will."

II

I reported to Lucia.

" How much is thirty thousand dinars?"

" One dinar is worth fourteen new francs. That makes . . ."

" Four hundred and twenty thousand."

" Yes." I had forgotten about her mental arithmetic.

" I would have taken that," she said.

" I'm sure that he has the authority to pay more. Besides, even if I had accepted, we couldn't have set up the meeting for to-night. It's too late now for the doctor and the cinema. Did you call the clinic?"

" Yes. They stay open until eight-thirty."

" That makes it easier for to-morrow. I said I'd call him at eight to-night. Can you be here before then?"

" Of course."

" You don't sound happy."

" I'm getting frightened. It is too near."

" What's too near? The meeting?"

" No. Success."

" If I had said that, you would have accused me of hoping to fail."

She laughed.

III

I had a drink and ran the vacuum-cleaner over the living-room floor. At six o'clock I called the Travelodge Motel Côte d'Azur. Skurleti answered promptly.

" I am taking your advice," I said. " The same arrangements as last night."

" Excellent. And the same time?"

" Yes, the same time, too. Nine-thirty."

" Everything is in order. I shall see you later then."

When Lucia arrived, she brought two bottles of champagne along with the food supplies and a package containing the duplicate copies of the reports.

The champagne wasn't really cold, but we opened a bottle anyway.

I telephoned Farisi.

He picked up the phone himself this time.

"It is as I thought, Brigadier," I said. "The Italians are determined. They offer four hundred and fifty thousand. That is thirty-two thousand dinars."

"Very well. We will pay thirty-five."

"A moment please." I turned to Lucia. "He now offers thirty-five thousand dinars."

For a split second her face was still. Then she said: "That is four hundred and ninety thousand francs."

"Do we accept?"

"Yes."

I turned back to the phone. "That seems satisfactory, Brigadier."

"There are conditions," he said curtly.

"Yes?"

"This offer must not be reported back to the Italians and used to raise the price further. I must be assured that the transaction is agreed. There must be no further haggling or I will be forced to the conclusion that you are not to be trusted, and inform the French Government through our Chargé d'Affaires in Paris of what is taking place. Those are the orders I have been given by my superiors."

"I understand, Brigadier. You have made your offer. It has been accepted by my principal. There will be no further dealings with the Italians, or with anyone else."

"Very well. I have also been instructed that no payment of any kind is to be made, and no money drawn from the bank, until I have satisfied myself that the material is genuine."

"There should be no difficulty about that. Do you know Colonel Arbil's writing?"

"I do, yes."

"I can show you specimens of the material so that you can satisfy yourself."

"When?"

"To-morrow night."

"Where and how? I think I should tell you that after our conversation earlier to-day I took steps to see if we are in fact under surveillance here. Your assumption that we would be proved correct."

His pomposity was catching. "The plan I propose for the

meeting was made with that assumption in mind, Brigadier."

"Very well."

I told him what he had to do. The doctor, the cinema and the pharmacy drew no comment from him; but when we got to the clinic he began to ask questions.

"Colonic irrigation? What is this?"

"A treatment, Brigadier. A perfectly ordinary sort of treatment. A kind of enema."

He didn't know the word. I had to explain it. When he understood, he became indignant.

"Why must I submit to this?"

"You don't have to submit, Brigadier. I was trying to explain. You only have to make an appointment. Your interpreter will tell you what to say."

"He can say it himself."

"Oh no. I'm sorry. We must have this meeting alone."

"Major Dawali is my official aide."

"I can't help that. He'll have to wait in the pharmacy. In fact it might be a good thing if he did. He can appear to be looking over the things for sale while you are waiting for your prescription to be filled. It would look well from the street."

"And you will be in the courtyard."

"Yes, at eight o'clock."

We went over it again while he made notes. Then I had to go over it a third time with Major Dawali, the interpreter-aide. Finally, he said that the Brigadier wished to speak to me again.

"All right."

The Brigadier had been thinking. "Assuming that I am satisfied after our meeting to-morrow," he said, "how do you propose that we complete the transaction? I cannot go to his clinic again."

"No. We'll arrange something different. We can decide that later."

"Very well. There is only one further thing I wish to say to you," he added grimly. "I am an excellent shot with a pistol. Kindly bear that in mind."

"I will. If we run into any kind of trouble, Brigadier, I shall leave all the shooting to you. Good night."

I told Lucia what he had just said.

She shrugged. "A military man."

" What's he look like, I wonder? He sounds tall and thin
to me, an ulcer type."

" Ahmed said that he was short and fat. Does it matter?"
She poured more champagne, drank some of it and sighed.

" Still worried?" I asked.

She nodded. " I expect it is because I have nothing more to
do."

" You could think what you are going to do with all that
money."

" Oh, that I know."

" What?"

She kissed me lightly on top of the head. " I'm going to
buy houses, of course. What did you think?"

IV

I got to the Relais at nine-fifteen and parked in the same place
as before, behind the filling station. It was a cloudy night and
quite warm. I could well have done without the plastic raincoat and the hat, but I thought it better to keep them on.
However, I left the revolver on the floor of the car; it was
easier to move about without that encumbrance.

It took less than five minutes to wire the TT plates into
place so that they covered the normal registration numbers.
That done, I sat in the car and smoked a cigarette. Somewhat
to my surprise, I didn't feel unduly nervous. I wondered why.
It might be, I thought, that Lucia's anxiety had somehow
exorcised my own. Perhaps I was becoming accustomed to
the *ambiance* of conspiracy and clandestine meetings. Or was
it just that I had accepted Mr. Skurleti in the role of totally
trusted father-figure? Upon reflection, I had to admit that
the third was the most likely explanation.

He arrived, punctually, as he had arrived the night before
and stopped in exactly the same place. To-night, he was
alongside an Italian furniture van from Genoa. As soon as
he had switched off his lights I walked over to his car, approaching it from the rear as I had done before.

The same head turned towards me from the same angle;
the same teeth gleamed; the same glasses mirrored the glow
of the Relais sign. There was no one crouching in the back
of the car waiting to pounce on me as I opened the door.

We said " Good Evening."

" A slight change of plan this evening, Mr. Skurleti," I
went on. " My car is over there behind the filling station
office. Will you join me?"

" Of course." There was no hesitation. He picked up a
briefcase from the seat beside him and got out.

We walked back to the Citroën. He did not so much as
glance at the TT registration plates ; he was too eager to get
to the car first and open the door of the driver's seat for me.

" No, no, please." I pressed him into the front passenger
seat.

When I got into the back, he shifted round to face me.

" Oh, I see. We are to do our business here." He sounded
disappointed.

" You don't think it safe?"

" Oh yes, it is safe enough, I am sure. But I had thought
that, as this would be our last meeting and that mutual confidence had been established, you might have decided to take
me to the house in which you have been living." The teeth
showed. " Beaulieu is, after all, only a little way down the
road, and Cagnes is on the way back to Antibes. Besides, I
should so much have liked to meet Miss Bernardi."

" I think this will do well enough." But I must have let
him see that I was disconcerted.

He laughed gently. " Surely, Mr. Maas, you do not think
that I wasted my time on Monday? As soon as I realised
who you really were, naturally I looked again at the list of
addresses which you so thoughtfully sold me, and realised
that it might not be as full as it could be. So, I went back to
the archives in the Hotel de Ville and completed the list."

" I see."

" I was a little *vexé* at the time, of course. All the driving
about and knocking on doors that I did on Saturday and
Sunday was really quite tiring."

" I'm sorry."

" Oh, I don't blame you," he said hastily ; " I truly don't.
I have a high regard for your intelligence. I would have done
the same in your place. Well now, shall we get down to
business?"

He opened his briefcase and took out a bulky envelope
and held it up.

" One hundred thousand francs, Mr. Maas."

" *One* hundred?"

" I have another envelope here of the same size. While yo
are counting the contents of this one, perhaps I can be ex
mining the package that I see you are holding. I think tha
will be an equitable arrangement."

" All right."

He handed me the envelope. I handed him the report
The magnifying glass and the flash-light came out of th
briefcase and he set to work.

Counting the money was easy. It was in wads of ten fiv
hundred franc notes, some fairly new, some old, pinned t
gether at the corners in the way customary with French bank
There were twenty wads.

I put the envelope in an inside pocket and waited while h
examined the reports. It took him quite a long time. Whe
he had finished, he switched the flash-light out and leane
against the door. He looked at me thoughtfully.

" Satisfied, Mr. Skurleti?"

" With the reports? Oh yes."

" Then . . ."

" But I am a little troubled on one score," he continue
slowly. " Or let me say that my principals are troubled. I hav
informed them that I regard you as a completely trustwortl
person, and that you have told me this is the only copy of tl
Arbil reports in existence—the only copy known to you, tha
is."

" Yes." I was glad it was too dark for him to see my fa
clearly.

He cleared his throat. " Now, I must explain something
a confidential nature to you. I know that I can rely on you
discretion. Why? Because you could not make a newspap
story out of what I will tell you without revealing the exis
ence of this little transaction." He tapped the report; the teet
appeared. " I don't think you would want to do that."

" No."

" Then I must tell you that my principals *may* decide, whe
they have considered these reports, I repeat, they *may* decic
to allow Operation *Dagh* to continue. It is possible, yo
understand, that it might be in their interests to do so. I
fact, I may tell you that, following our interview last nigh

nd as a result of what I was able to report, I was instructed
to place myself in touch with the members of the Committee
ow here in Nice and give them certain assurances."

I was beginning to feel quite sick. I managed to say " Oh
es?" with reasonable indifference.

" So you must see," he went on gently, " that the certainty
hat this is the original and only copy of the report, and that
here is no chance of another copy or photostat of the report
eing conveyed to Brigadier Farisi or any other representative
f the Iraqi Government, is a matter of vital importance to
y principals."

" I can see that, yes. But as I told you . . ."

" Yes, yes, Mr. Maas. As you told me, and as I reported,
verything appears to be in order. But while my principals
re prepared to accept the fact that you may believe what you
ay, they are still not entirely convinced. There is Miss Ber-
ardi, you see. Supposing you are not wholly in her confi-
ence."

" I believe that I am."

" Naturally you do." He was grinning broadly now ; a man
f the world. " But with women how can one ever be sure?
1r. Maas——" he tapped the back of the seat—" it will be
eeds that count from here."

" How do you mean?"

The grin became a grimace. " *If* this is the original and
nly copy of the report," he said, " then, after we have con-
luded our transaction here, you and Miss Bernardi will have
one all the business you had to do which called for privacy
nd secrecy. Am I not right?"

" I would think so, yes."

" And then?"

" It was our intention to go to the police."

" And tell them what?"

" That I had persuaded Miss Bernardi that her fears for
erself had been hysterical and groundless, and that the docu-
ents belonging to Colonel Arbil in her possession should be
anded over to the police."

" Are there such documents?"

" Yes. There are files removed by Colonel Arbil from se-
urity records in Baghdad prior to his asking for political
sylum in Switzerland. I understand that they concern high

government officials in Iraq, and could be embarrassing to them if published. Colonel Arbil had relatives in Iraq. He took the files as a form of insurance against reprisals."

"Ah yes. I see." He thought for a moment.

I was thinking, too. I had to be prepared for what was coming next.

"That seems satisfactory," he said slowly. "When will you go to the police?"

"In the morning, I thought."

"Why not to-night?"

"Miss Bernardi will want to get this money into a bank first."

He thought again. "Yes, I can see that it might be inconvenient to have to explain it to the police. That is reasonable. But now——" his voice hardened—"I must make you aware of some disagreeable facts."

"Yes?"

"First, Brigadier Farisi has arrived in Nice and is under close surveillance by agents of the Committee. Every contact he makes will be noted. I must also tell you that if you and Miss Bernardi do not go to the police to-morrow, as you say you intend, you, too, will receive the Committee's attentions. If you should go so far as to attempt to establish contact with Brigadier Farisi, that would be taken as evidence of bad faith on your part and hostility to the Committee. The consequences for you would be most unpleasant."

I did the best I could. "Mr. Skurleti, when you have given me that second envelope you mentioned, we will have no conceivable reason for contacting Farisi, or anyone connected with him."

"I am glad to hear it." He took the second envelope from his briefcase. "It has been a great pleasure meeting with you, Mr. Maas. You are an amiable as well as an intelligent young man. I foresee a great future for you. I very much dislike the thought of your becoming involved with these men of the Committee." He handed me the envelope and his eyes sought mine. "For if you should become involved with them, then you would have no future."

I made a show of counting the second lot of money.

"In my profession," he went on ruminatively, "one encounters many persons whom one would rather see behind

ars—the bars of a prison cell or those of a circus cage. If
ne is old-fashioned one thinks of them as evil. Nowadays
psychotic ' seems to be the word. It gives me no comfort.
1ad or bad—when I am with such persons my flesh crawls.
ut I will tell you something. Seldom have I had such an un-
leasant sensation as in dealing with this Kurdish Committee
nd those who are now working for them. They are clever,
angerous, highly disgusting animals." He paused. " Is that
atisfactory? "

The question referred to the money in the envelope ; he had
oticed that I had stopped counting it. In fact, I was trying
ery hard not to throw up.

" Yes, quite satisfactory," I said.

He closed his briefcase. " Then I must be getting back."
Ie held out his hand. " Again, Mr. Maas, a pleasure."

I managed to press his fingers.

He got out and walked away.

CHAPTER VIII

stuffed the rest of the money into my pockets and waited
ntil he had driven away. Then I lighted a cigarette.

After a while my hands stopped shaking and I was able to
hink. When I had thought, I got out, unwired the TT plates—
pathetic little deception *that* had been—and left them behind
n empty oil-drum. Then I drove slowly back towards the
eaulieu house.

Just before I reached the track down to the house I saw a
ar parked near the entrance to a small villa. Its lights were
ut, but there was a man at the wheel, and I could see the glow
f a cigarette. He could have been waiting for someone at
ne villa, but I was fairly certain that he wasn't. I drove on
own past the track for about five hundred metres. The road
ore right sharply there. I stopped alongside a high, stone
etaining-wall and got out.

By standing on the roof of the car I could look over the
all and see, on the hillside above, the roof of the house in
hich Lucia was waiting, and the lights of its neighbours. In
etween, there was a triangle of very steep, broken ground that

had once, long ago, been terraced for grapevines. I had see
part of it from the bedroom window. To one side of it, the
was a small square concrete hut with a red "Danger" sig
on the metal door—something to do with the electricity suppl
As I knew it to be immediately below the patio of the hous
I could use it as a reference point when I could no long
see the house itself.

Getting over the wall was not too difficult; there wer
drainage holes in the masonry big enough to provide foo
holds, and the drop on the other side was less than a metr
But climbing the hillside had looked easier than it prove
Rain had carved deep gullies in the old terracing, brush ha
grown over them, there were loose rocks. I didn't dare to u
the flash-light and the moon wasn't much help. I had to tak
a zigzag course, blundering along one terrace for a little wa
then clambering up to the next. I fell down twice. By th
time I reached the brick wall that marked the property lin
of the house, I was exhausted. Luckily, the wall was a lo
one, put there to keep the winter rains from washing th
garden soil away without obstructing the view from the pati
There was a line of potted plants on the top. I remove
three of them and climbed over.

Lucia heard my footsteps and had the light out and th
door open before I got to it.

"Are you all right?" she said. "I didn't hear the car

"It's down the road."

Then we were inside the house, the light was on again an
she had seen the mess I was in. As I was out of breath, to
she could only think that I had been running away fro
someone.

She stared at me wordlessly.

"It's all right," I said, "I've got the money." I took out th
two envelopes and gave them to her. "There it is. I loo
like this because I've been climbing the hill."

"But why? What's happened?"

"I'll tell you as soon as I get my breath back."

She looked inside the envelopes. "Did they try to take
from you?"

I shook my head and sat down. The second bottle of cham
pagne was in an ice-bucket on the coffee-table and there wer
two glasses waiting. I opened the champagne and filled th

glasses. She sat beside me; but as soon as I began to tell her what had happened she got up and walked about the room.

"They are watching this house now?" she asked when I had finished. "Are you sure?"

"I'm certain. And I'm certain that they are watching your house in Cagnes, too. It would make sense from their point of view. From now on, until we go to the police, they'll try to watch every move we make."

She stopped and faced me. "What do you want to do?"

I refilled the glasses. "I can see three possibilities. We can go to the police to-morrow morning, as I said we would. We could bank this money, also as I said we would, though I wouldn't recommend that. Almost certainly we'd be recognised in the bank, and then we'd be in trouble of a different kind. I think that if we're going straight to the police we should hide the money first here or in Cagnes. We would have to decide what we are going to do then about the second copy of the report—hand it over to the police, or hide that, too, and try to sell it to Farisi later."

"He would not buy later," she said impatiently. "He would not be here. He would assume that we had sold to the Italians for a higher price, and go away."

"We could always get in touch with him."

"Then he would believe that we had not been able to sell to the Italians after all. He would offer us nothing. Or, worse, he would tell the Iraqi Chargé d'Affaires in Paris to complain to the Quai d'Orsay that we were in illegal possession of the property of an Iraqi citizen. The only reason he has not done that before is because he is afraid we will sell the reports to someone else."

"All right. That brings us to the second possibility. We put this money somewhere safe for the moment, go to the police in the morning and mail the second copy of the reports to Farisi as a free gift."

There was a silence. I wasn't looking at her, but I sensed that she was examining me quite carefully.

"Is that what you want to do, my friend?" she said at length.

I looked up. She had her fists planted aggressively on her hips. At any moment, I felt, one of them might reach out to hit me.

"That depends."

"On what?"

I knew as I prepared to answer that I was committing myself to a course of action that terrified me. In a way, it was
like the moment when I had taken the sleeping pills. The act
of swallowing, of washing them down with brandy and water,
had been almost automatic, as if the hands and throat were
operating independently of the body to which they belonged,
in order to implement a judgment.

"It depends," I said, "on how much of that Skurleti money
you're going to give me. I need one hundred and fifty thousand. If that's all right with you, then we can have an early
night and be up with the lark to interview the police."

She said something so ingeniously indecent that it made me
smile.

"All right," I said, "we'll consider the third possibility. It
amounts to this. Somehow, we have to lose these people—
Skurleti, the agents he's employed, the Committee men—and
keep that appointment with Farisi at the clinic to-morrow.
Then—if we're still alive by then—we have to remain alive
long enough to get our hands on the money. How do you
feel about that?"

Her fists unclenched a trifle, but she still wasn't sure of me.

"What I wish to know is how *you* feel about it."

"If you mean, ' does the prospect frighten you?' the answer
is 'yes, it does.' If you are asking me what I think we ought
to do, I have already told you."

She scowled. "I don't understand you."

"I left the car on the road down the hill. I crawled all the
way up here on my hands and knees practically. I didn't do
that for fun. I did it so that the man watching the house would
not know that I had returned, and would not know, if we
didn't want him to, that we had decided to leave."

"Ah!" She came over and sat down beside me again.
"You ought not to have made those bad jokes."

"I wasn't making jokes. If we were wise we would forget
about Farisi and be satisfied with what we have. But it seems
we are both too foolish and too greedy for that."

She smiled and patted my knee. "Foolish and greedy perhaps, *chéri*, but also intelligent and charming."

" Charm won't be much use to us at the moment. We have to disappear for twenty-four hours at least."

" So let us be intelligent."

" Let's try anyway. We have to assume that the house in Cagnes is also being watched. All the same we've got to get back into it, and to-night."

" But why? I could stay here. After to-morrow, the cleaning woman . . ."

" You're forgetting. Once they realise that we've given them the slip and are *not* going to the police to-morrow, they'll be looking for us everywhere. If they can find us, they'll kill us. We'll be on the run. What about the files that we're going to have to turn over to the police when we *do* go to them? Where are they?"

She smacked her forehead with the palm of her hand. " I am an imbecile!"

" They *are* in that house, aren't they?"

She nodded. " There is a storage room under the terrace. The suitcase is there."

" We have to get them to-night or we may not be able to get them at all. Is there a way of approaching the house without being seen from the street?"

She thought for a moment. " There is a path at the back, by an old stone cistern. Adèle said it may have been built by the Romans. There is a spring. The market-gardener who owns the olive trees keeps some goats. The water from the spring has become saline by now, but it flows into the cistern still and the goats drink it."

" If we could get into the olive grove could we get into the house?"

" There is a fence to keep the goats out, but it has a gate. Adèle pays the man who milks the goats to water the plants."

" Do you know how to get to the olive grove?"

" No, but there must be a way. We will find it."

" First we have to think about where we're going afterwards."

" There is the apartment at Roquebrune."

" What apartment is that?"

" Adèle gave me the keys of three places," she explained ; " the house at Cagnes, this house, and an apartment in Roquebrune. They are all rented for the summer, but until May they are unoccupied. This house and the apartment in Roquebrune she gave me in case I would have to move quickly, and because no cleaning woman takes care of them at present."

" How many houses do the Sangers have?"

" About twenty, I think."

" How many occupied at this time of year?"

" Three or four."

" Well, you can be certain that Skurleti knows about the apartment in Roquebrune. It wouldn't take him very long to find us there."

" It took him two days to go through the list you sold him."

" He has help now," I said.

We sat for a moment in gloomy silence. Then, suddenly, she straightened up. " There is one place they would not think of looking for us. Patrick's own house in Mougins!"

" There's a maid living-in there."

" She can stay with her sister in Cannes for a few days. Adèle could send her on holiday."

" You know where the Sangers are?"

" Of course. They are just along the coast, in Italy near San Remo. I can telephone."

" I don't think they'll be particularly ready to help us at the moment."

" Why not? We are going to the police soon. It will be very inconvenient for Patrick if we are not discreet about the way they helped me before. Shall I telephone now?"

I thought for a moment. It was most unlikely that Sy would still be covering La Sourisette; and Skurleti would almost certainly have scratched it off his list as being occupied. If the Sangers could be induced to send the maid away—the maid he had described as " used to discretion " in their absence—the thing might work.

I nodded. " All right. It's worth a try."

Lucia had to get the number from the operator. It was that of an inn. " They have a business there," she explained to me while she was waiting; " a soft drinks bottling factory. The local people know them and it is logical for them to be there now. New machinery is being installed."

When the call came through she asked for " *La Signora* Chase."

"Adèle? This is Lucia . . . yes, very well . . . you have read the papers? . . . yes, but there are certain difficulties . . . it is a matter of only two more days, and then no difficulties . . . no, no more, if there is just one more place to go . . . you understand? . . . if Marie could go for two days to her sister . . . no, no, Adèle . . . darling, listen . . . it would then be better for everyone, you understand . . . no scandals, no publicity . . . Adèle listen . . . yes, yes, of course . . . he will understand."

She grinned at me. "She is consulting with Patrick."

Half a minute went by, then I heard Sanger's voice on the phone.

Lucia said: "How are you, Patrick? Yes, I am very well. Yes, he is here. One moment." She handed me the telephone. "He wants to speak to you."

He wasted no time asking after my health, but came to the point at once.

"Is what she is asking necessary?"

"Very necessary."

"Then you haven't made the deal yet?"

"What deal?"

"Oh, come *on*," he said irritably; "I can add two and two. Just because I made a chump of myself the other night, that doesn't mean that I do it all the time. I kept wondering why you turned down that thirty thousand bucks. The one thing I didn't think of was that you might have bigger fish to fry."

"I didn't, then."

"But you do have now, eh?"

"In a way."

"How big is it?"

"Twice the size."

He whistled. "And you need forty-eight hours to wrap it up? Is that it?"

"That's it."

"What's in it for me?"

"Immunity."

"You'll have to do better than that this time. You're in a spot."

"Wait a minute."

Lucia had been trying with only partial success to follow the conversation.

"What does he want?" she asked.

" He's guessed that there's money coming. He wants his share."

" Hah! " She flung up her hands in disgust. " You see what he is?"

" He thinks that there's about sixty thousand dollars involved. What shall I tell him? Ten per cent?"

" Six thousand dollars!"

" It would be worth it under the circumstances. After all, you'll still be getting your half-million clear—a bit over in fact. We have to have *somewhere* to go, Lucia."

" It is blackmail." Then she shrugged helplessly.

" Immunity plus ten per cent," I said to the telephone.

Sanger chuckled. " That's more like it. When does the deal actually go through?"

" The day after to-morrow."

" I'll tell Marie to leave the keys in one of the flower urns by the front door. She'll take the eight o'clock bus to Cannes in the morning. You can go in any time after that."

" Can't we get in earlier? It'll be light by then."

" As tough as that, is it? All right. I'll tell Marie to leave the garage doors open. Just drive in and stay there until she's gone. You can trust her. She'll just pretend you're not there. But it'll be safer for everyone if she doesn't recognise you. The less she knows the better. Okay?"

" Okay."

" I'll see you."

11

We put the money from Skurleti and the second copy of the reports in my suitcase, along with the few things I had. Then we unmade the bed and tidied the place up to remove the more obvious traces of my occupancy. Although Lucia was very bitter about Sanger's " blackmail," she still meant to keep faith with his wife. If Adèle were not to be compromised, our explanations to the police would have to include the story they had concocted between them when Adèle had first agreed to hide her. Lucia told me about it hastily as we worked.

She would say that she had never set eyes on Adèle Sanger and that she had leased the house in Cagnes by letter, using the name Berg, from Switzerland before Arbil's death. She and Arbil, she would say, had expected to spend the spring months there. She had paid cash in advance for the rent.

Adèle Sanger, if questioned, would say that Madame Berg had unexpectedly arrived ten days early, and telephoned with a sad tale of plastic surgery and a request that the date of the lease be brought forward. Madame Sanger had seen no reason to make difficulties. The house had been empty at the time anyway. The rent was already paid. The housekeeper had been told to permit poor Madame Berg to move in at once. Madame Sanger had never set eyes on Madame Berg.

"That's all very well," I objected, "but how do we explain why the housekeeper didn't see me when I'm supposed to have moved in with you? I know she has bad eyesight, but even so . . ."

"She is only there in the mornings. In the mornings you locked yourself in the storage room."

"The police won't believe that."

"They will have to believe it. They can't prove any different. Are we ready now?"

It was past midnight.

We turned off all the lights and let ourselves quietly out of the house. Lucia was wearing slacks and had no trouble getting over the boundary wall. I replaced the potted plants, and we started down the hillside.

I led the way, but I was hampered by the suitcase and could not do much to help Lucia. Half-way down she slipped in a gully and her wig came off. We had to stop and find it. Then I wrenched my ankle ; not badly, but enough to make the rest of the descent even more difficult. When we got to the re-taining-wall at the bottom we had to rest before attempting the climb down to the road. While we were resting, I dis-covered that the two drainage holes I had used as footholds to climb up from the roof of the car could not be seen clearly from above. So we had to use the flash-light. Luckily no cars passed while we were getting ourselves down, but it was a nerve-racking minute.

I locked the suitcase in the boot of the car and got into the driving seat. I switched on the lights, but did not start the car immediately.

Lucia looked at me. "What is it?"

" I was wondering which way to go."

It was only partly true. What I was really wondering was whether the meeting with Skurleti, which had undoubtedly frightened me, had so frightened me that I had begun to imagine things, that I had begun, as it were, to see Committee men hiding under the bed. No doubt the physical exertion of scrambling up and down the hillside and the all-too-real pain in my ankle had something to do with it ; but suddenly I felt that I *had* to see if the man who had been waiting in the car up the hill was still there. If he were not, then I was behaving like a clown, and making Lucia behave like one, too.

" Through Beaulieu," she said, " by the Pont St. Jean."

" It would be quicker if we went back up to the Corniche."

" What about the man watching the house?"

" As long as we go straight past it, he won't take any notice of us. Besides, it might be a good idea to have a look at him."

She made a comic grimace at me. " You want to see if that *chichi* you made up there was for nothing?"

There was no sense in protesting. " Yes, I do."

" All right."

I started the car, turned and drove as fast as I could round the bend and up the hill.

We were about fifty metres from the track down to the house and I could see the end of the crumbling stone walls that marked it, when the headlights of the stationary car came on.

For a moment, I was blinded. I was aware that Lucia had flung her arms up to screen her face. Then we had passed the lights and were coming to the hairpin turn at the top. I kept my foot down on the accelerator. As we had passed the stationary car I had seen that there was a second man there now. He had been sitting astride a motor-cycle with a half-eaten sandwich in one hand and his mouth open. In the rear-view mirror I had seen him drop the sandwich and stamp on the kick-starter.

We skidded violently around the hairpin into the crossroad just below the Corniche.

Lucia shouted: " To the left!"

I turned to the left. Almost immediately the road seemed to be falling away beneath us—we were going down hill again.

I braked hard and the weight of the car bore down once more on to the suspension. There was a series of hairpin bends, which I took much too fast, and then we were in the outskirts of Villefranche above the port.

Lucia was looking behind us. " I think he must have gone on up to the Corniche," she said ; " I don't think he saw us turn down. Shall we stop and make certain?"

We were on the lower main road now, going towards Nice.

" I think we'd better keep going," I said.

I was bitterly angry with myself. My weak-kneed yearning for reassurance had increased the danger for both of us. We had effectively demonstrated not only that we were aware of being under observation, but also that we were trying to avoid it. Skurleti and his temporary allies on the Committee would not now have to wait until the late morning for evidence of our " bad faith and hostility." I had handed them the evidence in advance.

Lucia said: " Well, now we know."

" Unfortunately, so do they. I should have had more sense."

" Ah, *chéri*, don't blame yourself. They had not seen you return to either of the houses. They would have begun to look for us soon anyway. It makes no difference."

" It'll make a difference if they find us."

" We will see that they don't."

Earlier, we had decided to enter Cagnes from the Vence direction and leave the car well away from the Rue Carponière. Lucia directed me through Nice. The streets were practically deserted and we made good time. Just outside Cagnes, I slowed down and she began to look for the side road that led to the market-garden.

We found it without much difficulty. It served a small farm and two or three cottages, then straggled on, getting rougher as it went, up the left side of the valley. The market-garden was a narrow, lozenge-shaped strip of flat land with the olive grove sloping up behind it. We passed a long fenced area with ordered rows of glass *cloches*, then came to some greenhouses. Beyond, there was a two-storey house with outbuildings.

I stopped by the greenhouses. It was obvious that the road ended at the house. The sound of a car there would start dogs barking. Lucia thought that we were already too near. I

G

reversed as quietly as I could down the road past the fencing to the edge of the property. Then I turned the car and parked under a plane tree.

It was all very quiet there, but the olive grove possessed a special stillness of its own. The trees were old, and the light breeze did not move their thick, twisted limbs. Only the leaves moved, fluttering softly. Once, as we walked up, the black shape of a goat stirred, and the chain that tethered it made a clicking noise. Then the bulk of the cistern loomed ahead and there was a sound of trickling water. A moment or two later, we had found the path.

We followed it up to the garden gate. We could see the house now. Lucia unlatched the gate quietly. There was a strong spring on it and the hinges were dry. They squeaked as we eased our way through into the garden.

Inside, all I could see was a brick pathway with shallow steps leading upwards, and some tall bushes. Lucia led the way. As we neared the house, the bushes thinned and the pathway ended on a paved platform with a long rustic trestle table in the middle and a slatted sun-roof overhead. In the warm weather that would be where the people of the house dined.

Three steps up and we came to a crosswalk below the terrace. The door to the storage room was on the right.

Lucia fumbled in her bag. " One little moment," she said ; " I have the key here."

" Do you need some light?" I had brought the flash-light with me.

" No, I have it."

We really were very lucky. We kept our voices down. Of course, we knew or assumed that there were men watching the house from the street in front, but the street was some distance away. It was the darkness that made us whisper.

It wasn't until the door was open that I switched the flash-light on, and then I directed the beam inside. We went in.

Most of the space was taken up by garden furniture and tools. There was a deep shelf across one wall on which the garden-chair cushions were stacked. I could see no suitcase.

" Behind the cushions," Lucia said.

She took the flash-light and pointed the beam at one end of the shelf. I began to remove the cushions there. A moment later I could see the suitcase. It was a relic of the days before air travel, made of metal with lines of rivets showing and thick leather caps on the corners. It was right up against the wall at the back of the shelf under the rafters. I stood on a chair so that I could reach it.

At that moment the terrace floor above us creaked.

I heard Lucia catch her breath, and she switched the flash-light out. Neither of us moved. The floor creaked again. Someone was walking slowly across the room above. Then there was a murmur of voices—men's voices, though it was impossible to distinguish words.

Lucia switched the flash-light on again and pointed it at the shelf.

I stared at her. She mouthed the word " Quick."

I eased the suitcase off the shelf and got down from the chair. Lucia kept the light on until we reached the door.

We were on the crosswalk again and Lucia had turned to relock the door, when there was a sound of voices from the side of the house.

I grabbed her arm and hurried her down the steps to the paved platform. Then a beam of light flickered on the path-way ahead of us and I pulled her into the shadow of the bushes.

The light flickered again and then became stronger as the man holding it reached the crosswalk. He said something to the man with him and began to walk forward. As the light disclosed the open storage room door, he let out an exclama-tion and moved forward quickly.

We could see them now. The man with the light was wear-ing a motor-cycle crash-helmet. The other man had on a hat like mine and was carrying a gun. The man in the helmet went into a crouch, then darted into the storage room.

I didn't wait to see what the other man did. I pressed Lucia's arm and we moved quickly down the pathway from the platform to a place where the bushes were thicker. We hid ourselves again.

We were out of sight of the crosswalk now, but we could still hear the two men. I didn't know what they were saying, but it sounded as if they were discussing the situation. Then their voices began to recede.

I had Lucia's hand in mine and she was trembling. I picked

up the suitcase and led her down to the gate. We opened and closed it very slowly this time. It made hardly a sound.

We didn't speak until we had reached the car again.

" Those men," she said as I put the suitcase in the trunk, " they were the ones who killed Ahmed."

" Are you sure?"

" Oh yes. I could make no mistake about that. Did you understand what they were saying?"

" No. But I think I know the language they were speaking. I think it was Czech."

Half an hour later I drove into the garage of the Sanger house in Mougins. The light outside the front door was on, but the rest of the place was in darkness. It was a quarter to three. We had over five hours to wait before Marie left to visit her sister in Cannes.

The garage was a converted stone barn, part of which had been boarded off and binned for use as a wine cellar. There was no corkscrew, but I found a bottle of whisky with a screw-cap that could be opened by hand.

We sat in the car and drank whisky for a time. Then Lucia put her head on my shoulder and went to sleep.

III

We slept most of the day, too, on the bed of the Sangers' guest-room. Marie had left a note indicating which room we were to use, and reporting that there was food in the refrigerator.

We had a meal late in the afternoon. When she had cleared away after it, Lucia suddenly began to watch the clock and to worry. Had Farisi understood exactly what he had to do? Was I sure? It was five o'clock now. Had he already gone to a doctor for the sleeping-pill prescription? Soon he should be starting for the cinema. Did he know what he had to say when he went to the clinic?

Quite a lot of her anxiety was due, I realised, to the fact that the plan for the meeting was very largely hers. She was feeling responsible for it. And our experiences of the previous night had made the danger seem to her again as real and present as it had been in Zürich.

I did my best to reassure her, to appear relaxed and confident, but it was not easy. I had been trying *not* to think about
the meeting with Farisi. Her anxiety was infectious.

I had one drink—one too few, it seemed to me—before I
set out.

We had judged it advisable for me to arrive at the clinic just
fifteen minutes early. In that way, we thought, there would
be no risk of my being spotted by the men shadowing Farisi ;
at the same time, I would not be exposed for very long to
accidental recognition by persons using the courtyard.

I arrived there at exactly a quarter to eight.

It had been during a week-end when I had reconnoitred
the courtyard and there had been only two cars parked there.
Now there were three, and a motor-scooter. I managed to
back the Citroën into the space left, but it was a tight squeeze
and I was sweating by the time I had finished. I smoked a
cigarette and tried to cool off. I wanted to appear calm and
unflustered when I met Brigadier Farisi.

At five to eight things started to go wrong. A car drove into
the courtyard and stopped in front of me with its headlights
shining on my face.

A large red-faced man wearing a cap and a bow tie got out
and came towards me waving his arms.

" What are you doing there?" he demanded angrily. " That
is my place."

I switched on my headlights to make it more difficult for
him to see my face, and called to him that I was leaving at
once.

It made no difference, he still came on.

" Three times this week," he bawled. " It is too much. This
is a private place." He pointed at the parking sign. " Can you
not read?"

I started the engine and shouted again that I was going.

" I will inform the *concierge*." He started towards the office.

His car was blocking the way out. I could think of only one
thing to do. I drove the Citroën forward to intercept him. At
the same moment I leaned out of the window and snarled at
him.

" I am a doctor. I was called here on an urgent case, and
must now, at once, return to the hospital."

He hesitated.

" So," I went on sharply, " if you will have the goodness to move your car, we can both be about our business."

He was staring me straight in the face. I could only pray that he didn't read the newspapers carefully, or that he had bad eyesight.

Suddenly, he threw up his hands in a sort of oh-what-the-hell gesture, made a throaty, French noise of disgust and climbed back into his car.

As he backed into the street, I drove out past him and his headlights again shone in my face. I tore down the street and made the first right turn I could before I stopped. I waited for a moment or two, to make sure that he had not recognised me at the last moment and tried to follow. Then I found a parking place outside a shop that had closed for the day, and started to walk back. There was no sense in hurrying ; I didn't want to arrive back at the courtyard before he had finished parking his car. In any case, my legs didn't feel like hurrying, except in the opposite direction.

It was exactly eight o'clock.

I walked into the courtyard with my head bent and my stomach churning and went straight across to the clinic door. There was nobody there yet ; so I waited, wondering if anyone were to challenge me, if I could pretend to be one of the clinic's professional personnel, and trying to think what to do now about Brigadier Farisi, if and when he arrived. Should I walk him back to the car, or would it be better to transact our business by flash-light in the courtyard?

The clinic door opened suddenly. The sound made my heart jolt. A tall, emaciated old man came out, brushed past me with a word of apology and hurried with quick, loping steps across the courtyard and away.

He had startled me, but his departure had given me an idea. As the clinic door had opened I had seen there was a well-lighted staircase inside, with a tiny lobby at the foot of it. If the Brigadier could be induced to keep his voice down, it might be possible to hold our conference there. At least, he would be able to read the specimen pages easily ; other departing patients would be incurious and disinclined to linger ; the place could have a peculiar sort of privacy.

I opened the door an inch or two, to have another look at

the lobby, and heard someone descending the stairs. I opened
the door a little more and looked up.

Lucia had said that he was short and fat; the man coming
down the stairs was short and square, but I was fairly certain
that it was Brigadier Farisi. He had the tentative, self-con-
scious air of a military man unused to wearing civilian clothes.
The suit was good—made in Rome probably—but all the
buttons were fastened and the tie was too bright. He had a
smooth, olive complexion, close-cropped hair, an arrogant nose
and a small black moustache touched with grey. His eyes
were dark and alert.

When he saw me, he paused on the stairs.

"Brigadier Farisi?" I asked.

He continued down. "Mr. Maas?"

"Yes. Brigadier, there has been a hitch in the arrangements.
There was no room in the courtyard for my car."

The dark eyes assessed me briefly. "Then where do you
suggest we go? I must tell you I am very closely followed."

"Would you object if we stayed here?"

He thought for a moment and his eyes strayed up the stairs.
"We could be interrupted."

"If we speak quietly, I think we will be quite safe here."

"Very well."

I handed him the file of specimen pages.

He put on a pair of reading glasses. For two minutes there
was complete silence.

Then we heard voices above. Another patient was leaving.
There was stertorous breathing at the top of the stairs and a
slow descent began.

The Brigadier's eyes met mine questioningly.

"Perhaps we might wait outside for a moment," I said.

He nodded and shut the file. We went out into the courtyard.

Some moments later the door opened and a sturdy, broad-
shouldered man emerged, breathing painfully and leaning as
he walked on a leather-tipped cane. He left a smell of stale
urine behind him as he moved away.

The Brigadier and I returned to the lobby.

We had no further interruptions. When he had finished the
reading, the Brigadier nodded. "So far, so good," he said.
"When may I have the whole document?"

" To-morrow, Brigadier."

" And where?"

" I will telephone you later to-night."

" Can't you tell me now?"

" Later."

" We have to exercise extreme caution." The dark eyes assessed me again. Was I really to be trusted?

" You need have no fear of that," I said firmly. " Will the money be in French francs?"

" Yes. I take it that when you have the money you and this woman will be leaving the country?"

" No. She will surrender to the police."

" With a reasonable explanation?"

" Exactly. It will not, of course, include any reference to our business. She will surrender Colonel Arbil's personal papers."

" What papers?"

" I understand that they consist chiefly of an unfinished history of the Kurdish people."

He seemed satisfied. " It is time that I was going." he said. " I shall be at my hotel waiting."

With a nod he turned away and walked back up the stairs.

I waited until he was out of sight and then went out again into the courtyard. Everything seemed as before. I started to walk towards the *porte cochère*. I was even beginning to feel relieved. Then I stopped.

Standing beside his motor-cycle just inside the big doors of the *porte cochère* was the man in the crash-helmet. As I saw him he was in the act of easing the machine backwards on to its rest. Then he left it and began to walk forward into the courtyard, peering about him intently. It was obvious what had happened. The Brigadier had been out of sight for too long. Someone had been sent to check the rear of the building.

I was in the shadow. For a moment I considered trying to work my way around the parked cars and then making a dash for it, but then I realised that that would be hopeless. Even if I could beat him to the street, I still had to get to the car ; and he had a gun as well as a motor-cycle. My only chance was to get back inside the clinic before he was far enough

ito the courtyard to notice the light that spilled through when
opened the door.

The moment I was inside the lobby again, I looked at
ie lock on the door. It was something like a Yale, with a
:ver on it which could be set to prevent the latch engaging
vhen the spring closed the door. There was a bolt, too, but
 didn't bother with that. I turned the lever and eased the
itch into the slot. The patients would still be able to get out
ut the man in the helmet would be unable to get in, if he
iought of trying to do so.

That was a short-lived advantage, though. I knew that I
ouldn't stay there long. Not only would the last patients be
oming down, but it was already twenty past eight and the
ersonnel would soon be leaving, too. I had no valid reason—
o one in his senses *could* have a valid reason—for standing
t the bottom of those particular stairs. If I were seen there
 would certainly be questioned, and just as certainly recog-
ised. I had to move.

There was only one way to go—up.

At the head of the stairs there was a short, narrow passage
ading into a corridor. A man in a white smock—a doctor or
 male nurse—passed by along the corridor as I hesitated,
ying to work out the geography of the building.

I *had* to keep going. I set my teeth, walked briskly to the
orridor and turned left.

I had guessed right; that was the way to the stairs leading
own to the pharmacy. Next to the reception booth there were
vo waiting-rooms with rolled glass partitions, and an obvious
ntrance door. Unfortunately, the receptionist was there, too ;
 tall, angular woman in a white coat. She was energetically
praying the air with disinfectant from a device like an old-
ashioned Flit-gun.

The flooring of the corridor was rubber. She did not notice
ie until I was almost level with her. I passed through a cloud
f disinfectant. As I did so I murmured a casual " good
ight," and headed for the door.

I had my hand on the knob of it when I heard her call to
ie : " *Ah non, Monsieur, la porte est encore fermeé. Il
aut . . .*"

I didn't hear the rest of it. The door was indeed locked, but

the key was still there and I had it unlocked in a second. As
the door closed behind me I crossed the landing outside and
ran down the stairs. Mercifully, the door at the bottom lead
ing into the pharmacy had no lock, only a pneumatic closer

Through the small circle of glass with the name of the
clinic lettered on it, it was possible to see part of the shop
including the doorway to the street. There were still several
customers at the counters.

The three minutes which had elapsed since I had left the
courtyard had not seemed like hours, but they *had* seemed like
ten or fifteen minutes. I had assumed, without really thinking
about it, that Brigadier Farisi must have long ago left the
pharmacy, taking his shadowers with him.

I slipped through into the shop and started towards the
street. I was within ten feet of the doorway, when I saw that
Brigadier Farisi was still there in the shop.

He was standing by the prescription counter, still waiting—
very properly, I suppose—for the sleeping-pills that he was
ostensibly there to buy. Beside him was a cadaverous, brown
suited man with a pendulous upper lip and the eyes of a
confused bloodhound—Major Dawali, the aide, no doubt.

I had a moment of stark terror, then did the first thing that
came into my head: I turned away from the doorway, walked
towards the other side of the shop and became engrossed in
the nearest counter display that would mask me from those
watching from the street.

It happened to be a display of toilet paper at discount prices
I couldn't stare indefinitely at that without attracting atten
tion, so I explored the alternatives furtively. The scent counter
was near by, but there was a salesgirl there. I edged over to
a display marked OCCASIONS, which had trays full of plastic
soap-dishes, toothbrush-holders, toy ducks and shower caps
A woman was picking over the soap-dishes; I tried to look
as if I were with her and bored. Then, as she made a choice
I turned and peered intently into a glass-enclosed show-case
full of bandages and elastic stockings, " *pour les varices.*

I could see Farisi from there. He had his pills at last and
with Major Dawali's assistance, was paying for them.

The lights in the shop were brilliant. Everything in it seemed
white and bright, even the floor. The sweat was pouring down
my face. At any moment, I was sure, someone was going to

look at my face, look away, then look again and start point-
ing me out to someone else. Until Farisi left, I had no way
of escape, except back up to the clinic, the entrance door of
which had certainly been relocked.

Farisi had finished at the prescription counter now and, with
Dawali, was on his way out. Even so, he didn't hurry. He was
busy giving a performance for the benefit of the shadowers.
He paused at a display of vitamin pills and made some sort
of joke about them to Dawali. Then he looked at the soap
counter. Finally, he did go, ostentatiously holding the paper
bag with his box of sleeping-pills in it.

But still I couldn't leave ; I had to wait until they were well
away. By shifting slightly to the douche bag side of the show-
case, I could see through the doorway to the street. They were
standing on the kerb and Dawali was waving frantically, presumably for a taxi. My heart sank. It is not easy to find a
cruising taxi in Nice at that time of night. But, incredibly,
they had found one. As it drew away, I began to move slowly
towards the door, counting under my breath as I went ; I had
decided to give them a full minute to get clear.

Then I was through the doorway and in the street. I kept
my head down and turned right, away from the side-street and
the courtyard. I walked slowly at first, then gradually increased the pace. There were quite a lot of people about ; it
would have been difficult to find out if I were being followed.
And risky, too ; the streets there were very well lighted. I
trudged on, hoping for the best. Ten minutes later I reached
the car.

I would have liked to have sat there for a moment and
given myself time to recover. I didn't dare. Instead, I wiped
my sweaty, shaking hands on my handkerchief, and drove back
to Mougins.

There were lights on in La Sourisette and, when I drove
into the garage, I saw why. In the space for the second car
there was a Lancia Gran Tourismo.

Phillip Sanger, as well as Lucia, was there to welcome the
hero home from the wars.

IV

Lucia ran to meet me. Sanger followed at a more leisurely pace.

"Was it all right?" she asked breathlessly.

"Yes. All right. Not exactly according to plan, but all right. No casualties so far. What's he doing here?"

Sanger was near enough to hear the question. He grinned.

"Well," he said breezily, "since I now have a small piece of this joint enterprise of yours, I thought I might as well see if there was anything I could do to lend a helping hand."

"He has come," said Lucia tartly, "to make sure of getting his money."

Sanger chuckled. "Now, now, children. A little respect, eh, for my grey hairs?" He looked at me. "I expect you'd like a drink."

"Very much indeed."

"Let's go inside."

He led the way. Lucia shot me a warning glance which I didn't need.

He watched me closely as I took off the hat and raincoat, and said "Tut, tut" when he saw the revolver. I handed Lucia the specimen pages file.

"The property?" he asked.

"Just the front gate to the property."

We went through into the living-room.

"Let me see," he said; "it's Scotch and soda with ice for you, isn't it?"

"That would be fine. Thank you."

He went to the drink table in the alcove. "Lucia has been telling me about our enterprise," he said.

"Not everything," she said pointedly, and looked at me again. She meant that she had not told him about Skurleti, nor how much Farisi was going to pay.

"Naturally, not everything. After all, I am only a junior partner. But what I have heard has been very interesting." After a moment or two, he came back and handed me a drink. "I hear that you have been having adventures."

"He has been wonderful," Lucia said challengingly, as if he had been attempting to criticise me.

"I'm sure he has." He sat down. "What happened to-night?"

I drank half my drink and then looked at her.

She shrugged. "It doesn't matter if he knows now."

He seemed unperturbed by her hostility; his own attitude was one of good-natured tolerance.

I told them what had happened at the clinic.

By the time I had finished, Lucia was looking appalled.

"It is too dangerous," she said flatly.

"Well, *that* was too dangerous, maybe." The whisky was helping a lot. "We'll have to think of something better for to-morrow night. I promised to let him know this evening. At least there is one thing we don't have to worry about."

"What?"

"The Brigadier himself," I said. "He's a very cool customer. He's not going to lose his head or do anything foolish. And he obeys orders to the letter. The only thing we have to decide now is what orders to give him. I was thinking about it on the way back. Is it possible to charter a light plane at Nice airport?"

"I suppose so. Why?"

I got to my feet the better to express it. "Here's what I thought. To-morrow morning he goes to a travel agency and books on a scheduled flight to Paris leaving early in the evening. The surveillance will know about that reservation at once. Next, he goes back to the hotel, calls the airport on an outside line and charters a plane to take him to Cannes at roughly the same time. The surveillance won't know about that until it's too late. They'll follow him to the airport, of course, but by the time they realise what's happened he'll be in the air. At Cannes he takes a taxi and meets me near here—somewhere on the golf course possibly. How about it?"

She thought it over and then her face brightened. "It's perfect."

"Well, I don't know about that. We have to find out first if the charter plane part of it is practicable. And we'll have to choose the rendezvous carefully. We don't want the taxi-driver getting curious or suspicious."

Sanger had been silent until then, watching us; but now, suddenly, he began to laugh.

Lucia glowered at him.

He went on laughing. It became tiresome.

" May we share the joke?" I asked.

" It's you," he said. He choked slightly over his drink, pu
it down and mopped his face with his handkerchief. " I'm
sorry, but it really is very funny."

" The plan?"

" No, no. That's very ingenious. I was laughing at you."
He started again.

" Oh?" I was getting annoyed now.

" Please forgive me." The paroxysm seemed to be subsiding
" It was just hearing you. First, there was this clinic affair o
yours this evening, and then the plan." He shook his head ii
wonderment and smiled up at me. " Have you any idea, any
idea at all, my friend, how much you have changed during
the last few days?"

" I've had other things to think about," I said impatiently
" I still have."

He took no notice. " When one compares," he went on
wide-eyed with amazement, " the brooding young man with
the haunted eyes and the aura of death, the man who sat in this
very room a week ago apologising for the iniquity of his
existence—when one compares that man with the arch con
spirator hunted by the police, who risks assassination by hire
gunmen and makes daring, ingenious plans to sell secrets to
the representative of a foreign power, one can only . . ." He
broke off, overcome again by helpless laughter.

Even Lucia laughed then. In the face of all that merriment
I summoned a sour smile.

" The circumstances last week were rather different," I re
minded him.

He shook his head vehemently. " Oh no," he said when he
could speak again. " Oh no, that's not the answer. I though
I knew what made you tick. ' A new kind of anger,' I said
How wrong I was! Your kind of anger is as old as the hills
You've just bottled it up all these years—just like the man
who becomes a policeman instead of a crook. Or is that sub
limation? It doesn't matter. The point is that you have a
taste for larceny. It agrees with you. Therapy!" He started
to giggle. " Instead of giving you all those shock treatments
you know what they should have done? They should have
sent you out to rob a bank!"

To my astonishment, I found that the idea amused me, too.
It was Lucia who brought us back to earth. She looked at her
watch.

" It's getting late," she said. " We have to decide what to do.
We have to find out about the plane."

I said: " I think most of these charter services run a twenty-
four-hour service. I'll call the Nice airport and check. In fact,
I might even book the plane for Farisi. Then all he has to
do is pay for it—and make the Paris reservation, of course."

" You have another drink," Lucia said. " I'll call the airport."

As she started towards the telephone, Sanger held his arms
up high in the air.

" Wait a minute, children," he said ; " just a moment."

" Pierre has to call Farisi soon."

" I know, I know. He can call him in a minute. But first let
us consider." He took my glass and went to refill it. " Let us
consider carefully," he added slowly.

Lucia shrugged. " What is there to consider?"

" I said that Pierre's plan—may I call you Pierre?—was
ingenious. It is, but it is far from being safe or foolproof. In
fact, I think it could be highly dangerous. Let me tell you
why."

We waited until he resumed his seat.

" First," he said, " I think you are underrating our oppo-
nents. From what you tell me it is clear that we are not
dealing merely with a small political group having limited
resources. There are powerful forces backing them. Pierre was
lucky this evening. We cannot rely upon luck again. We cannot afford to be amateurish. Consider this plan in detail.
Pierre says that, once in the air, Farisi will be out of their
reach. Why? Even for so short a flight as that from Nice to
Cannes, there must be a flight plan filed. Farisi's destination
will be known immediately. How do we know that they don't
have an agent farther along the coast to whom they can telephone instantly?"

I thought of Skurleti in Antibes.

" They have agents on motor-cycles, you say," he continued. " With the taking-off and night-landing procedures added
to the actual flight time between Nice and Cannes, a fast
motor-cyclist could be there as soon as the plane. Choose

another small airfield you say? One much farther away?
Digne? Aix-en-Provence? Pierre then has to drive hundreds
of kilometres, some in daylight perhaps, to get to the rendez
vous, and every kilometre he drives creates an additional risk
from the police. This is not sensible."

He paused. Lucia was looking gloomy.

Sanger went on: " Now let me tell you something else. If
I were Brigadier Farisi, I would not accept this plan. It is
one thing for Pierre to receive the money and hand over the
documents in exchange. It is another for Farisi to take the
documents and deliver them to his government. Where does
he go after the rendezvous? Back to his chartered plane? He
would never reach it alive."

" He would be foolish to try," I said. " But surely it's up to
Farisi to make his own arrangements once he has what he
came for."

" Perhaps. But I don't think he would regard the middle
of a strange golf course as an acceptable point of departure
And who could blame him? In any case, it is all quite un
necessary."

" What's unnecessary?"

His hands fluttered and he hunched his shoulders. " All this
—all this elaboration."

" You have a simpler plan?"

" Oh yes, of course." He looked mildly surprised. "
thought you realised that."

" No."

" The only question is "—his eyes went deferentially to
Lucia—" whether or not you will find it acceptable."

Her eyes had narrowed. " Let us hear about it, Patrick."

He thought for a moment, then began, ticking the items off
on his fingers as he went.

" Pierre has taken frightening risks," he said. " You, my
dear Lucia, have taken risks also. Surely, your luck must soon
run out. On the other hand, you have also acquired a partner
who has taken no risks at all, so far."

He paused. Lucia's mouth was tightening.

He gave her a warm smile. " Lucia always distrusts her
friends, even when they have proved themselves by helping
her."

She turned on him, her face pink with anger. " I said that would protect Adèle, and I will!"

"And me, too, I hope." He threw me a humorous glance. These women!

" Let's hear what you have in mind," I said shortly.

"All right." He settled himself. "To business. Lucia has explained what you mean to tell the police. That's fine. I think you should go to them first thing in the morning."

Lucia and I both started to object at once. He threw up his hands.

" Wait, children! Listen! Do you want to hear it or don't you?" He was suddenly a man much misunderstood, and tired of the injustice.

We were silent.

After a moment, he went on quietly: " The minute you go to the police, several things will happen. First, the Committee agents will be thrown off balance. They will question the reason for this move, and they will become alarmed. If you have given these documents to the French police, very soon they will have found their way to the Iraqi police, with terrible consequences for the *Dagh* conspirators and for those who associated with them. Instead of attacking, they will be suddenly on the defensive. If, at the same time, Brigadier Farisi makes a reservation on the first connecting flight to Ankara, Aleppo and Baghdad, their fears will be confirmed. They will conclude that he has been ordered home. True, they will maintain the surveillance over him, but probably with fewer men and certainly with less conviction. You agree?"

"Go ahead."

"You are being questioned by the police. Brigadier Farisi has reserved his air passage home. What then? All seems to be concluded. Who will notice that a Monsieur Sanger has taken a suite on the same floor of Brigadier Farisi's hotel? Who will know if Brigadier Farisi, on his way to the elevator, makes a little detour and spends a few minutes with Monsieur Sanger? Nobody." He spread out his hands. "The transaction is completed."

I looked at Lucia. She looked at me and sighed wearily.

"He makes sense, *chéri*."

"There's one thing he hasn't thought of," I said. "Farisi

will have to go to the bank to get the money. That'll alert them, surely?"

Sanger grinned. "I am prepared to bet," he said, "that Farisi went to the bank to-day and arranged for the money to be delivered by messenger to-morrow. That is what I would do in his position. It would be an obvious precaution. Of course, I can't be sure. There remains a certain element of risk in any case. Which brings me to the final question."

"Your share?"

"Exactly."

Lucia didn't even sigh. She had given up.

"What do you suggest?"

"A third?"

Lucia moaned. I moaned too, silently but in sympathy. Now he was going to have to know the price I had agreed with Farisi. I did my best to negotiate.

"Fifteen per cent," I said.

"But I already have ten per cent," he protested. "Surely you cannot expect . . ."

"Fifteen per cent of four hundred and ninety thousand francs," I said. "That's what Farisi has agreed to pay."

I had the minor satisfaction of seeing his jaw drop for an instant, then he recovered.

"*Tiens!*" he said mildly.

"And fifteen per cent is . . ." I started to work it out.

"Seventy-three thousand, five hundred francs!" This was Lucia, of course. "Seventy-three thousand—just for taking a room in a hotel!"

"And thinking of the idea, and taking a certain amount of risk."

"Risk? After what Pierre has done? It is an insult!"

"Then I withdraw the offer," he said cheerfully. "Pierre shall take the hotel room."

"*Espèce de chameau!*"

"Do we have a deal or don't we?"

She looked at me. I nodded.

"Yes, we have a deal," I said.

Five minutes later, after we had discussed details, I telephoned Farisi and told him the proposed arrangements. He approved of them heartily. It occurred to me that he had not enjoyed the visit to the clinic any more than I had. He had only one question to raise.

"This man, when he calls, how will I know that it is not a trick? How will I know he is genuine? There should be a code. He should give a password."

"Yes, he should. The password will be 'Ethos'."

I had to spell it out, but it was worth it. However, only Sanger was amused.

v

Ten minutes later, after further discussion, I called Sy Logan at his apartment in Paris.

His wife answered the telephone; they were obviously in bed. I heard her say to him: "It's that rat Maas."

Several seconds went by before he came on. He was switching on a tape-recorder, I suppose.

"Well, Piet," he said affably, "long time no see."

We were to dispose, it seemed, with the recriminations—at least for the present.

"I thought the story looked good," I said. "I hope the repercussions haven't been too embarrassing."

"They haven't exactly been fun. Where you speaking from?"

"The South. I thought you might like a follow-up on the story."

"We might." He sounded non-committal.

"If you're not enthusiastic, I'll give it to *Paris Match*."

That stung him. "No you won't, Piet. Not if you want to stay out of the courts, anyway. You're still under contract to us. Remember us? Your salary's still being paid and it'll go on being paid until your contract's expired. That's an order from New York."

I had to laugh. "Oh, I see. It wouldn't look good if you fired me, would it?"

"That's our business. The point is that legally you're still working for us. Now, what's this follow-up you're talking about?"

"Is Bob Parsons still down here?"

" Yes. Why?"

" I've persuaded Miss Bernardi to turn herself in to the police, together with the papers she took from Arbil's villa."

" Listen, you son-of-a-bitch, if you're trying to pull something else . . ."

" I'm not trying to pull anything. If Bob Parsons—just Bob Parsons, nobody else—will have a car waiting at a place I nominate at nine o'clock to-morrow morning, he can drive us to the Commissariat at Nice and have the whole story first hand."

" Are you on the level?"

" Of course. I've been working on this all the time. She wouldn't have given me the time of day with you or the police around."

" Will she co-operate now?"

" Now that I've persuaded her to do so, yes. Naturally, she'll be nervous."

" You say only Bob Parsons. What about a photographer?"

" Okay, one photographer. But nobody else."

" Who needs anyone else? Where's the place to be?" He was excited now.

" In Cagnes-sur-Mer. But you'd better let me talk to Bob Parsons about that, so that there's no slip-up. Where's he staying?"

" The Negresco. I'll speak to him now. Can he call you?"

" I'll call him. In case I can't reach him, the place will be the north side of the square in Bas-de-Cagnes. Got that? There's just one other thing. It might be a good idea if he has a lawyer on hand at the Commissariat. I have a sound logical explanation for what has happened, but the police may be bloody-minded. And Miss Bernardi could use some protection, too. She's in a pretty bad state of shock still. It's been a sort of nightmare for her, this whole business. You can understand that." I managed to sound an emotional note.

He responded to it beautifully. " Don't you worry, Piet. We'll have the Marines there, and a whole platoon of lawyers with them to run interference. You just deliver."

" I delivered the interview, didn't I?"

" Yes, Piet. But just don't go bad on us again, eh?"

" I'll see Bob Parsons in the morning. Good night."

This time I had pleased both members of the audience.

" They will send lawyers?" Lucia asked incredulously.
' Lawyers to help us with the police?"

"They will."

"You thought of this?"

" I don't want us spending to-morrow night in jail. Besides,
we have an appointment with our friend here to-morrow
evening to collect some money."

Sanger beamed at her. "You see? It is as I said. He has
a natural talent for these affairs. You should be very happy
together."

CHAPTER IX

Next morning, Sanger drove us in the Lancia, with the Arbil
suitcase, to within a kilometre of Bas-de-Cagnes. He was unwilling to take us any nearer to the square, and became irri-
table when we suggested that he should.

" I have work to do for you in Nice to-day," he reminded us
sharply. " If Pierre's newspaper friends have decided to improve their relations with the police by notifying them in
advance of your surrender, there might be considerable em-
barrassment for all of us."

So we got out and walked the remaining distance. We
passed several people on the road, but nobody took any notice
of us. We were just a man and a woman with one heavy
suitcase between them. Lucia was wearing her wig, and I my
hat. We were some distance away from the house in the Rue
Carponière, and the men watching it, but there was no sense
in taking needless risks.

Bob Parsons was standing by his car at the appointed place,
looking this way and that; and the photographer had his
cameras draped around his neck ready for action. Neither of
them recognised us until we were within a few metres of them;
it was incredible.

The photographer saw us first and immediately went into
action. Bob ran towards us.

I introduced him to Lucia. She managed to appear aloof,
pathetic and slightly mad all at the same time. She refused to
take off her wig for the photographer, insisting that every

moment she stood there she was in danger. It had been my idea to go to the police, she said ; perhaps I had been wrong. I saw that Bob Parsons was getting worried. When I suggested in an undertone that it might be as well to call off the photographer and get going, he agreed immediately.

I had always liked Bob Parsons. He was from San Francisco, fortyish, with a long, thin face and a quiet sense of humour. He was also a very clever reporter. While he was driving in to Nice he managed to extract from us the whole story that we had prepared for the police, and, moreover, to expose a few holes in it that we hadn't realised were there. Between us, Lucia and I managed to cover the holes up again ; but it was an unnerving experience, though invaluable, we were to discover later, as a dress rehearsal.

With Lucia's consent, Bob stopped just short of the Commissariat and sent the photographer on ahead to get shots of our arrival. She also shed her wig and scarf at that point and put them in her handbag. I discarded the hat.

From the moment of our arrival, the day was sheer hell.

True to his promise, Sy had managed to retain no less than three lawyers to represent us and protect our interests ; but it soon became clear that the police were having no nonsense of that sort. The lawyers were told that, since we had reported to the police voluntarily in order to make statements as responsible persons, and since no charges against either person existed or were even contemplated (yet), our interests required no protection. Since we were not under arrest (yet), we needed no legal representation. If they, the lawyers, felt that their clients might be guilty of some offences, let them speak.

The lawyers decided to hold their peace, at least for the moment. We were on our own.

Lucia was magnificent, and so convincing that I became concerned. One impressionable deputy Commissaire, suffused by compassion, proposed that the interrogation be postponed and that a doctor be called to administer sedation. Somewhat hastily, she toned down her performance. A grim-visaged matron from the women's jail was brought in for consultation instead. She prescribed a cup of hot chocolate.

Soon after that we were separated. I had to tell my story all over again. *Why had I not secretly contacted the police?* I was in a position of trust *vis-à-vis* Mademoiselle Bernardi.

But if I believed her fears to be irrational it was my duty to inform the police, was it not? I had no way of knowing at first that her fears were irrational. *Had I not read the documents in the suitcase?* No. *Why not?* I could not read Arabic. *Did Mademoiselle Bernardi describe the contents to me?* No. *What had I thought to be the basis for her fears?* The things she had been told about the documents by Colonel Arbil, and the fact that he had been murdered by men seeking the documents.

It seemed to go on interminably. My watch had stopped and I lost all sense of time. At one point food was brought in. The questioning continued.

I had stayed in the house at Cagnes, had I? Was it not strange that the femme de ménage *had noticed no trace of my presence there?* Not strange at all; the *femme de ménage* had bad eyesight. *Where had I slept in the house?* In the storage room. *Where in the storage room?* On the seat cushions of the garden chairs. *How had I shaved that morning?* Mademoiselle Bernardi had lent me a razor. *Had I perhaps shared the lady's bed, too?* They should ask the lady herself that question. *Would I object to a search of my person?* Not in the least. On and on it went.

It must have been late afternoon when they took me into a sort of waiting-room and left me there alone. After a few minutes, Bob Parsons came in. With him was one of the lawyers, a chubby little man with an imperious air.

Bob looked weary. " Well, Piet," he said, " as far as the police are concerned you're not exactly smelling of roses, but I think you're off the hook. Maître Casier here says they won't hold you."

" What about Lucia?"

" A couple of cops from Zürich flew in about an hour ago. They're with her now. Has she any more to tell them than the stuff that was in the interview?"

" Not a thing."

" Then she'll be released soon, too. But there's a problem."

" What?"

" Our colleagues on the newspapers. There are about fifty of them waiting outside."

" Oh God!"

" I've talked to Sy. He's talked to New York. The story's

too early for us, and too hot. So we're putting it out to the
wire services about an hour from now. The pictures we took
this morning went to Paris by plane earlier. They'll put some
of those out, too. We'll just keep a couple of the best for
ourselves."

"What about the people outside?"

"Well, you'll have to let them take a few pictures of you
with the girl, but as for statements the police have hinted
pretty strongly that they'd prefer to do the talking themselves,
and only after those papers of Arbil's have been examined by
the Deuxième. So your lips are sealed."

"Well, that's something. When do we get out of this place?"

"As soon as they're through with Lucia, I guess. That
shouldn't be long now."

Maître Casier intervened. "There is one small difficulty,
Monsieur Maas. The police have expressed a wish that both
you and Mademoiselle Bernardi remain in the area and report
daily to the police. This is at the request of the intelligence
authorities. They may wish to ask more questions later, when
the Arbil documents have been translated and assessed."

"I see. Very well."

"Which brings us to a different kind of difficulty, Piet."
Bob Parsons was suddenly looking embarrassed. "At least I
assume it's a difficulty." He smirked self-consciously. " *You'll*
have to tell *me*. You see, I had your bags picked up from
that station hotel, and I've got you a room at the Negresco.
Now Maître Casier tells me that Lucia intends to go back to
that house in Cagnes to-night. She says the rent's paid in
advance anyway. The police have no objection. Well, it
seems that she's sort of expecting you to go along with her.
Some sort of prior arrangement you had. I don't know."

"She states," said Maître Casier firmly and rather accusingly,
"that you, in persuading her to report to the police, definitely
promised to stay with her and protect her from further journa-
listic intrusions. On the basis of that promise, she trusted
you."

I had trouble keeping a straight face. I said, as hesitatingly
as I could: "Well, yes, I suppose I did say something like
that."

"And since you must, in any case, hold yourself available

r further questioning by the police, there seems no reason
hy you should break that promise."

He was very stern now; clearly Lucia had made a deep
pression on him.

I tried to look dubious. " Well . . ."

" I need not remind you," he went on primly, " that, in view
 the suggestions about your relationship with the lady which
.ve already been made in the press, your abandonment of
r at this moment would make a very bad impression. She is
Frenchwoman. It is, after all, an American publication that
u represent."

" *L'Amérique perfide*," Bob Parsons murmured sardonically.
He took her story from her, and then threw her to the
olves."

His eyes met mine; I hadn't been able to fool *him* for long;
 had no doubts at all now that Lucia and I had been sleep-
g together.

I turned to Maître Casier.

" Very well," I said manfully; " if that's what she wants, so
 it. I have no car, of course. If we have to report to the
lice daily, I'm going to need one."

" You can take mine," Bob said promptly. " Your bags are
 the boot already. I'll be going back to Rome to-morrow.
e can get everything squared away with the rental people
fore I leave in the morning."

He had a broad grin on his face. He was thoroughly en-
ying himself. So was I, though for a different reason. If
aître Casier hadn't been there, I would have been grinning,
o.

II

was seven o'clock before we managed to get away from the
ommissariat and the photographers. We were both consider-
·ly dishevelled. Some of the photographers followed us in
rs and on motor-scooters. When we reached the Rue Carp-
ière there was another group already there waiting for us.
ore photographs were taken. After about twenty minutes,
wever, the crowd thinned and I was able to get the car
side.

At nine o'clock I drove the car out, shutting the gates behind me. There were only two photographers left, and a solitary reporter. Mademoiselle Bernardi was exhausted, I told them, and had retired for the night. A nurse, summoned earlier, I added gravely, was in attendance. Nobody troubled to ask me about my plans for the evening. Now I was just another inconvenient competitor.

I drove down the hill on to the Vence road, then took the turning which led to the market-garden.

Lucia was waiting at the bottom of the olive grove, where we had parked two nights previously. She was wearing her wig and scarf again. I had retrieved my hat. We had had a bottle of champagne to celebrate the occasion, and Lucia was in an exuberant mood. We had a merry drive along the back roads to La Sourisette.

Sanger received us with the confident affability of the specialist who has studied the X-rays and concluded that the disease is not, after all, as serious as you had been led to believe.

" Quite a day you must have had, children," he said, " quite a day. I've been listening to the radio." He went away to the drink table.

Lucia gave me a look.

" Quite a day, indeed," I said. " However, since you've already heard all about our day, how about telling us about yours? Did you get to Farisi?"

" Certainly I did." He came back with a brandy for Lucia. " And?"

" The meeting was brief but interesting. A very able man that. Very able."

We waited while he mixed my drink, and a Campari-soda for himself. At last, he came back.

" And?"

He shook his head sorrowfully. " Children, we miscalculated."

" Did you get the money?" Lucia demanded.

" I got some money." He breathed heavily.

" How much?"

" As I said, we miscalculated." He sipped his drink. " You should have gone to the police later. As it was, that second-in-command of his . . . what's his name?"

" Dawali."

" Yes, Dawali. He'd heard the story on the radio. Secret
documents turned in to the police. Farisi suddenly decided
you'd short-changed him. As a result, he reneged on the deal
you'd made. I had quite a tough time fighting him."

I got to my feet. " That's nonsense! He already knew that
we were turning in some of Arbil's papers. I'd told him about
'An unfinished history of the Kurdish people.'"

He shrugged. " The radio said secret documents—documents that have been passed to the Deuxième Bureau. Naturally, he was upset. Naturally, he thought he'd been given a
raw deal."

Lucia, too, was on her feet now, her eyes glittering.

" How much, Patrick?" Her voice rose. " How *much*?"

He sighed. " Half," he said quietly.

" Liar!"

" Half. Two hundred and forty-five thousand francs. I'll
show you." He went to the safe.

" Liar!" She snatched off her wig and flung it at his head.
It missed him and fell with a faint " plop " on the Aubusson.

" Now, now, children."

" *Espèce d'ordure!*"

" Let's be reasonable."

" *Merde, alors.*"

" Pierre, can you persuade her to stop yelling?"

" I feel like yelling myself," I said. " I also feel like calling
Brigadier Farisi and finding out exactly what he did give
you."

" He left by the five o'clock plane." He smiled reproachfully.
" Come *on*, kids! Two thousand and forty-five thousand
francs, less my seventy-three thousand, nets you close on forty
thousand dollars. And all for a bundle of yellow paper
that . . ."

It took another deafening ten minutes to reduce his commission from seventy-three to forty-three thousand. He re-
mained good-tempered and reasonable throughout. Since, almost certainly, he had the other half of the purchase price
safely stowed away in another part of the house, this was
scarcely surprising.

He could also be frank. " Honey," he said plaintively at
one point, " you're being stupid. For you, I didn't have to

come back here to-night. If it hadn't been for Pierre and a
those wicked things he might have said about me in prin
maybe I'd have gone straight back to Italy. As it is, Pierre
in on the deal, too, so he can't say anything. So we are a
friends."

He didn't ask what my share was going to be ; I don't sup
pose he cared, but when he had given Lucia the two hundre
and two thousand and watched her cram it grimly into he
bag, he did give the matter of my future some thought.

" You know," he said, " that magazine proposition o
Pierre's is not bad—not bad at all. From an investment stan
point, I mean. There should be a steady return when it ge
going. I wouldn't mind having a piece of it myself. There
one problem, though. If he starts up again, he must do s
with a limited liability corporation. Otherwise, the person
risk is absurd. As a foreigner in France, however, he woul
be in a difficult position. In French law the principal shar
holder of a limited company registered here must be a Frenc
citizen. That means that he would have to find someone l
could trust."

She thought for a moment, then shrugged. " That is h
affair." She glanced at me significantly. " Don't forget, Pierr
you left some things in the bedroom."

" Oh yes."

Sanger came towards me smiling. " I took the revolver.
hope you don't mind. It belongs to Adèle. And her ca
keys, too."

" Of course. Don't bother to come up. I remember th
way."

For a moment I was afraid that he was going to insist o
going with me, but Lucia saved us from that. She upset he
brandy.

" I am sorry," I heard her saying severely as I went upstair
" but it is no wonder that I am nervous. When one has be
lieved that one was dealing with a friend, and then discove
that there is no true friendship but only hard self-interest, one
hands are apt to tremble a little."

I found the two envelopes stuffed with the Skurleti mone
where we had hidden them under the carpet in the gues
room. I put them in my pockets, packed the suitcase an
carried it down.

Sanger was his usual happy self as he saw us off the prem-
es.
"Bless you, my children," he said, "bless you. I will give
ièle your love."

III

e were out of Mougins and on the road to Vence before
icia mentioned the Skurleti money.
"Was it safe, *chéri*?" she asked.
"It was safe." I patted one of my pockets.
There was another silence.
Then she said: "Is it true what he said about companies in
ance, that the principal shareholder must be a French
tizen?"
"I don't know, but we could find out."
After a moment or two, I took the envelopes, one by one,
om my pockets and gave them to her.
She leaned over and kissed me on the cheek.
"Four hundred thousand," she said thoughtfully as we came
Vence.
"Four hundred and two thousand," I corrected her.
"No. There is the matter of the cleaning woman's eyes. I
omised to pay for the operation."
"So you did."
I saw her smile, and felt her hand on my knee. "I never
rget a promise, *chéri*," she said, and then added reflectively:
That lawyer, Maître Casier, was very understanding to-day.
rhaps we should ask his advice."

Eric Ambler

A world of espionage and counter-espionage, of sudden violence and treacherous calm; of blackmailers, murderers, gun-runners—and none too virtuous heroes. This is the world of Eric Ambler. 'Unquestionably our best thriller writer.' *Graham Greene*. 'Ambler is unequalled in his artful reconstruction of the way things seem to happen.' *Guardian*. 'He is incapable of writing a dull paragraph.' *Sunday Times*. 'Eric Ambler is a master of his craft.' *Sunday Telegraph*

The Light of Day *30p*

The Intercom Conspiracy *30p*

Dirty Story *30p*

A Kind of Anger *25p*

The Night-Comers *25p*

Passage of Arms *30p*

The Mask of Dimitrios *25p*

Judgment on Deltchev *30p*

The Schirmer Inheritance *30p*

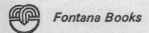 *Fontana Books*

Winston Graham

'One of the best half-dozen novelists in this country.' *Books and Bookmen.* 'Winston Graham excels in making his characters come vividly alive.' *Daily Mirror.* 'A born novelist.' *Sunday Times*

His immensely popular suspense novels include:

Angell, Pearl and Little God *40p*

After the Act *30p*

Greek Fire *30p*

The Little Walls *30p*

Night Journey *25p*

The Sleeping Partner *25p*

Fortune is a Woman *30p*

The Poldark Saga, his famous story of an 18th Century Cornish tin-mining community:

Ross Poldark *35p*

Demelza *35p*

Jeremy Poldark *35p*

Warleggan *35p*

And his historical novels:

The Grove of Eagles *40p*

Cordelia *40p*

 Fontana Books

Fontana Books

Fontana is best known as one of the leading paperback publishers of popular fiction and non-fiction. It also includes an outstanding, and expanding section of books on history, natural history, religion and social sciences.

Most of the fiction authors need no introduction. They include Agatha Christie, Hammond Innes, Alistair MacLean, Catherine Gaskin, Victoria Holt and Lucy Walker. Desmond Bagley and Maureen Peters are among the relative newcomers.

The non-fiction list features a superb collection of animal books by such favourites as Gerald Durrell and Joy Adamson.

All Fontana books are available at your bookshop or news agent; or can be ordered direct. Just fill in the form below and list the titles you want.

—————————————————————————————

FONTANA BOOKS, Cash Sales Department, P.O. Box 4, Godalming, Surrey. Please send purchase price plus 5p postage per book by cheque, postal or money order. No currency.

NAME (Block letters) _____

ADDRESS _____

_____

_____